JAMI GRAY

HUMAN
AUTHORED

SIGN UP FOR FREE READS FROM JAMI!

Join Jami's newsletter to be the first to hear about new releases, free books, special prices and other nifty events.

Sign up at: https://www.subscribepage.com/jami-gray-books

WHAT READERS SAY...

About Arcane Transporter:
"Taking a refreshing approach to fantasy magic, this fast-paced, economical thriller is told from a highly likable perspective." —Red Adept Editing

About PSY-IV Teams:
"This story is an emotional roller coaster, from betrayal, anger, fear, love..." —InD'tale Magazine

About the Kyn Kronicles:
"...a fantastic paranormal action novel is quite possibly the best book I've read this year. I could not put it down, and had to exercise serious self-control to keep from staying up all night to finish it." — The Romance Reviews

About Fate's Vultures:
"...if you like your characters with a bit more bite, with secrets, with hidden agendas, and all those sorts of things, and your worlds are a far more deadlier place, then this is for you." — Archaeolibrarian

ALSO BY JAMI GRAY

ARCANE WONDERLAND

Last Call

Bitter Spirits

Rune & Tonic

ARCANE TRANSPORTER

Ignition Point (*Prequel Novella*)

Grave Cargo

Risky Goods

Lethal Contents

Collision Course

Blind Spot

Terminal Drift

THE KYN KRONICLES

Shadow's Edge

Shadow's Soul

Shadow's Moon

Shadow's Curse

Shadow's Dream

Shadow's Fall

Tangled in Shadows (*Short Story Collection*)

FATE'S VULTURES

Lying in Ruins

Beg for Mercy

Caught in the Aftermath

Fear the Reaper

PSY-IV TEAMS

Hunted by the Past

Touched by Fate

Marked by Obsession

Fractured by Deceit

Linked by Deception

BOX SETS

PSY-IV Teams Box Set I (Books 1-3)

The Collapse: Fate's Vultures (Books 1-4)

The Kyn Kronicles Box Set (Books 1-6)

Arcane Transporter Box Set I (Books 1-3)

Arcane Transporter Box Set II (Books 4-6)

ACKNOWLEDGMENTS

This last year was difficult on multiple levels, and like, I'm sure many of you have experienced, when life decides to throw curveballs, they tend to be a hell of a curve. For me, the later half of 2023 hit me with a doozy. Like losing traction on black ice, spinning into a hairpin curve with a sheer drop-off on one side, and solid rock on the other, while handling the wheel blind-folded, kind of doozy.

Terminal Drift would not have come about if not for all of you and your continued support and enjoyment of Rory and Zev's stories. While I have to pull off to the side and take a break until the road conditions clear up, I'll be back at full throttle by mid 2024. I'm just not sure who is going to be hitching a ride.

Hopefully it will be someone we all love and adore, but until then remember to hold your loved ones close and take joy in the small things because they can flit away before you know it.

Love to all—Jami

"You win some, lose some, and wreck some."
~ Dale Earnhardt

For all those who spun out, hit the wall, then got up and walked
away…

ONE

"WEREN'T YOU JUST HERE, RORY?" The question was accompanied by the slap of a coaster that was tossed in front of me and pinned in place with a chilled glass.

I picked up my preferred mix of half tea, half lemonade and lifted it in a mocking toast. "Missed me, did you, Cass?"

My wiseass remark earned an amused snort. "Like a damn rash." She gave an exasperated headshake that threatened to dislodge her precariously perched topknot as she wiped down another glass. Then she filled it with ice and made quick work with a soda gun and a bottle of whiskey. "You need an office."

Pearl of wisdom delivered, she wandered away to hand the glass to a customer a few seats down. When she came back, she continued with her unsolicited advice. "Not sure if you noticed, but with the alcohol"—she waved to the bottles lining the wall under the mirror behind her then swept that same hand out to indicate the space behind me—"the pool tables, the music, and the sticky floors…" Her hand flattened against the bar's top as she eyed me, laughter glinting behind the purple-tinted lenses of her glasses. "This is a bar, not an office."

I widened my eyes and gasped. "No? Really?" She chuckled as I took a sip of my Arnold Palmer.

"Seriously, girl, I've seen more of you in the last few months than, well… ever." She cocked her head, and a sparkle of sympathy replaced her amusement. "When's your probationary stint over?"

I set my glass carefully back on its thin piece of cork. "Two and a half weeks."

"Just around the corner, then." When I didn't respond but continued to fuss with my glass, she pressed, "Why don't you sound more excited about that?"

Because I wasn't, and the reasons why were too complex to get into with the slightly strange but definitely sweet bartender. I forced a smile and shrugged. "I'm excited. It's just been a long day."

She stared at me for a moment, clearly not believing me, but instead of pursuing it, she circled back around. "Which brings me back to, why are you here? You left…" She looked to the clock hanging on the wall. "Like an hour ago."

That was a much easier question to answer. "Got a friend who wanted to meet up for a drink, so I suggested the best place in town, Wonderland."

"Aww, that's sweet. Maybe I can get you a part-time gig as our social media manager."

I suppressed a shudder. "I'll pass, thanks."

Someone called Cass's name, and she excused herself to answer their summons. I sipped my drink and stared unseeingly at the mirror. It was midweek and closing in on eight at night, so the crowd was quiet enough that I could still make out the lyrics of the song crooning through the speakers.

"*Matches in my back pocket, I'm the queen of burnin' bridges…*"

Oh yeah, I could totally relate.

Close to six months ago, while on a job for the Arcane

Council, I'd set fire to a bridge and watched it burn. Now, when only a few nails were left to completely restore it, I was reconsidering its necessity—probably because the vestiges of previous bridges dotted the gorge underneath, a visceral reminder of my track record.

Nearly two years ago, the first bridge went down in a blaze of glory after I took an off-the-books job that generated a surprisingly large payment from a very unexpected source. That influx of cash had jump-started my entrepreneurial plans, and within six months, I had left the protective arms of the Western Arcane Guild and hung up my own shingle as an Arcane Transporter. It was slow going at first, then a body dropped on my doorstep, my roommate disappeared, and I got tangled up with Zev Aslanov.

A year and half later, the body was long gone, along with the person who'd dumped him there. My roommate was currently canoodling with her geeky electro mage snuggle bunny, and Zev had a drawer in my dresser. More importantly, the connections Zev had encouraged me to forge in those initial months were the only things keeping me in the black now. I wasn't as deep into the black as I had been when the Arcane Council was on my roster, but enough to hold the bill collectors at bay and cover my half of expenses.

Hence my current decision conundrum. Did I really want to take the Council contract back on, and the convoluted strings it brought with it?

In my heart of hearts, where I tucked my most personal things, the current answer was a resounding no.

Granted, the suckiest thing about the Council cutting me off for six months was losing access to the associated Guild resources, like their fleet of various magically protected vehicles and steady stream of Transporter assignments to fill the gaps in my schedule. The insurance rates for even a class-one Arcane-provisioned vehicle were astronomical, and without the Guild's discount, it really cut into my profits. Not to mention that some of the Arcane Families had decided that doing business with me was too risky while I was under Council censure for not following their dictates.

Of course, that had been inevitable the moment the Council handed down their judgement. It hadn't taken long for word to get out that I was no longer the Council's preferred Transporter. Initially, it was a huge hit to my bottom line, but I wasn't stubborn for nothing. After clawing back my professional reputation and patching it back into shape, I'd managed to restore my earnings to survivable levels by taking a wide variety of jobs from an even wider variety of clients. Over the last handful of months, I'd kept more than busy, which meant less time to sink into the rabbit hole of what-ifs, as I was currently doing.

Granted, there had been a few black moments when I'd given serious consideration to a couple of murky assignments for even murkier clientele, but I'd already learned that lesson once and didn't need a repeat. No sense in tempting fate (again) with something that would make me Zev's, or another Arbiter's, target. Getting on someone's most-wanted list— and not in a positive way—would not be good for my heart on a multitude of levels. Plus, I wasn't a fan of lying to Zev or putting him in any more corners, so I chose assignments that might skim the gray line but never crossed the threshold to black.

That was the most appealing thing about being an independent operator. I was the one who got to decide which jobs I took and how much I was willing to risk for my clients. Not to mention there was something to be said for not having to justify my professional decisions to the Council or document the events with the mounds of paperwork their hoops required. The last few months had been blissfully free of such patience-straining discussions, and honestly, I was over putting my life on the line for a group of people who believed that sacrificing the one for the many was a viable option. An even bigger bonus, my medical copays had all but disappeared.

And that brought me back to my original question—did I really want to be connected to the Council again?

A heavy hand landed on my shoulder, and so deeply involved in my introspective reverie, I startled. Hard.

The weight disappeared, and deep voice said, "Whoa, Rory! Relax, woman."

I twisted in my seat and came face-to-face with a thick-chested, beefy bald man in well-worn jeans and T-shirt with a faded logo of a long-gone gas station. His hands were up in effort to show he wasn't a threat.

"Wheelz, hey." I got up to give the man a hug. "Sorry, didn't see you come in."

His return squeeze was gentle and completely at odds with his appearance. "Obviously." He let me go and eyed me. "You good?"

I waved off his worry. "Totally. I was just thinking about something." My attention shifted to the man standing next to Wheelz. "Hello." I held out my hand. "Rory Costas."

He shook it and smiled politely. "Toby Wilson."

The name rang bells, and once the notes connected, I asked, "As in Wilson's Custom Rides?"

That earned a chuckle. "One and the same."

"Nice, I love your work."

"Thank you."

"Can I get you gents a drink?"

At Cass's question, both men turned to the bar and placed their orders.

I picked up my glass and waited until they were done. "Let's grab a table."

I led them over to a booth on the far wall, where the music didn't drown out conversation. I slid into the side facing the room, leaving the other side to the two of them. I scooted in and set my drink in front of me.

Rather than squeezing in next to Toby, Wheelz snagged a chair from a nearby empty table and set it at the booth's edge. "Thanks for meeting us on such short notice."

"Of course." I didn't bother pointing out that I hadn't expected Wheelz to come with a friend. "Are you two working on something?" It was a logical question, considering Wheelz was a mechanic and Toby's custom designs were all the rage with high-end clients.

"We are, but that's not why we're here."

"Okay." I drew out the word.

"The thing is—"

A server came over to deliver the two men's drinks, cutting Wheelz off. I waited while she did her "Will there be anything else?" spiel and waved off Wheelz's offer to share cheese-smothered fries.

When the server left, Toby resumed the conversation. "I'm in a bit of a bind, and when I was talking to Henry, he suggested that you might be able to help me out."

Henry? It took a second for it to click that he meant Wheelz. My lips twitched because that name did not fit the night racer I knew. When I caught Wheelz's gaze, I mouthed, "Henry?"

He gave me a small headshake even as red slipped along his cheekbones.

I coughed away my humor and asked Toby, "What kind of bind?"

"You know I do custom rides and restorations?" He waited for my nod. "I've got an order I need to get to a client in Vegas, but my normal delivery driver is currently unavailable, and I'm looking for a reputable replacement."

Not that I didn't want the job, but… "I'm flattered, truly, but I have to ask, why me?" I looked between the two men. "There are plenty of drivers out there that would jump all over this." That was an understatement—I was sure Toby had an exhaustive list of people more than happy to get behind the wheel of one of his rides, including the man next to him.

Wheelz lifted his glass and tipped it Toby's way. "Told you that would be her first question, so drinks are on you, buddy." He downed a healthy amount from his glass.

"Yeah, yeah." Toby blew out a breath, sat up a little straighter, and met my gaze head-on. "Normally, your assumption would be correct, but in this case, my client... has... well, he's a bit..." The man was clearly struggling with finding the right words.

Wheelz took over. "Damn, dude, just tell it to her straight. She's good—hell, she's dealt with worse."

My eyebrows rose at that rather-cryptic praise, and my curiosity came to quivering attention, but I waited for Toby to make his decision.

He drummed his fingers against the tabletop for a few seconds then sighed. "Look, my client, who prefers to remain anonymous, is concerned that a professional rival may try to interfere with this delivery since they ended up in a bidding war."

There was a lot to unpack in that statement, but I went with the most important because a lot could go wrong on a five-hour road trip. "Interfere how?"

"I don't know. However they could, I guess."

"Right, that doesn't tell me much, Toby." I shifted in my seat and leaned in to emphasize my point. "I'm trying to determine what threat level I need to anticipate. Would your client's rival stick with being an annoyance or something more substantial?"

He frowned. "What do you consider substantial?"

"On a scale of one to ten, with one being a flat tire and ten being run off the side of a mountain in a fiery crash, where would you rate this run?"

He blinked at me. "Who would rate a simple transport run a ten on that scale?" Thankfully, he didn't wait for my answer.

"I was thinking more along the lines of stealing it. You know, maybe causing a flat or waiting until you stop to fuel up."

I cocked my head and blandly pointed out, "Basically, a carjacking, which, you know, could also end up with me dead."

He shook his head adamantly. "No, no way. They might steal the car, but they wouldn't want you dead. These two are highly respected professionals. They would never go that extreme over a car."

Wheelz snorted. "Brother, that's why they have fancy, high-priced lawyers. That way, shit doesn't stick when it hits the fan."

"Not these two," Toby said. "They aren't the type. I would never put my driver at risk if I thought that was a possibility."

"Good to know." I sat back. "So which car are these two fighting over?" It had to be something good to cause this much concern for Toby.

"A restored 1955 Mercedes-Benz 300 SL Gullwing."

"Mercedes-Benz?" I let out a low whistle, impressed. "There were—what? Only fourteen hundred or so of those made in like three years?"

"Yep, between 1954 and 1957." Toby's smile was small but smug. "But this is one of the twenty-nine that has an alloy body."

Stunned, I blinked. "Original body?"

He nodded. "And the original numbered engine."

"Wow, that's a hell of a find." When it came to classics, finding an intact body, much less the original stamped ID plates that were put on frames and engines, was like finding a unicorn munching grass in your backyard. "No wonder you're not worried about an accident." No one who appreciated cars would dare hurt such a beauty.

He laughed. "Like I said, at worst, they'll try to take it from you before you hand over the keys."

No doubt, because once it got handed off to its owner, that precious piece of history would likely get locked down in a fancy, climate-controlled personal showroom somewhere. *What a waste.* As for me, I wasn't about to pass up a chance at this once-in-a-lifetime opportunity. Excitement stirred. "What's the delivery window?"

"Tomorrow by three." Then he proceeded to name a fee that elicited even deeper excitement from my bank account.

I did a bit of mental rearranging of my schedule. "I can make that work."

"That's great news. I'm assuming manual won't be an issue for you."

"Not at all."

That last bit of his hesitancy disappeared as he sat back with a relieved smile. "Good." We then proceeded to work out a time to meet in the morning so we could review the various business pieces, like the nondisclosure agreement, payment venue, and necessary insurance documentation. In the end, we were both grinning.

When I finally sat back, Wheelz tipped his half-filled glass my way. "You owe me, girl."

I snagged one of the few remaining cheese-covered fries from the plate. "I'll take you out for a nice dinner when I get back." I popped the fry into my mouth.

He dragged a fry through the cheesy goodness, brought it up, and asked, "How about that cordless Milwaukee impact wrench instead?" The fry disappeared.

"Seriously?" Toby asked.

I eyed Wheelz as I chewed and swallowed. After using my Arnold Palmer to wash down the last bits of carbs, I lowered my glass and asked, "With the recharge charm?"

"Oh yeah." An avaricious light hit Wheelz's eyes as Toby shook his head. "Yeah, that would work."

That was an IOU I could get behind. "Deal."

TWO

EVEN THOUGH I had to be at Toby's garage early the next morning, I was still up, camped out on my couch and flipping through channels, when someone knocked on my door as midnight closed in. I popped my head up so I could see the softly lit entryway. The muted snick of the locks had me scrambling out of the comforting confines of my sofa. I managed to find my feet as I heard the door open and felt the brush of magic as the security wards flared in warning. By the time I rounded the couch and headed to the entryway, the wards had gone quiet, indicating they had been deactivated. There were only three people who could do that, and two were shacked up elsewhere.

A contented sort of joy swept through me, and I was smiling as I stepped into the arms of the dark-haired man kicking off his boots in my entryway. "Hey, you."

I waited until he was done before I wrapped my arms around his waist and rose onto my tiptoes to meet him as he bent his head to kiss me. And just like every time he kissed me, I melted. Zev was a hell of a kisser. He started out gentle, sometimes with a lip touch or a soft nibble, then he would coax me inside. Then boom! The next thing I knew, I was caught up in his whirlwind, my hands buried in his shoulder-length black hair and holding on for dear life.

His hands drifted from my hips, along my ribs, then up my spine, where he caught the back of my head in one palm then revved my hormones into overdrive by following up his devastating kisses with a sneaky, but lovely, move that got to me every time. He brushed his lips along my neck and nuzzled in where it started to curve. The soft rasp of his closely cropped goatee and mustache lighting up every nerve ending and igniting a wave of goosebumps as he murmured, "Hey back."

I sank into him with a soft hum of appreciation and arched my neck to give him more access. The hint of sandalwood and spice that was uniquely him wrapped around me, and I curled my bare toes against the cool hardwood floor. "I didn't think you'd make it tonight."

He pressed one more kiss against my neck then lifted his head, shifting his hold until he had an arm around my waist. "Neither did I," he said, shuffling me out of the entryway, "but Locke said he'd finish things up with Emilio."

"That was nice of him." I stepped back and caught his hand as I led us farther into the condo.

Zev grinned as he padded along behind me. "I don't know about nice, but since he owed me one, I had no qualms cashing in."

I stopped by the island counter and looked back. "You want a drink or something?"

"Water's good. Too late for much else."

We let each other go and split directions. He headed to the couch, and I went to the kitchen.

He glanced at the frozen screen and picked up the remote. "What are you watching?"

"Nothing in particular." I grabbed a glass out of the cabinet and hit the ice maker in the refrigerator door. Once the clatter of ice was done, I turned to the spigot in the sink for filtered water and filled it up. "Wasn't ready to sleep, so was channel surfing."

I got to the couch and handed him his glass as the low murmur of the TV regaled us with the latest and greatest must-have gadget.

He muted the TV, took the glass, then settled back into his lounging position in the couch's corner—one arm along the back of the couch and his long legs propped on my coffee table. "How'd things go with Wheelz?"

I stole the remote and hit the off button. "Good, actually."

"Yeah?"

"Yeah." I curled up next to him. "Found out his real name is Henry."

That got me an amused eyebrow lift as he wrapped his arm around me. "Henry? Really?"

I grinned then settled in next to him. "Yep."

"Uh, yeah, I get why he sticks with Wheelz, then."

I laid my head against his shoulder. "He brought along a friend."

Zev's fingers nudged under my T-shirt so he could stroke along my ribs. "A friend? Who?"

I put a hand on his chest and angled my head so I could see him—well, the underside of his jaw—as he took a drink from the glass. "Do you know Toby Wilson?"

"Doesn't ring a bell." He held the glass against the armrest before angling his head so he could see my face. "Should I?"

"Not unless Emilio decided to pick up a classic-car-restoration hobby." That was a hell of a long shot since Zev's cousin was plenty busy leading the intimidating Cordova Family through the shark-infested Arcane waters, chomping on whoever got in his way.

Zev chuckled. "Yeah, that's not a hobby that would fit him."

Curiosity about Emilio sent me on a minor detour. "What would be?"

"For Emilio?" He shrugged. "When we were teenagers, he had a hell of a weapons collection."

That did not surprise me. Zev's cousin was an intimidating force, professionally and personally, so I could see him acquiring tools that matched that persona. Of course, that description could also fit the man currently serving as my pillow. "Arcane or mundane?"

"Both."

I thought back to the last time I was at Emilio's and had dared to nose around in the many rooms that made up his spacious home, but I couldn't remember seeing a weapons collection hanging around. "What happened to it?"

His gaze lifted as he looked over me, his brow furrowed. "You know, I'm not sure." He gave me a gentle squeeze, and his gaze came back to mine. "But I'm sure it's still around."

Hmm, next time we're at Emilio's estate, I'll make sure Zev gets me in to sneak a peek. It would be interesting to see what Emilio thought was worth collecting.

"So, this Toby guy," Zev said, getting us back on track. "He restores classics?"

"Not just any classics." I grinned, unable to hold back my excitement. "High-end classics. He runs Wilson's Custom Rides, and his stuff tends to dominate the car shows each year."

"Wilson's Custom Rides," he murmured. "That actually sounds familiar. I'm just not sure where I heard it."

"Probably from someone who knows Emilio since Toby tends to cater to those with deep pockets."

Humor sparked in Zev's voice as it rumbled against my ear. "You sound a little jealous."

I tilted my head back, my cheek against his chest. "I'm a little green around the edges. His work is beyond stunning, but it's way out of my league, so I'm stuck coveting from afar."

That earned me a chuckle as Zev reached out and tucked a

curly strand of hair behind my ear. "I'm guessing he offered you a job."

I nodded eagerly and pushed up off his chest until I was sitting on my knees, facing him. "Catch this." I curled my hands into his T-shirt as my excitement spilled out. "He asked me to deliver a 1955 Mercedes-Benz 300 SL Gullwing."

His dark gaze studied me, humor lighting the depths. "Sounds like it's the shit."

"Oh my gods, Zev, it's like a freakin' unicorn of classic cars." Because I was such a gearhead, my enthusiasm sent my words tumbling over each other. "These coupes had Sonderteile engines, which increased their two-hundred-and-fifteen horsepower by fifteen, which, back then, was amazing for an inline six-cylinder engine, four-speed manual transmission. Even though they were intended as high-end street rides, they held their own against the racers. This one"—I pushed and pulled on his T-shirt then leaned in—"has an alloy body, and there were only twenty-nine of those made. I think the last one at auction got like four or five million. I never would've thought I'd get a chance to get behind the wheel of a beauty like this."

Zev's smile deepened, and he covered my hands with his, probably so I wouldn't rip his shirt. "I'm guessing you took it."

"Oh, heck yeah. I meet with Toby tomorrow morning to go through all the paperwork before he hands off the keys."

His smile faded around the edges. "Tomorrow?"

"Yep."

"Isn't that a little… I don't know… rushed?"

I wasn't offended by Zev's implied paranoia. I got it. His job as the Cordova Arbiter meant he typically interacted with those with nefarious intents as he doled out judgement and punishment, but this had nothing to do with the Arcane Families. It was just a cool transport job. In an effort to alleviate that suspicious glint in his eye, I explained. "It is, but

Toby said his normal driver ended up in the hospital unexpectedly, and when he was sharing the situation with Wheelz, Wheelz suggested he connect with me, see if I was available."

Zev eyed me for a moment before he relented. "Where are you taking it?"

"Vegas."

"Vegas? Really?"

I nodded.

"Huh."

"Huh what?"

He gave a slight shake of his head. "Nothing."

I knew better than that. I caught his face between my hands so he couldn't look away. "Spill."

His free hand went to my hip as he consciously chose his words. "A car like that, that's worth millions, why on earth would anyone risk it on the open road? Forget about what could happen in the long stretches between here and there, just getting through local traffic would be tricky enough. Why not use a transport company and have a truck haul it up? Wouldn't that be cheaper?"

I managed a half-hearted shrug. "I don't know. Probably."

"So why have you drive it up directly?"

I really needed to convince Zev to take a vacation here soon so he could rebalance his perception of his fellow humans, because his first instinct was to search out potential ulterior motives for every-freakin'-thing. I might not like it, but I understood it, especially after I spent the last couple of years trying to swim with the big fishes, only to be churned into chum. Surviving that had required a combination of luck and Zev's help. I had to admit, even if it was only to me during the darkest depths of night, that I was actually relieved when the Council had cut me loose. The very first thing I'd done was vow to stay clear of the whirlwind drama that typically spun around the Families and their business. It was the only way I could ensure I would keep breathing. "It's not like I was the first choice here, babe. I'm getting lucky because someone got sick."

Zev's gaze narrowed. "And you know for a fact the driver's in the hospital?"

"Okay, Mr. Paranoid, take a breath. This is a transport job for some business hotshot with too much money that likes to collect cars. That's it." My mind kindly pointed out Toby's disclosure about the owner and his rival, which came remarkably close to the kind of Family drama I'd been avoiding, and I flinched the tiniest bit. *Okay, fine, whatever, so there's a good chance I'll encounter a few stray breezes. But it's a 1955 Gullwing for goddess's sake.*

His powers of observation were on point, because he asked, "Uh-huh, so what was that?"

"What was what?" I tried to play innocent, but when he continued to stare at me, I blew out an aggrieved breath. "Fine. There was a bit of a bidding war on the car, and the winner is concerned the loser won't let go gracefully."

All of Zev's humor winked out like a switch being thrown, and the hard-ass Hunter rose to the fore. "How dangerous is this run?"

I petted his chest, knowing my answer wouldn't help, but I was confident in my skills as both a Transporter and a Prism. "It's got some risk, but nothing I can't handle." I held his gaze, letting him see I really wasn't overly concerned. "I'll be fine, Zev."

"If you run into problems—"

I cut him off with a quick press of lips, and when I drew back, I said, "You'll be my first call, promise."

Knowing that was as good as he was going to get, he let it go. "Are you flying back?"

"Most likely." There was no way I was taking a bus, so I would sacrifice a few coffee runs and maybe pencil in a night race to cover the ticket home.

"Text me your flight info once you have it. I'll pick you up."

"Not sure if it'll be tomorrow night or Friday morning," I warned.

"Either one. I'll be there."

I flattened my hands against his chest and leaned in until I was lying along his side, our faces close. I tried batting my eyelashes, which probably looked ridiculous, but still… "Pick me up on your Harley?"

The last bits of grimness drifted away as he tugged on my hair. "I'll bring the Harley, and we'll take a road trip up north."

I grinned. I loved Zev's bike. I loved it even more when he relented and let me drive instead of ride, but I wasn't pushing my luck tonight.

He stopped playing with my hair and drew a finger alongside my jaw, his gaze roaming over my face. When it came back up to my eyes, he switched topics. "You give any more thought to my suggestion?"

It was my turn to study him, and as I did so, I felt his body still. "I have."

His gaze sharpened. "And?"

I settled deeper into him. "I shared it with Lena, and she's considering it."

A few weeks ago, Lena got an offer for our condo, and it had sparked an unexpected conversation. Right now, it was a seller's market in the valley, so she knew she could make bank on it. Good for her, not so much for me.

I got lucky with this place when she asked me to move in when her last horrific roommate bailed with no notice. Lena was one of the top Keys for the Western Arcane Guilds, and her curse-breaking skills were in high demand, a truth reflected in her paychecks. Still, rent on a two-bedroom condo was a bit hefty, even with us splitting the costs, but since my previous apartment wasn't the greatest, I'd jumped all over that offer. A newer place, with tighter security I could never afford on my own, located in the heart of downtown Phoenix, and my bestie as a roomie? Yeah, that had been a no-brainer, even knowing that getting my solo Transporter gig off the ground would keep my finances on the lean side of things for a bit.

That was two years ago, and now, things had changed. The biggest one was my take-home pay. Even with the loss of the Council's fees, I was still in a much better financial position than when I'd first moved in. Granted, there were a few weeks where my business overhead could get a bit daunting, but that was what savings accounts were for. Unfortunately, I didn't have enough set aside yet to make Lena a competitive offer on the condo.

That was where the second-biggest change came into play.

Both of us now had significant others. Lena's lovebug was Evan Fields, the premier electr omage for the Guild who somehow managed to pull off the messy-but-sexy-professor look without trying. Most nights, she ended up at Evan's place in an older neighborhood in the nearby Biltmore area, leaving the condo to Zev and me. The fact that her stuff was slowly migrating into Evan's house was playing a big part in her consideration to sell.

As for my snuggle bunny, he lived with his cousin Emilio in the very spacious Cordova estate at the northern end of the valley. It made his trips to see me a haul. Even when we switched it up and I went to the estate, it was still a challenge, mainly because when Zev was there, a part of him remained "on-duty." As the Cordova Arbiter, his primary objective was to keep the family safe, especially the head of his family. He never really relaxed, and over time, that low-level vigilance took its toll. It was also why he preferred spending time at my place.

I wasn't much better when we were out at the estate. I was never really able to relax either. So when I mentioned my worry about possibly having to find a new place, especially in a market where "affordable" was debatable, Zev had made an unexpected offer to go in with me on a down payment, either for a new place or to buy the condo from Lena. My first reaction was shock, but the more I thought about it, the more I wanted it. Still, I had learned to be cautiously optimistic about huge life changes. Zev had employed some pretty heavy-duty convincing to mute my anxiety enough to give his idea serious consideration.

Zev's voice nudged me out of my thoughts. "Hey, you okay?"

I blinked. "Yeah, I'm good."

He studied me. "You sure? You were thinking about something pretty hard. Did Lena say something?"

I shook my head. "Lena was relieved, actually. I guess Evan's been after her to move in with him for months." She'd kept that from me because she thought I had enough to worry about and she had her own concerns to work through. "She was going to tell him about your proposal tonight."

"So we're doing this?"

"Looks like it." Hearing the words out loud made my pulse pick up speed.

Whether Lena agreed to let us buy or we ended up house hunting, life was about to change in a big way. My experiences with change weren't always positive, which left me a bit leery. I curled my hand until it fisted above his heart. "Are you sure about this?"

"Wouldn't have asked if I wasn't."

No, Zev was not the type to make meaningless offers of any kind. "Okay."

"Okay," he repeated softly, then he leaned up to kiss me.

I got lost in his taste and the hunger that rose at his touch. I buried my fingers in his hair, holding him close as our tongues tangled, and my body lit up like an overzealous Christmas tree. When he finally let me surface, I was breathing hard. My vision was a little hazy, but I didn't miss his wicked smile or the glint in his eye.

He leaned in and softly nipped my lower lip before he pulled back just enough to whisper, "Wanna go celebrate?"

I held on tight and breathed, "Oh, hell yeah."

THREE

SINCE ZEV SPENT THE NIGHT, he offered to drop me off at Wilson's Custom Rides so I wouldn't have to worry about my precious rebuilt 1968 Mustang Fastback making it back to my place. He knew me so well, because leaving my baby unattended would drive me nuts. There was a chance that Toby would have a secured garage I could use, but truthfully, I wasn't the most trusting of souls when it came to my ride, as evidenced by the high-dollar, custom-spelled security system I had installed shortly after winning the pink slip from an overconfident frat brat with more money than sense.

Typically, that would be enough to deter any of the nefariously curious, but there were times, especially during the last six months, when my job took me to some truly sketchy neighborhoods. Those denizens weren't easily scared off, which was why I'd had Lena reinforce it with her uniquely intimidating touch a few months back. Still, the memories of those earlier attempts lingered, which meant I would continue to worry about my baby being jacked instead of being focused on the assignment.

And Zev wanted me focused. Despite my reassurances

last night, he remained unconvinced that this would be a straightforward job, so as we got ready, I did some more feather smoothing before we headed out to brave the steady stream of morning commuters as rush hour was just getting underway.

I gave a silent snort. *Rush hour, what a misnomer. More like rush hours.*

The multiple suburbs that surrounded Phoenix meant traffic was a snarly beast from just after six and typically didn't let up until near ten. It made driving in it a test of patience and luck. On the plus side, it provided justification for an additional surcharge on any contracted job that required dealing with it.

This morning, however, I ignored the headache-inducing crush of cars and let Zev handle it. We managed to sneak in an early-morning coffee run, for which I was eternally grateful, especially since I had a five-hour drive ahead of me. I had tucked my cup of joe into the console's holder and was scrolling through emails on my phone when a text flashed across my screen. Seeing the sender, I flicked over and read it. "Uh, that's wild."

"What?" Zev asked a bit distractedly as he navigated traffic.

My fingers flew over my phone as I typed and talked. "Sabella had a change of plans. Initially, she was scheduled to be back in the Valley on Sunday, but now she'll be in Vegas on Friday then coming home next Thursday."

"I thought she was back east with some kind of advisory board or something?"

"Board of directors, actually," I correctly absently while I texted my great-aunt that, funny enough, I would be hitting Vegas tonight. "Something about a merger in Europe or something."

Just another day in the life of the worldly woman that was Sabella Rossi-Giordano. As the head of the Giordano

Family, one of the original twenty-seven Arcane Families, Sabella was an indisputable force, both magically and financially. In some cosmic twist of irony, she also happened to be my great-aunt on my mother's side, a family connection that I'd only learned about when I started to wade into the Arcane Family waters. Initially, we'd both shied away from being too public with that tie for a plethora of reasons on both sides, as Sabella hadn't risen to her position by being nice and polite. Then, when a narcissistic ex (Zev's, not mine) lost her mind and tried to assassinate the head of another prominent family in front of the Council, that little tidbit came to light, and to this day, I continued to check my rearview for unexpected fallout.

"I thought her son handled the European businesses." He maneuvered around a lumbering school bus caught behind a street sweeper then smoothly slid back into the right lane that branched off to the freeway exit.

"He does." My message left with a soft swish. "But she offered to step in on this side, said it gave her an excuse to visit friends back east. Her words, not mine."

"She needed an excuse?"

"I didn't think so, but what do I know?" An incoming text dinged, and I read out loud, *"Che buono!* Let's make it a weekend. Stay with me at the Four Seasons. I'll switch my reservation to a two-room suite so you can check in before I arrive."

"Is that a request or an order?" Zev merged on to the interstate and fought his way over to the carpool lane on the far left.

I waited until we finished our real-life game of Frogger before I answered. "A request." At least, I hoped it was, because I wanted to spend my weekend with Zev and his Harley. We were closing in on the end of May, which meant the summer's brutal heat was creeping back in with a vengeance. "I'm letting her know we had plans."

I was still typing when he said, "I'll make you a bet that she insists you stay."

"Sucker's bet, babe." I hit Send. "And she'll resort to the tried-and-true weapon of every matriarch ever."

"Guilt?" Zev asked dryly, making me laugh.

"Guilt," I agreed. Three dots appeared on my screen as Sabella crafted her response. "Though I guess I should take it as a compliment."

"Why's that?"

"Because it's exactly how she manages her kids." And those kids were a good ten to fifteen years older than me and just as inclined as the next person to buckle under Sabella's pressure. My text dinged, and I huffed out an amused noise as I read it.

"What?"

Without looking up, I started to type back, but told Zev, "She says you should come join me."

Instead of brushing it off as I expected, he made a soft *hmpf*.

My fingers froze midstroke, and I lifted my head and saw he was watching the traffic studiously. I narrowed my eyes. "What was that?"

He managed a credible blasé "What was what?"

"Mm-hmm." I angled in my seat, resting my phone face down against my thigh as I watched him closely. One of his fingers tapped the wheel absently, but his white knuckles and blatant attentiveness to driving belied his studied indifference. I stifled my grin and asked casually, "Zev, dearest, did you want to go Vegas with me?"

His finger missed a beat, but he didn't look at me as he met my question with one of his own. "If I said yes?"

Truthfully? A road trip with Zev hit the top of my list any time. Throw in the custom classic ride, and it was a shoe-in for best idea ever, but there was his Harley and… "You sure Emilio would cut you loose on such short notice?"

This time, he shot me a look before he rolled his shoulders. Then he flexed his fingers on the wheel and resumed watching the road. "Emilio's not an ogre, babe. Besides, Locke's in town this weekend, and he doesn't do well when he gets bored."

My lips twitched as I thought of the combat mage who was Zev's friend and backup when it came to protecting Emilio's ass. The Locke I knew could laze around a pool with the best of them, making me think boredom wasn't really the issue. "You're doing this for Locke, then?"

He grinned. "Nope, not just Locke's ass I want to keep out of trouble."

It was easy to read between the lines. Instead of taking offense, I folded my arms and mock-glared at him. "Are you insinuating that I'm trouble?"

He chuckled. "Babe, you are a trouble magnet. You hit Sin City, no telling what the hell will follow you home. I'm just offering to tag along to make sure that trouble thinks twice."

There was a smidgen of truth to what he said, which made getting pissed hypocritical. "Whatever." Yeah, it was a lame comeback, but it was all I had.

"All kidding aside..." He got serious. "After what you shared last night, let's just say that I'd feel better if you didn't do this run solo."

I had to admit, having him ride shotgun would be nice. Toby might balk at the idea of truly felonious activity from his wealthier clients, but greed and selfishness had zero to do with what was in a person's wallet. Plus, bonus for me would be getting to spend a weekend away with Zev in a ritzy-ass hotel room I wasn't paying for. I could think of it as a mini vacation. Not that I needed much convincing.

"You should probably let Locke know he's on Emilio duty." I picked up my phone and quickly texted Sabella, letting her know Zev and I would take her up on her offer, no guilt required.

He waited until I was done before asking, "Is it going to cause problems? 'Cause if so, I can meet you up there."

"With who?" I asked absently. "Toby?"

"Yeah."

"Nah, I think we'll be fine," I reassured him, appreciating the offer. "I'll just let Toby know that after the concerns he shared last night, I decided to utilize reinforcements." And if he pushed it, I would point out that having a combat mage of Zev's caliber ride along at no extra cost would tip the odds of a successful delivery in my favor. I downed that last bit of coffee and resettled in my seat as the GPS warned our exit was coming up.

Traffic had increased, which made working our way back across the four packed lanes a trial of patience and courage with no room for conversation beyond "Watch that truck" and "I see it." I didn't dare check my phone again until we hit the less nerve-wracking surface streets. "Sabella's thrilled. She's going to set up reservations for Saturday night for dinner."

"Maybe we can catch a show afterward," he suggested.

That would be way better than hanging out at the tables losing money I didn't have. "Oh! I heard there's a new one that just opened up. Something-something menagerie, I think."

"Don't recognize that name," he teased as he slowed to turn in to a small street that stretched into a series of squat buildings and large fenced lots with an industrial vibe. The buildings were painted in the shades of beige that was the dominant color scheme in the desert. The only real differentiation were the signs above the tinted-glass-door entrances.

"Aren't you the funny one?" I murmured as I leaned forward, checking out the names. When I spotted what I was looking for just beyond the stop sign ahead, I pointed toward it. "There, on the left. See it?"

"Yep." He took the first left that would get us into the parking lot. We rolled down the asphalt and to the end, where Wilson's Custom Rides stretched over the far end of one line of buildings. There was the main entrance, a garage door in a mix of glass and steel and a brick fence with a reinforced gate topped by barbwire right next to it. The parking spots in front were mainly empty, probably due to the time. Zev nabbed one by the main door.

I undid my belt as Zev shut off the SUV and checked the time, noting we were about ten minutes early. "You want to call Emilio and Locke first, make sure things are copacetic before I tell Toby what's happening?"

"Yeah." Zev grabbed his phone and tapped the screen.

I set my now-empty cup in the console then got out. I could hear him talking to Emilio as I shoved my sunglasses up to the top of my head and got my lightweight suit jacket from the back seat. I stood in the back passenger door and used the reflective surface of the dark-tinted window to adjust the steel-gray linen jacket so that it lay smoothly over the deep-red silky shell with the Mandarin collar. I grabbed the battered leather backpack from the floor and swung it onto one shoulder. Ready to go, I closed the door, dropped my sunglasses back down, and went to wait for Zev on the sidewalk. While I waited a few feet from the main entrance, I scratched at a faint, irritating itch. When it didn't go away, I realized it was my Prism's innate reaction to the magic securing the lot just beyond the cement walls and barbwire and forced myself to stop.

Thankfully, Zev made short work of pulling out an overnight bag from the back of the SUV. When he stood next to me, he beeped the locks and gave me a look. "You good?"

I studied his face, but he had his professional blank mask in place, and his dark sunglasses hid his eyes, making him even harder to read. "I'm good. You ready?"

He dipped his chin. "Yep."

Taking him at his word, I led us over to the door. The shop's logo was etched into the glass door, and the hours of operation were listed on a metal sign secured to the wall next to it. The handle was wrapped in padded fabric, a trick many businesses used to prevent their customers from walking away with third-degree burns in the height of Phoenix's summer. I tugged on the door, and it swung open, emitting a two-note chime. I crossed the polished cement floor and headed to the mechanic's table that served as a reception desk.

The man behind it looked up from his computer, caught sight of me, and smiled. "Good morning. Can I help you?"

"Morning. My name is Rory Costas. I'm here to meet Toby Wilson."

"Of course. If you wouldn't mind having a seat, I'll let him know you're here."

I returned his smile with a polite one of my own and turned to head over to the sitting area. I didn't bother to sit, but I did check out the works in progress on the other half of the floor. The second section with the garage door held two cars in various stages of work. One looked to be a newer Dodge Hellraiser, with a deep, dark-green paint job that appeared almost black and had pearlized white racing stripes. The passenger door was open, revealing an interior sans seat and a streamlined console housing the gear stick.

The other project would look much less impressive to someone who didn't know what it entailed. The paint was faded to a dull, dirty white, interrupted by a couple of primer spots and missing pieces. Likely, those pieces were either being refurbished elsewhere in the shop or were on their way in from a supplier. Sitting off to the side was a bench seat wrapped in soft ivory leather, and the color matched what I could see of the headliner inside. It looked to be a late-1950s Chevy truck, and once it was done up, it would be gorgeous.

A door opened along the back wall, and Toby strode

through. He headed toward me, a polite curve to his lips, but when he caught sight of Zev, it faded to a wary frown. He didn't say anything until he was standing in front of me. "Morning, Rory."

"Morning, Toby. How are you?"

"I'm good." His gaze went to Zev, and he held out his hand. "And you are?"

Zev shook his hand. "Zev Aslanov."

The frown lightened but didn't disappear. "Zev, Rory, why don't we head back to my office."

It was clear he had no idea who Zev was but he wanted to ask. I would fill Toby in once we were settled in his office. We followed the shop owner back through the door that led into a much more impressive garage. An amalgam of scents wrapped around me—dust, motor oil, exhaust, and rubber. The magical echoes went from irritating to annoying, but with years of practice, I tucked my reaction away. All part and parcel of being a Prism. Curiosity was actually harder to ignore, but there wasn't time to check out the cars in the garage because Toby was standing in an open doorway, waving us inside.

FOUR

FORTY MINUTES LATER, I was settled behind the wheel of the Mercedes-Benz, wearing a big-ass grin. The passenger door was up, and Zev, his bag over his shoulder, was shaking Toby's hand as the reinforced gate rolled back into place. Toby had not only been cool about Zev coming along but clearly relieved. He lost his earlier wariness and offered to keep Zev's SUV in their secured yard until Locke could pick it up. Zev dropped Toby's hand and started over. Behind him, Toby lifted a hand to me, and I raised mine in return.

Zev got to the car, braced a hand on the raised door, and bent down so he could see inside. "Babe, seriously?"

My lips twitched as I tried not to laugh. "Seriously, what?"

"You didn't tell me I wouldn't fit."

"You'll fit." *Maybe.* I leaned in and shoved the passenger seat back as far as it would go. The Gullwing was a two-seater, and between the raised door sill, vertical-lift doors, and low bucket seats, getting in could be a challenge. For someone over six foot, that challenge was a *challenge.*

He sighed, shrugged his bag off his shoulder, and passed it over so I could stuff it next to mine in the storage space behind the two seats. Then he gingerly folded his long body into the passenger seat while muttering a few choice words under his breath. Once in, he shifted around, adjusted the seat back so his head wasn't brushing the roof, then pulled down the door. He reached for the seat belt and pulled up short when he found nothing.

Trying not to laugh at his disgruntled expression, I settled my sunglasses in place. "You ready?"

"Where's the seat belt?"

"There isn't one." I turned the key, and the car rumbled to life.

"The hell?"

I couldn't stop my giggle. "Car safety wasn't even a gleam in automakers' eyes until the late 1950s. In fact, Mercedes didn't introduce seat belts in passenger cars until 1958, and even then, it was considered an option. But never fear, Toby's client wasn't a diehard originalist." I touched the third knob to the right of the steering wheel and murmured, "Safety saves."

A flare of magic burst bright and sharp, and my Prism shivered in response to the activated charm. Invisible bands slipped from my left shoulder to my right hip and across my waist, holding in me place.

Zev frowned as he was pulled back into his seat. "What was that?"

"A protective charm, basically mimics a safety harness."

He tested the invisible bonds. "That typical?"

"Nope, it's a serious upgrade." It took a skilled Key to create such a spell.

"Right, well, at least it's something." He didn't sound impressed, but he did relax back into his seat. "Am I stuck here until you let me go?"

"Nah. If you touch your waist and say, 'Release me,' it'll unbuckle." I grabbed the tall gear stick, pushed in the clutch, and manually shifted us into Drive. I flexed my fingers on the wheel, and at the same time, I stretched out that innate part of me that made me a Transporter and stroked it over the car.

My magic slid over the mechanical soul of the Gullwing, forging that connection that was so hard to explain. My fingers curled around the narrow steering wheel, and like a switch had been flipped, my mind settled into a crystalline clarity as energy wound from me to the car and back. There was a zing of excitement, followed by the need to move, to test myself against the ribbon of asphalt that spiraled in front of me.

This is what I lived for, this unique space where me and the machine became one. A Transporter's relationship with vehicles utilized magic and inherent skill that slipped into place as easily as breathing. It was instinctive, and it needed to be because it allowed the driver to anticipate at an unexplainable level critical adjustments required to get the best performance from their mechanical beast.

Ready to ride, I rolled out.

⁂

We were passing the exit for Tolleson and about to hit the turn off for the 303 that would link us up to the Phoenix-Wickenburg Highway taking us west into Wickenburg when I checked the rearview mirror mounted on the dash and caught sight of a now-familiar sedan switching lanes a few car lengths behind. "Well, damn."

Zev lost his causal demeanor and came to attention in a blink. "What?"

"We've got a tail." I sped up just enough to get past the work truck on my right.

"Are you sure?" Since space was tight, he didn't bother trying to check the slope of the back window. Instead, he glanced into the side mirror.

"Yeah. It's the gray Civic on the left." I hit my blinker then glided into the middle lane. "We picked them up just after we got on the freeway."

Zev split his attention between the side mirrors—his and mine—and the dash-mounted rearview mirror. "And you didn't say anything earlier?"

"No point since I couldn't be sure it was us they were tailing or they were just heading in the same general direction."

But any lingering doubts were erased once they tagged along with my last few lane changes. They stayed just a couple cars behind, a typical practice, but if you were looking for it, it became obvious.

"You planning on losing them?"

It would be easy to shake them once I hit the surface streets of Goodyear, but... "No point. They know we're heading to Vegas, and it's not like there's a lot of options to get there from here."

"And you want to know what they want," he added, proving how well he knew me.

My lips curved. "I know what they want, but I'm more curious as to what they're planning to do to get it."

"You just can't help yourself, can you?"

"What?" I sank every bit of innocence I could into that one word.

He simply sighed and settled back as I took the exit that curved into the 303. "How high are the odds they'll try something by Wickenburg?"

"If it was me, low to negligible." The highway was two lanes in both directions, split by a wide swath of dirt and broken up by the occasional traffic light. It was long and fairly straight, and there were only a few feeder intersections. But it was nowhere near as desolate as Highway 93, the road between Wickenburg and Kingman. If I was planning on attempting dastardly deeds with no witnesses, I would wait for my target to get past the blip on the map between those two points known as Wikieup before I made my move. "Too many eyes, and it's easy access to phone service."

"You're thinking they'll make their move on 93," he murmured. "No cell service, no cops, minimum traffic."

"Yep."

I kept an eye on our new friends, not making any obvious moves to give away the fact we knew they were there. No sense in spooking them—they would just back off and try again. I would much rather know where they were than be left guessing.

Zev reached back and grabbed his phone, which was sitting on top of his bag. With no glovebox and very little by way of storage or room, it was the only place to put anything.

I waited until he'd finished texting before asking, "What did you do?"

"Called in a friend." He tapped his fingers against his knee. "Or two."

Hmm, not ominous at all. "Do I want to know?"

"Nope."

"Okay, let me rephrase. Do I need to know?"

"You're good." Even though I wasn't looking at him, I still caught the flash of his grin. "Just keep on keeping on. We'll be fine."

That meant our shadows would not. We were coming up on an intersection with a light when he asked, "How fast does this thing go?"

"Top speed is a hundred and sixty."

"Can you hit that quick?"

"Well, there are two hundred and fifteen horses under the hood, so it can go zero to sixty in eight and half seconds." *I might be able to nudge it to seven, but still…* "So not in a snap, but I can get us there."

"You might want to work on that."

Heeding his advice, I slid a little deeper into my connection with the car, coaxing its horses to dig in. Our followers lost whatever subtlety remained and worked to maintain their two-car distance. There was a slim opening ahead that would allow me to slip in front of a semi with just enough space to spare. Our shadows did their best to keep up but couldn't get around the van in front of them.

I took the narrow gap, the rpms ticking steadily upward, and continued to put space between me, them, and the semi. At the same time, I felt the invisible whisper of power as Zev flicked his fingers at the windshield. Just ahead, the green light switched to yellow. I didn't need him to tell me not to slow, and the speedometer's needle continued to creep up with each heartbeat.

We hit the outside edge of the intersection's box when the light flashed to red. Grinning madly, I roared through it, hearing the semi's brakes engage behind me. Safely on the other side of the light, I checked the side mirror and chuckled. The Civic was stuck at the light, caught behind the van and unable to get around because of the semi beside it. I leveled off on my speed as I threaded between the other cars.

"Shouldn't you be going faster?" Zev asked.

"Unless you can do your invisible thing with the car, no."

"My invisible thing?"

"You know, that thing you do where you all but disappear when you're tracking someone."

"Yeah, that doesn't work with a two-ton car going eighty," he said dryly.

I didn't think so, but it was a nice thought. "Bummer." Something fast and bright was coming up behind me, and I caught sight of a low-slung, vibrant-yellow sports car that came out of nowhere and was quickly closing in. "Those your friends?"

Zev twisted his neck and looked back. "Nope."

"Right, then." I found my opening and got out of their way by moving into the right lane behind a battered SUV with out-of-state plates and slowing down. The sports car blazed past me as if I were doing twenty instead of just shy of eighty, and I shook my head as the wake of their passage rocked my ride.

Zev muttered something uncomplimentary under his breath.

"If it makes you feel better, in about three, maybe four miles, we'll be able to wave at them as they argue with the state trooper." With the left lane clear, I retook my original spot and gave the Mercedes its head. The speedometer needle rose steadily, and when it hit seventy-five, I held it in check.

"Speed trap?"

"More than one. Cops like to run this stretch because everyone goes at least twenty over the speed limit while playing leapfrog with the semis. By the time the drivers clock the troopers tucked under the mesquites, it's too late, and there's nowhere to turn off and hide."

"And our shadows?"

"They'll catch back up, but they'll have to play nice until we get clear of Wickenburg."

We both fell quiet, and the only interruptions was the occasional buzz of Zev's incoming texts. As he dealt with whatever was going down on his screen, I split my attention between evading potential tickets and regaining my Civic shadow.

The road went back to two lanes, and while traffic wasn't heavy, there were enough semis interspersed with boat haulers and campers that it kept my speed in check. I came around a soft curve just past a rest stop and eased off the gas. There was no stopping my amused snort when I spotted a familiar yellow sports car pulled off on the side, a silver SUV marked with State Trooper in black behind it.

At the sound, Zev looked up then shook his head as we passed karma doing what she did best.

I had just slid around a slow-moving fifth wheel, when I clocked the Civic. "They're back," I warned Zev.

He checked his side mirror. "Where?"

I drifted to the right so he could see back behind us. "Three cars back, behind the brown SUV. See 'em?"

"Yeah." He straightened and tapped on his phone. "Map's showing orange through the turn to North 93."

"It'll be slow, but nothing like the endless wait if it was Friday." That was when everyone tried to escape the valley and get up to Lake Powell.

"I'm thinking we have… what? Maybe an hour before we hit no-man's-land?" Zev asked.

"Sounds about right," I confirmed.

He typed something out, set his phone back behind me, then shifted in his seat, digging into his pocket.

"What are you doing?"

"Making sure our backup won't miss us." He resettled in his seat, his hand cupping something I couldn't see. "Sorry, babe, but you're going to have to brace."

Since I was driving, I couldn't watch what he was doing, but I sure as hell felt it. Magic filled the interior until the air was heavy with it. The sensation nipped along my skin like fire ants, leaving stinging bites behind. Sensitivity to magic was both a curse and a blessing of being a Prism, and stuck so close to Zev, I couldn't escape the uncomfortable sensation if I tried. With that first wash of power, my Prism slid around me, coming to attention as it held back the press of Zev's magic. Even though I wasn't under attack, tension still locked my jaw and tightened my grip on the wheel until my fingers were bloodless.

"Hurry up," I gritted out.

Zev murmured a phrase I couldn't catch, and the burn of magic spiked then winked out with a startling quickness. He shook out his arm, his hand fisted over the object. "Done."

In front of me, brake lights lit up as we hit the city limits of Wickenburg. I downshifted as everyone started to slow. Next to me, Zev rolled down his window, and air swept through the interior, carrying away the lingering echoes of spent magic. The change in air pressure along with the breeze whipping through the interior had me cranking down my window to level it off before my ears popped.

When my hair started whipping around my face, I caught what I could in my left hand so I wouldn't be blinded and thought I should've pulled it back this morning. I shot a look at Zev to see his hair was doing something similar with the long strands escaping the band at his neck, but he had his arm out and curved up as if holding on to the roof.

"What are you doing?" I asked.

He pulled his arm back inside and opened his fist. "Checking to see if there was someplace I can put this."

I waited until we were passing the fast-food joint with familiar golden arches to glance at what Zev held. It looked like flat clay disc. "What is that?"

"It's a marker. If I can get it on the roof, it'll make it easier for backup to pick up its signal."

Damn, the man has all the nifty toys. "So basically it's a magical GPS?"

"Yep," he confirmed. "I was hoping to get it on the roof."

"Yeah, that's not going to happen." The Mercedes's gullwing design meant there was very little roof space that wasn't part of the door. "Your best shot is putting it just above the windshield."

He ducked down as he tried to look at the top edge of the windshield from the inside. "Where?"

I let my hair go then switched hands on the wheel so I could hold out my right. "Here, give it to me."

He dropped the disc into my hand. "It's active. We just need to get it in place."

Magic buzzed against my palm, like brushing a live wire. I spit out a mouthful of hair that blew into my face, switched the disc to my left hand, then took the wheel with my right. "How do you make it stick?"

"Set it in place and say, '*Luciérnaga pegajosa.*'"

Thankfully, we were going under forty, so when I leaned forward and reached out with the marker, I was able to get it in place just above the edge of the driver's-side windshield in the narrow band of metal that was the frame. I held it in place and murmured, "*Luciérnaga pegajosa.*"

Power flared, and I hissed at the slight burn against my fingers, but I felt the marker lock to the car's frame. I held my breath as I let go, a little concerned the disc would fall off. It didn't.

"Done." I pulled my arm back in, dragged my hair out of my face, then rolled my window back up as Zev did the same on his side. "Now what?"

He pulled out his hair band and regathered his hair to pull it back into a tail. "Now we wait for the show to start."

FIVE

THANKS to the Mercedes's thirty-four-gallon gas tank, stopping for gas wasn't necessary at least until Henderson, so instead of going full-out, I kept my speed at a sedate eighty-five whenever possible. We left Wickenburg behind, and traffic thinned as everyone took advantage of the passing lanes to get ahead of the slower vehicles. I didn't go out of the way to lose the Civic, but I made sure to keep plenty of space between us. They could see us, but if push came to shove, I could hit the gas and leave them in the dust.

For the next thirty minutes, I caught glimpses of the Civic whenever I checked my mirrors, but eventually, the distance between us stretched. I found my place ahead of a couple out-of-state plates and did a mirror check as we blew past the turnoff for the Burro Creek campground. Nothing. No sign of silver anywhere behind me. I waited for the road to curve then did another check, this time trying to see if they were stuck somewhere farther back. *Semi, pickup, van, sedan, sedan, boat hauler... no sign of silver.* "Huh."

Zev, who had been shifting in small increments for the last minute or so, asked, "What?"

"Not sure, but I think our friends disappeared." And that

worried me. *Where the hell would they go? The only things out here are rocks and scrub.*

"Maybe they're stuck behind a truck or something."

"Maybe." But the longer I went without seeing them, the more I doubted the explanation was anything so simple. "Or your backup caught up with them."

"Nope, they're hanging back until I call them in."

That was not what I wanted to hear. Tension crept in and took a seat in my gut. "I don't like this."

"We knew it was going to happen."

"Doesn't mean I'm not nervous."

He made a noncommittal sound as he twisted in his seat yet again.

For a man with infinite patience, especially on a hunt, his twitchiness was unusual. "Zev, seriously, you good?"

"I can't feel my ass."

His grumpy complaint triggered a soft snort of amusement on my part. "I can pull off at the next rest stop if you want."

"Yeah, I definitely want." He adjusted his position yet again. "Did they not believe in padding when they built this thing?"

"It was meant to race, not road-trip."

That was why this little beauty liked to test her drivers. It was light and fast, with good visibility all the way around, but the interior was pared way down. The only drawback, besides passenger comfort, was its cornering. It didn't take me long to realize that to compensate for the rear-axle geometry changes, I had to go hard into corners, lift off the throttle so the back end would step out, then reapply the gas to shift weight rearward and power out of the turn. Still, while it might not be the best for riding, the car was fun to drive.

"Then maybe we should switch positions when we stop," Zev suggested.

"Not going to happen." Spotting a double-trailer semi ahead, I hit the turn signal to move to the left lane.

"Didn't think so." He checked his phone. "Maps says there's a rest area by Wikieup."

"Rest area or rest stop?" I did another check to see if our shadows had reappeared but didn't spot them. However, there was a lifted SUV barreling my way, so I guided the car past the semi and the two slower cars in front before I moved back to the right lane. The SUV roared past.

"There's a difference?"

"Yep, one has bathrooms. One is just a place to pull over."

"Huh, learn something new every day." He studied the map. "Says rest area."

"If you don't need the facilities, I can pull over, and you can walk around. Otherwise, we'll need to wait until we hit Wikieup."

"I'm good with hitting the rest area."

"Got it."

We kept driving, both of us quiet, until Zev said, "It should be coming up soon."

"You sure?"

"That's what the map says."

I was thinking Zev's map was wrong when a small sign indicating a historical marker appeared on the left side, marking a bump out of cracked asphalt that created an artificial shoulder. "No way."

"What?"

I waved a hand at the quickly approaching pullout. "That is the rest area?"

"Looks like it," Zev said. "Let's keep going. I can hang until Wikieup."

Truthfully, even if he'd said to pull over, I wouldn't have. No way would I risk pulling into that with a car like this. We drove on and soon hit Wikieup.

As an unincorporated community sitting on the edge of

lands held by the Free Nations, there wasn't much to it, and most travelers drove through never realizing it was more than a name on a signpost. That included me since my time was usually tight when I was on a run between Phoenix and Vegas, which didn't allow a chance to meander through the temporary shop stall set up alongside the road. There were a couple of the requisite gas stations with restrooms and attached stores that sold all sorts of trinkets and snacks, along with the desiccated remains of what had once housed the popular Wikieup Trading Post Market.

A little farther down were two unimposing restaurants. One served Chicago-style hot dogs that did not fit with the arid landscape or nearby Free Nations lands, and the other had gained a reputation for its homemade pie. Both were hidden gastronomy gems that those in the know didn't like to share, but a couple had shared with me.

It was late morning, heading into lunch, and since we weren't crunched for time and could afford to enjoy our pit stop, I asked Zev, "You want to stop and grab a bite?"

"Are you really hungry, or are you hoping our friends will catch up?"

I could feel his gaze but kept mine on the road even as my lips curved at being read so well. "Both?"

"Mm-hmm." He didn't say anything for a long moment, but he did check his phone again then tapped out a message. When he was done, he said, "Fine. Let's stop, see what happens."

Needing no further encouragement, I decided to head for the pie instead of the hot dogs. Caffeine and sugar, I could do.

I slowed down as we bypassed the gas stations and made our way through the signs of life. Just before the sign for Kingman, I made a left at the stop sign, crossed the highway down to the frontage road, made another left, and pulled into the parking lot that fronted a hacienda-style building complete with wooden support posts and actual hitching posts out front.

Alongside the empty hitching posts, there was a dusty truck, a battered compact, and a newish sedan. On the side, a large truck hauling a speedboat had angled in. Just behind the restaurant was the tall metal structure meant to hold hay, and there was a motley collection of farming and construction equipment scattered behind a wooden, weathered fence.

On the left, before a house half-hidden behind mesquite, was an old windmill and oversized discs decorated with traditional art from the Free Nations. Half-ranch, half-trading-post, and pure tourist charm, its kitschiness drew road-trippers in like honey.

I shut down the Mercedes, released the seat belt charm, and lifted the door. Zev and I met on the wooden planks that lined the storefront. Between the windows and screened-in doors, the adobe walls were adorned with artwork. A peacock sitting at the foot of a statue was ceremonially dressed as a Free Nation member. The peacock watched us with beady eyes, daring us to come close.

"That's a hell of a watchdog." Zev put a hand on my hip, nudging me a little closer to the wall and keeping his body between me and the bird.

"Right?" I murmured back as we steered clear.

I pulled open the main door, which jingled the bell above it. Zev grabbed the door's edge just above my head as we walked through.

"Hello there," a friendly voice said.

Zev's hand landed on the small of my back as I shoved my sunglasses up to the top of my head and pasted on a polite smile. "Hello."

I blinked a couple of times so my eyes could adjust to the light change then blinked again. The wall behind the Formica counter was covered in colorful metal artwork. There were coyotes, hummingbirds, turtles, quail, geckos, and various renditions of suns plastered all over the wall. The only places not sporting the artwork were the service window through which I could see a young man in an apron working in a kitchen, the doorway with swinging wooden slats, and the three framed documents above the coffee maker.

"Hi," Zev said as we moved through the tables set out in front of the counter.

A young family took up the space right next to the clear glass display of pies, and an older couple was settled in a small booth over on the far wall to the left. Just beyond them, a couple of middle-aged men in worn jeans, chambray shirts, and stained straw cowboy hats were enjoying coffee.

My attention went to the right, where a long wooden counter topped by heavy glass held a plethora of pretty, shiny jewelry. The planked walls behind the counter held more discs decorated in local art, along with more wall hangings in colorful enamel shapes of moons, parrots, and the all-too-familiar geckos. Long, ornate belts of leather and turquoise hung just underneath, and gorgeous hand-woven blankets were draped over display rods.

"You're welcome to wander," the clerk offered, clearly reading my interest.

"Thanks," I murmured.

I drifted along the counter, stopping every now then to check out whatever caught my fancy—a thick silver bracelet set with a deep-blue crystal stone, a pair of delicate dreamcatcher earrings of silver and rose gold, and stunning rings for all genders.

I could feel Zev behind me, keeping close, but he let me look to my heart's content, probably happy to stretch his legs. I wandered toward the back of the store, where there was a display of hand-carved animals from a local artisan. I found a stalking wolf carved from polished wood that I couldn't resist and claimed it. I carried it with me as I continued on to look at the gorgeous vases from another artist then the collection of handmade dolls in traditional garb safely tucked inside a locked glass case.

By the time I made it back to the clerk, I was definitely ready for coffee and pie. I set the wolf on the counter and consulted the list of fresh homemade pies posted on the top of the display case.

The clerk picked up the figurine and scanned it. "Will that be it?"

I turned to Zev, who was standing behind me. "What are you getting?"

He eyed the list. "Lemon cream."

Perfect. "Could we get two coffees, a slice of your lemon cream, and banana cream, please?" I pulled out my wallet and got my card.

Her professional smile warmed. "Of course." She lifted the wolf. "Did you want this wrapped?"

"No, thanks." I grabbed Zev's card, which appeared above my shoulder, and stuck it back in his face with a soft "Nope. This is mine."

He glared and opened his mouth, but I gave him a look he knew well, so he closed it.

I handed my card to the now-grinning clerk. She slid it through and asked if I wanted a receipt. When I declined, she handed me the wolf and two stoneware coffee mugs. "You're welcome to help yourself to the coffee over there"—she motioned to the left—"and take a table. We'll have your order out in a minute."

"You have outside seating?" Zev asked.

She nodded. "Yep, just make your way out past the vases, down the short hall to the door at the end. We've got a couple tables set up around the garden and pond. If you want to take a seat, we'll bring your order out."

We thanked her, got our coffees, and made our way through the store. We pushed out the door marked Exit and found a hidden oasis. My steps slowed as a soft hum of magic whispered over my skin, but my Prism remained quiet. There was no threat here, just a little magical gift of scenery. Something this green and lush wouldn't do well in the debilitating heat that scoured the Arizona desert for at least four months out of the year, but add in a little magical help, and what would normally be a dusty, arid backyard would transform into a quiet piece of verdant heaven.

We crossed the planks that made up the back porch and held a couple of tables nestled against the building. Overhead, ceiling fans churned in lazy circles, nudging along the early-fall breeze. We stepped off the porch and followed the gravel path that twisted under tall palm trees and thick-trunk mesquites until we found an oval pond surrounded by a ledge low enough to serve as a bench. In the water, bright flashes of orange glided under broad-leaf lily pads.

I slowed and lifted my mug toward the pond, directing Zev's attention to the scaled inhabitants. "Check out the koi."

We stopped to watch the large fishes swim lazily through the water.

Zev asked, "What the hell are they feeding them?"

I kind of wondered the same thing. "Dunno, but they sure aren't starving."

They were hefty critters, for sure, probably made out like bandits from guests tossing in bits to see them surface. We stood there, mesmerized by the flowing movements of the fishes, shoulders touching, until Zev lifted his arm and tugged me in close.

I switched my coffee to my other hand so I could dig out the carved wolf I had put in my pocket. I held it up to him. "This is for you."

He looked down at me, his eyes hidden behind his sunglasses, a puzzled frown lining his forehead. "What? Why?"

I wiggled it in front of his face, pleased by my unexpected

ability to take him off guard. "Does there have to be a reason?"

His arm at my waist tightened then dropped away as he let me go to claim his gift. "No, I guess not." He took it from me, running his thumb over it as if petting it. "Thanks."

I flashed a grin. "You're welcome."

His answering smile was slow in coming, but he tucked the figurine into his pocket. "Why a wolf?"

Called out, I shrugged under the brush of embarrassment and turned back to the swimming fish. "I don't know," I muttered as I brought my coffee up. "Made me think of you."

He tugged gently on my hair, and I tilted my head back with a frown. "Hey—"

He cut off the rest with a quick press of his lips against mine. When he lifted his head, he teased, "Did they have a roadrunner?"

When I blinked owlishly at him, still under the influence of his kiss, his grin widened. That smug grin cleared the last bits of fuzz from my mind. "I can go back and trade it for a jackass if you'd like."

He chuckled and let me go. "Let's grab a seat, babe."

We claimed a round metal table for two tucked in a grassy area near a couple of wooden water barrels doubling as planters. We took our seats, and Zev stretched out his legs, lifted his arms, and arched his back in a long stretch.

I echoed his audible sigh with my appreciative one, which earned me a knowing smirk. I shook my head, sipped my coffee, and checked out the rest of the garden. A breeze swept through every now and then, keeping things comfortable, and with each passing moment, my shoulders lost a little bit of tension.

It was an eclectic garden, to be sure. Wagon wheels were leaned against wooden rails stretched between posts. Ceramic posts of various sizes were positioned throughout, adding to the garden's feel. Just beyond the shaded oasis protected by palms and mesquites, I could make out the outbuilding that belonged to the everyday operations. Still, it was a lovely spot, made even more so since it was Zev I was sharing it with.

The squeak of door hinges announced that our pies were incoming. A different young woman who shared some traits with the cashier approached with a smile. She set our plates in front of us and assured herself we were good before leaving us alone once again.

I took a bite of my banana cream and nearly moaned when the creamy goodness hit my tongue. *Damn, this is the shit!* Once I surfaced from my initial descent into the sugar euphoria and my brain clicked back on, a few things hit me. I held my fork aloft and shared the first thought with Zev. "You know, they're going to stop. Especially when they see the car out front."

"Yep," he agreed, clearly following my thoughts with ease. "They won't be able to resist."

Okay, clearly this was his plan all along. "The real question is, will they do something to the car, or will they come and confront us?" I dug into my pie for another forkful of goodness.

Zev took his own bite, and a soft sound of appreciation escaped as the tines of his fork reappeared, wiped clean of any evidence of pie. He chased his bite with coffee then answered, "It's going to depend."

I finished my bite as he took another, but when he didn't say anything else, I prodded. "On?"

"How many are in the car shadowing us." He set his fork down, picked up his coffee, and slouched a little more in the chair. "If there's two of them, one will stay with the car, and the other will come in to check us out. If there's only one person on our ass, they'll tag the car somehow."

Since my mouth was full, I made a noncommittal hum as I

studied his profile. As soon as I could talk, I murmured, "I don't know."

He paused with his coffee at his lip and slid me a look. "You don't know what?"

I licked some banana cream off the fork tines. "If your assumption is correct."

His dark eyebrows rode up in that intriguing way that always got to me. "Why's that?"

"Well, first off, tagging the car isn't exactly smart." I set my fork down in an effort to prolong the pastry experience. I leaned in, braced my forearms against the table's edge, and interlaced my fingers under my chin. "They know I'm a Transporter, which means the minute I get behind the wheel, I'd know if it was tagged."

Looking completely unconcerned, Zev shot me a predatory grin. "Which is why I'm banking on them coming in to give us a once-over."

I studied him for a long moment, recognizing the pose. It was akin to a tiger waiting lazily in the high grass for his stupid prey to make its move. I sighed, sat back, and picked up my coffee. "You really think they'd actually confront us here?" I lifted my chin in the direction of the store. "In front of witnesses?"

"I didn't say anything about a confrontation. I said they'd come in and check us out."

There was something in his tone that gave me pause, and I narrowed my eyes over the rim of my mug. "What are you planning?"

"Me?" He gave me mock-innocent eyes. "I'm not planning anything."

My answer was a disbelieving snort. I sipped my coffee because I knew that trying to talk him out of this approach was a no-go. Instead, I should probably enjoy this coffee while I could, because I had no doubt, once we headed back in, shit would hit the fan.

SIX

ZEV and I spent the next fifteen minutes finishing our pies and talking about nothing important. It was a lovely break, despite what lay in wait. When were done, I got up to take the plates back and stopped next to Zev. "You want me to get you a refill?"

"Nah, I'll come with." He pushed out of his chair, and together, we headed back in.

I dropped the plates in a plastic bin labeled "dishes here" at the end of the counter as Zev continued to the coffee area.

"You two want another slice?" the clerk asked as she finished ringing up a sale for a fresh-faced young woman with heavily highlighted blond hair and oversized rhinestoned sunglasses.

"No, thank you. That one hit the spot," I assured her and headed over to join Zev.

I'd just finished pouring when the bell over the door jangled again, and instinct had me looking over as two men walked in. One light, one dark, close in height, both were studiously trying to being casual, to the point that they weren't. The lighter one hid his eyes behind a pair of sunglasses under his short, styled hair. He wore jeans paired with an unbuttoned flannel over his T-shirt. The other kept his dark hair buzzed close his skull and was tucking his sunglasses into his tight-fitting black T-shirt tucked into a wide belt that held up his well-worn jeans. His thick-soled motorcycle boots created a beat across the floor.

The young coed gave the duo an appreciative look as she swept by them on her way out, but they ignored her. They should've been just two more customers stopping in on their road trip to Sin City, but I hadn't missed the glances of both as they clocked Zev and me on their way toward the register.

I immediately dubbed them Goon One and Two before turning back to my coffee. I added creamer and stirred as Zev stood next to me, not bothering to hide the fact he was watching the two newcomers as he sipped his refilled coffee.

"Down, boy," I murmured under my breath.

"Oh, this will be fun," he murmured back, hiding his response behind his mug.

Oh yeah, Zev was jonesing for a fight.

Not inclined to provide a show for the remaining customers, I finished with my coffee prep, took my mug, and led Zev back through the dining room and down the hall to the garden. If he was determined to do this, I needed to minimize collateral damage and witnesses. Instead of reclaiming our previous table, I took a seat on the low wall by the pond with a direct line of sight to the back door. Zev stood in front of me, sunglasses in place, casually drinking his coffee as we settled in to wait.

Before long, the two goons stepped out to join us. Goon One with the lighter coloring took the lead. Goon Two stepped through the door and half turned to pull it closed. Even though Goon One partially blocked my view, I knew exactly what was going on when an irritating abrasion of power nipped at me. Goon Two was spelling the door. Clearly, they didn't want witnesses either.

Tension sifted through the air. I set down my coffee but didn't get up. With a flex of magical muscle, I wrapped my Prism around Zev and myself, holding it at the ready, and left the initial pissing contest to Zev.

"Here." Zev handed me his mug without taking his attention from the two men who were now stepping off the porch.

I set his half-filled cup next to mine as the two began to separate in an obvious attempt to split Zev's attention. I managed not to snort in derision at the obvious ploy.

He was partially turned toward me, his back blocking the fact he was handing me a slim but lethal blade, indicating he thought they might have more than magic up their sleeves. In a low voice meant to carry only to me, he said, "Take this, as well, just in case."

Since his instincts were generally spot-on, I didn't hesitate to take it. When he turned back to the duo, I tucked it under my hip so it was out of sight. Zev remained in front of me, his stance disconcertingly relaxed.

As if that acted as a signal, Goon One slowly paced forward. Goon Two remained at the edge of the porch, his feet braced against the gravel path and his arms folded over his chest, his message clear. If we wanted to leave, we would have to go through him. Little did he know, Zev wouldn't even consider him a speed bump.

Goon One came to a stop about ten feet away, keeping well out of arm's reach. His sunglasses were aimed at Zev, but he addressed me. "You know, this doesn't have to be a thing, Ms. Costas."

Guess we're jumping straight into it. How refreshing.

I braced a hand next to my hip as I leaned around Zev and looked pointedly at Goon Two before meeting Goon One's sunglasses, my image a ghostly reflection in the shiny black lenses. "Doesn't it? Not me playing the heavy here."

His mouth gained a humorless curve as he tilted his head

toward Zev, his voice gaining a hint of condescension. "Thinking you have your own weight to throw around."

Heaving a beleaguered sigh, I got to my feet but kept Zev between me and Goon One as I tucked the blade into my back pocket. Stepping around my silent, self-imposed bodyguard, I took a position at his side. "He's not keen on me talking to strangers, says it courts trouble." I mimicked Goon One's insincere smile with one of my own. "Maybe you can reassure him you're not trouble."

"Not looking for trouble." He lifted his hands out from his sides in the universal sign that he was unarmed. "I'm simply here to pass on a request from my boss."

Uh-huh, and if I believe that, I bet he has a magic lamp with a resident genie to sell me too. "And who would that be?"

"He prefers to remain anonymous."

I just bet he does.

Goon One dropped his hands. "But it's an offer worth considering."

Sure it is. I wasn't a stranger to offers like these, but it amazed me how many people thought money would get them their way. "Let me guess…" I continued to play along, even as the waiting magic slowly suffocated the white noise of birds, insects, and faint traffic until only an anticipatory silence filled the space. "Your boss would like to offer me a cash incentive to hand over the car keys?"

"If I said you were correct?"

At the unspoken threat hovering just under Goon One's pleasant tone, a familiar power joined the party on the magical plane where my Prism waited expectantly for the incoming attack. Outwardly, Zev's stance didn't change, but if his magic were a holstered gun at his hip, his fingers would be dancing over the butt right about now.

I thickened my Prism just a tad more, even as I kept up the verbal game. "I'd have to ask, how much?"

"Fifty thousand."

He stated the amount as if I should be impressed. I wasn't. In fact, I simply stared at him as if waiting for a punch line. When the silence grew awkward, I blinked. "Oh wait, you're serious?"

He frowned. "It's a generous offer."

I held up a hand and shook my head, my lips curled in disgust. "Please, don't be insulting. That's chump change." I dropped my hand then propped both on my hips. "I not only know what that car's worth, but how much my fee is to delivery it safely to someone who is not your boss." I stressed the last.

Goon One's shoulders tightened, and he gritted out, "He'll triple it."

I gave him an insincere smile. "Look, I'm not sure how you and your buddy work, but there's a reason my services don't come cheap. Friendly word of advice—don't sell out, especially for pennies on the dollar. It never ends well."

When Goon One's jaw clenched, I knew my barb had found its mark. I didn't get much of a chance to enjoy my small win, because there was a sudden burst of movement from behind him as Goon Two decided he'd had enough with the chitchat.

Magic hurtled toward me as Zev took a step forward, meeting the attack with one of his own. Power collided, and small magical bullets ricocheted off my Prism. I barely had time to flinch at the stinging hits before a muffled grunt sounded off to my right. I chanced a glance in that direction to see Zev and Goon Two duking it out, magical style. In fact, Zev had drawn first blood with a hit to Goon Two's mouth, which had split his lip and left behind a deep-red mark. Zev dodged what looked like a thick metallic vine that slammed into the gravel, sending up a shower of broken rock.

Gravel crunched under a foot, drawing my attention back

to Goon One, who had raised his hands. A watery globe grew between his palms as he chanted. Pale-colored power churned between his palms until the globe glowed.

Great, I got the casting mage.

And here I was with only a knife. Not about to chance losing my one and only weapon, I thickened my Prism and charged. I got two steps in before Goon One threw his orb of burning water straight at my head. It didn't matter that I knew my Prism was in place. Pure instinct had me lifting my arms to deflect. His aim was spot-on, and the orb hit my Prism at face level, shattering on impact.

When nothing more happened, I dared to lower my arms. Goon One blinked at me owlishly, his mouth open, clearly not understanding why I was still there. He snapped out of his momentary disbelief and started to cast again. I knew I had only a handful of seconds to react. Time slowed as I counted down in my head.

One.

I took a step.

Two.

Then another, gaining speed.

Three.

The distance between us shrank rapidly.

Four.

I reached out, my fingers just inches away, when something coiled around my ribs, whipped around my hips, and yanked me back and off my feet. A squeak of surprise escaped as I was hauled through the air so fast my hair streamed around my face, turning the world into a dizzying blur.

There was shift in my movement, and the ground dropped away. My breath stalled as I was jerked this way and that, bumped up until sky filled my vision. Then I dropped back with a sickening speed that smeared the world around me. I was trying to find air to scream when I slammed into the koi pond.

In something close to a miracle, I managed to capture a lungful of air before water closed over my head. Whatever line I was hooked on dragged me deeper into the damn pond than the actual hole could possibly be. It had zero logic, which didn't mean much when I was borderline panicking.

Those invisible bands tightened with brutal intensity until I was sure my ribs would snap. Just when I was about to risk opening my mouth to scream out my pain, my magic shifted as my Prism kicked in with a vengeance, wedging itself between me and the magical restraints.

Magic surged into a concentrated blast, forcing the pressure to take a step back. The sudden relief made me sag, and I fought back the urge to suck in much-needed air. Instead, I thrashed around, my frantic movements turning the water opaque with bubbles and silt, but eventually, I got my arms free. I clawed at the bands still coiled around my hips and legs and was almost free when a large shadow zoomed out of the curtain of bubbles.

I jerked back, my hands up as I kicked free of the last of the binding spell and barely managed to roll out of the path of whatever was incoming. All I could make out were dull orange scales the size of my hand on a body much larger than mine. Weight slammed into my back with bruising force, causing me to lose precious air. Gray teased the edge of my vision, my heart pounded, my head pulsed, and my need for oxygen was critical. Something heavy crashed into my hip, and it clicked—I was being mosh-pitted by the damn koi. Before sanity handed the keys over to blind panic, it took one last shot at survival and screamed at me to kick, and kick hard. I shot up toward what I hoped was the surface, even as I kept an eye out for whatever was circling back around.

It was surreal what went through my brain as the last of

my air puttered out. The biggest question was how in the hell did a pond turn into a lake?

Another flash of orange triggered a visceral response, propelling me a few feet closer to my goal. I twisted in the water and barely managed not to gape.

Holy shit! The koi had tripled in size.

Adrenaline rushed through my veins, drowning out logic and leaving me in a bizarre underwater bubble. My brain stalled, and my lungs screamed for air, but my arms and legs kept up their desperate churning. It took me by surprise when my head broke the surface, but at least when I gasped, it wasn't water that filled my lungs but precious, beautiful air.

My chest ached as it frantically worked to restock on oxygen. My stomach rebelled, until I was doing a strange mix of coughing and gasping, all of it resulting in a harsh bout of coughing. I didn't know when things shifted, but it struck me that the koi circling me might make great fillets. None came close to the monster that had tried to make me its snack, though. On top of that, the pond lapped at my waist as I sat on my knees in the shallow, reed-choked waters.

Desperate to get the hell out of there, I crawled to the ledge and dragged myself out of the stinky water, coughing and sputtering the entire way. When my ass was sitting in the dirt next to the ledge, I couldn't help but check the churned-up waters to make sure that gargantuan koi wasn't about to resurface and turn me into dinner. All I found was a simple koi pond, though. No water portal to prehistoric hell in sight.

What the ever-living…?

Stunned by the incomprehensibleness of it all, my mind stuttered. Shoving aside the disconcerting insanity, I turned away and saw Zev looming over an unconscious Goon One, who was crumpled at his feet.

Okay, one threat down.

I searched the area for Goon Two. He wasn't hard to find. In fact, he was currently pinned against one of the painted oversized discs meant to showcase Free Nations art near the fence. The thick ropes that created the painted weave now bound him to the metal-framed disc, and he was clearly down for the count based upon the fact he wasn't moving and his head lolled forward.

Since Zev had things under control, I braced my palms against the rough surface of the ledge and got to my feet. Rivulets of water seeped from my clothes and over chilled skin. Something slimy slid from my hair and plopped against the back of my shoulder. I gave a violent shudder as I batted it away, and a clump of sludgy reeds hit the gravel, joining the growing puddle at my feet. A breeze drifted through the leaves overhead and curled around me, bringing a whiff of rotten-egg stench. *Lovely!* My lip curled even as another shudder ran through me.

"You okay over there?" Zev asked.

No, not particularly. I needed a shower and clothes. "Yeah," I muttered as I made my way to him, occasionally risking a glance back to make sure the koi stayed put.

"Good." He took me at my word and motioned toward Goon One's boots. "You want to grab his feet for me?"

With a sigh, I bent over, grabbed Goon One's heels, and waited for Zev to get his hands under Goon One's pits. "Where are we putting him?"

Zev used his chin to indicate a spot over to our left. "See that shed?"

I looked past him and spotted the dingy metal shed that had seen better days. "The one just past the fence?"

"That's it." He waited until my gaze came back to him. "Ready?"

I used my shoulder to wipe away a trickle of water above my eye and adjusted my grip on the boots. "Go."

We both lifted at the same time, and together, we hauled the limp body of Goon One across the yard. We weren't careful, and even though he groaned once or twice, he didn't rouse. We got to the fence, then it was my turn to drop his heels and duck between the split rails so I was standing on the other side. Between the two of us, we got Goon One through the fence and inside the stuffy metal structure. Taking up most of the interior space was a lopsided wheelbarrow propped against the right side filled with a crumpled tarp that had seen better days. The other side held a collection of rusted, dust-covered tools covered in cobwebs and what looked like engine parts. Not the car kind, more like equipment type. With a bit of juggling, Zev pulled out the tarp, and we dumped Goon One into the wheelbarrow. We made the return trip to retrieve Goon Two.

Zev fisted his hand in Goon Two's T-shirt then released the magical bindings. His body slid to the ground. Zev's grip was the only thing that kept him from adding another bump to his facial decorations. His lashes fluttered as he started to come around, but Zev moved quickly and shifted to a choke hold. Once Goon Two was back in la-la land, we did a repeat of our previous trek.

By the time we stuffed him next to his buddy, sweat had replaced pond water, and my skin had collected its own layer of dirt and grit. I stood outside the shed while Zev tossed the tarp over both goons then came back out and cast a lock spell on the shed.

I pulled at my clinging mess of a shirt, trying to find some sort of relief from my discomfort. "How long will it hold?"

He traced one more rune over the door and blinked away the blue glow that infused his dark eyes. "Long enough for it to be an issue to catch up with us."

He turned, and together, we headed back to the garden. Between the damp and the dust, things were starting to chafe. Zev muttered a curse, and I looked over to see him swipe at a seeping cut just over his eye, smearing blood and grime over his skin.

I grabbed his wrist, bringing him to a stop. "Stop it. You're making it worse."

He rotated his wrist until he was holding my hand then lifted it just enough to raise my arm. "You're one to talk."

I grimaced. "What the hell happened?"

"You mean the fish attack?"

"Yeah, and the pond that was bigger on the inside than it looked."

His lips twitched. "If I had to guess, I'd say it was some sort of divergent spell."

Not really up for a magical lesson on spell crafting, I groused, "Whatever it was sucked."

"I bet."

We started to walk again, and after my third squelching step, I asked, "Did you catch where the bathrooms were in there?"

He shook his head. "I don't think a bathroom is going to cut it for you, babe, unless it has a shower."

I eyed the building ahead. "Yeah, I don't think we're going to get that lucky." We ducked back through the split-rail fence then wound our way through the gravel path and to the wooden slats of the porch. "Maybe they have an industrial sink."

We stopped just under the eaves, and it hit me that whatever spell work Goon Two had in place earlier was now gone. There wasn't even an echo to ruffle my Prism's feathers. Thank all that was holy no one had decided to come out and enjoy the garden during our little tête-à-tête with the goon squad.

Zev used his fingers to swipe at his cut. "We can ask."

I stood next to him, unable to escape the stench wafting from my ruined clothes. My nose wrinkled as I looked him over. A thin layer of dust and a few smudges of dirt decorated his jeans and T-shirt. Along with the cut above his eye, red marks heralded incoming bruises along one cheek and half-hidden by his close-cropped beard along his jaw. Still, he was in better shape and less likely to raise eyebrows than me. "Probably best if you go in and ask. I can wait here."

He reached for the door. "Clothes?"

"In my bag in the car."

"Got it." He held out a hand. "Keys?"

I dug them out of my pocket and handed them over.

He pulled open the door. "I'll be back."

I waved him off. "I'll be right here. Waiting."

SEVEN

ZEV DISAPPEARED INSIDE, and I shuffled over to pull a metal chair out from one of the small tables. I sat down, and the moment my ass touched the seat, my muscles rejoiced. I braced my elbows on the table and dropped my head into my hands, enjoying the momentary reprieve.

What a cluster.

Even though I anticipated running into problems, I hadn't thought they would try to take me out in public. Then again, the fact someone would make such an attempt over a car, no matter how sweet it was, left me shaking my head. Though it shouldn't have been a surprise. The idiosyncrasies of those with more money than sense was beyond me, but there was no doubt that whoever this rival was, they were used to getting what they wanted without fear of reprisals.

Lovely. Just what I need, another arrogant jackass with entitlement issues.

I sighed and hoped Zev wouldn't be long. We needed to get cleaned up and back on the road ASAP, especially since Toby had indicated there was a delivery deadline. The thought barely finished when I sat up abruptly and shot my hand into my side pocket where I had stashed my brand-spanking-new cell. A plethora of curses ran through my head as I pulled it out along with a desperate prayer for a minor miracle as I thumbed the screen. Amazingly, it lit up, seemingly fine.

"Yes!"

The waterproof rune I'd paid extra for had worked, apparently. I couldn't wait to crow about it to Lena, who gave me such grief for going overboard on protection wards for my phone. Considering how much trauma my last one had endured and the resulting hefty replacement cost that had followed, I had no problem shelling out for serious aftermarket protection charms—which, since it seemed relatively unscathed after its encounter with the koi pond, had been worth the investment.

I checked the time then calculated cleanup and remaining road time. As long as we pushed a few speed limits and the two idiots were the worst this mysterious rival was going to throw at me, we should still hit Vegas with time to spare.

I left the phone on the table and dug out the rest of my pocket's contents. A hair tie that I would be using as soon as I got rid of the pond scum, my wallet (which would have to be replaced since leather never survived being drowned), a soggy pack of gum now destined for the trash, and my lip balm. I dumped the gum in the bin sitting under a tree.

I was missing something. I looked around and patted my pockets then my tangled mass of hair as my mind did a mental checklist. It stalled at *sunglasses*.

Right.

I left my little pile and phone on the table and retraced my path to the pond. I really hoped they weren't swimming with the fishes. Luckily, I spotted them lying in the gravel, where they must have fallen during my struggle with Goon One. I picked them up, happy to note there was nothing but dust on the lenses. The back door swung open as I retraced my steps to the table.

Zev stuck his head out and spotted me. "Come on. Stacy said we could use the employees' bathroom at the back."

"Stacy?" I grabbed my stuff from the table and joined him in the doorway.

He stepped back and held open the door for me. "The clerk. She said this business has been in their family for a couple generations." He proceeded inside and back down the hall. "Initially, her grandparents set up the store in the front part of their house. Over the years, when they needed to make room for family, they added on to the initial homestead. When her parents took over the store, they expanded the store to include the restaurant and moved their family into a new home they built in the back acreage when she was ten." He stopped at an unassuming door, used a key I hadn't noticed to unlock it, and disappeared inside.

I came up behind him as he strode through a narrow hall barely wide enough to fit his shoulders that was clearly part of the original homestead. An abstract pattern of shadowed echoes dusted the faded ivory walls, indicators that at some point in the past, they had been covered with a plethora of picture frames. He made a right, and I rushed to keep up.

The hall opened into a kitchen done in shades of decades past. The initial gold had become a dingy yellow. Even the fridge was done in the same color. The only difference was it had a handwritten sign taped on the front, warning, "If you didn't bring it, don't eat it!" A coffeepot rested upside down on a drainboard, along with a couple of mugs and spoons. Clearly, this was where staff took breaks.

We crossed the faded linoleum to another door near the back. For a moment, I wondered if he was leading me back outside, but when I followed him through, I realized that the original space had likely been a mudroom but now held a narrow shower in the corner, a toilet, and a pedestal sink complete with separate knobs for hot and cold. Despite the obvious age, everything was clean and neat, including the towels Zev was pulling out of a cabinet above the toilet.

He set them on the back of the tank then motioned to the other door on the far side. "Stacy said when you're done, you can just dump your towels in the washing machine through there."

I sat on the toilet's closed lid, bent forward, and started working on getting my boots off. "Dare I ask how you explained my need for a shower?"

"I shared that a couple of her customers got a little rowdy and accidentally knocked you into the pond." He came in close enough that his thighs brushed my shoulder, and he reached above me. "She wanted to come out and reassure herself you were okay, but I convinced her it wasn't necessary, that I'd taken care of it."

I looked up as he pulled a washcloth out of the cabinet. "She's probably worried about liability." I toed off my boot and peeled off my damp sock, wiggling my toes against the cool floor.

He shrugged as he turned to the pedestal sink, turned on the faucet, and ran the cloth under the water. "Or maybe, little miss pessimist, she was concerned about the well-being of her customer." He started scrubbing his face, a soft hiss emerging as he hit some of the open cuts.

Unable to sit and watch, I got the other boot and sock off then pushed up to my feet. I reached over and tugged on his arm. "Give me that."

"What?" He frowned at me.

I grabbed the cloth from his hand and ran it back under the cold water. "Did you tell her about her uninvited guests in the shed?" I turned back to him and grabbed his chin so I could angle him where I needed him. His dark eyes lit with a slight bafflement as, with much more care than he had used, I started to wipe away the grit and blood from his face.

His hands went to my hips, their warm weight comforting. He stared down at me and blinked. "Babe."

I stopped dabbing at his split lip and held up the cloth as my brows rose. "What?"

His gaze went to the washcloth then back to me. There was no missing his mix of amusement and warmth at my Florence Nightingale behavior.

I could feel blood rush to my cheeks. Flustered, I turned to rinse the cloth and muttered, "Whatever."

He chuckled but didn't drop his hands. "I told her the two idiots took exception to my request to knock it off, so I put them in her shed in a time-out."

I twisted back around to finish what I started, my fingers sinking into his beard to hold the uninjured side of his jaw at an angle as I cleaned. "And she was okay with that?"

"Not like she had much of a choice about it. It was already a done deal."

True enough, and it wasn't like they were dead, just out for the count. I sincerely doubted they would be filing a police report. I got the last bit of grime cleared and eyed what remained. "She didn't happen to have a first aid kit around, did she? We could use some ointment for your lip."

His hands squeezed my hips then gently nudged me back a few inches. "How about you get in the shower, I'll ask, then go grab your bag so we can get out of here before the two idiots in the shed wake up and start making a ruckus."

"Fine." I turned to the sink, rinsed and wrung out the washcloth, then folded it over the edge.

Zev went to the door and started through, only to stop when I called his name. His head came back through the door. "What?"

"Bring back the Neosporin."

"Aye, aye, captain," he drawled then closed the door behind him.

Once alone, I made quick work of getting out of my

clothes and into the tight confines of the shower. I went to work on my hair, and it took three rounds with the shampoo before I was satisfied that I wouldn't reek of eau du pond scum. The rest of me didn't need much more than a quick scrub and rinse. However, I did find a couple of lovely bruises coming up along one thigh and up high by my ribs. I was reaching for the towel when the doorknob rattled in warning. I whipped that rectangular terrycloth around me and barely got it tucked into place before Zev came in with my bag.

He set my bag on the toilet seat then turned, trapping me between him and the shower. The air between us took on weight as my hands went to his chest and my head fell back to watch him watch me. The low simmer of hunger warmed, adding a husky quality to my response of "Hey, you."

"Hey back." His voice was the quiet rumble that I'd come to adore. There, in the slightly steamy confines of a roadside diner bathroom, he traced one of my curls down to the edge of the towel that was wrapped around my chest, then he continued to follow that line, his finger leaving a trail of goosebumps in its wake on my damp skin.

Even knowing this was so not the place or time for such things, I couldn't stop my fingers from curling into his T-shirt as my body leaned into the warmth of his. "Zev." His name came out softly, but even I didn't know if it was a protest or encouragement or both.

His finger left the towel, trailed up to my chin and tipped my head back so I could meet his lips as they covered mine. His kiss was gentle and strangely comforting, something I hadn't realized I wanted or needed until he gave it. Maybe it was because the attack had left me a little more off balance than I realized. What little logic remained shimmied away as I followed his lead, taking and giving comfort and reassurance.

When he finally pulled back, I blinked up at him as my body did a mellow happy dance at his touch. "Um…" was the extent of my brilliance.

His slow grin held a tinge of wickedness. "Hurry up and get dressed before we get in trouble."

I bit the edge of my bottom lip as my brain slowly cleared. "I kind of like the trouble we were finding."

"We'll indulge in a longer visit later," he promised.

Sighing, I rescued my towel. "Fine." I held out my hand, palm up, and wiggled my fingers. "Hand it over."

He dug the Neosporin out of his back pocket and passed it over so I could play nurse. Once I was satisfied he was safe from flesh-eating bacteria, I gave it back and shooed him out so I could dress. He grinned as he left, and I hustled into a clean pair of jeans and a T-shirt. Not my normal business attire, but it would work.

I found a crumpled plastic grocery bag tucked in the side pocket of my backpack and used it for my damp clothes. I should probably just burn them, considering the lovely pond stench they sported, but there was a slight chance they were salvageable, so I tied up the plastic and shoved it into an outside pocket of my pack

Then I went to work braiding my clean but wet hair. After wrapping the tail end with my hair band, I crossed the tile in sock-covered feet and dumped the used towels in the washing machine that was barely younger than the kitchen. I tromped back to the bathroom, where I stuffed my feet into my still-damp boots but left the laces undone so I could kick them off in the car. It would probably take most of the remaining ride for them to dry out. Finally done, I picked up my stuff and headed back out to face the world.

Zev was waiting for me in the kitchen. "Here." He shoved a to-go coffee cup into my free hand. The contents inside were hot enough to heat my palm.

"Thanks." I blew across the top and took a testing sip. The blessed java juice chased away the last bits of chill as Zev finished with a text. *Which reminds me...* "Hey, whatever happened to your backup?"

"Oh, they'll be here shortly." He tucked his phone into his back pocket. "They managed to divert the second car that was tailing us, so I asked them to pick up the trash if it was still hanging around."

"Nice of you." I sipped my coffee as we headed back through the halls and out to the main area of the store.

We spent a few minutes thanking Stacy for her help and hospitality before waving our goodbyes. I got outside, shoved my sunglasses on to combat the bright light of the sun, and clomped over the wooden planks that made up the front porch of the store. Four cars besides ours were lined up in their spaces. I spotted a familiar sedan at the end.

I stopped just before stepping off the porch. Zev came up to my side, and I held out my bag. "Can you put this in the car for me?"

He took its weight from me and hoisted it over his shoulder. "Going somewhere?"

"Nope, just making sure our friends stay put for a bit."

"Make it quick." He started for the car.

"That's the plan." I headed for the silver sedan, my loose boots chafing my heels with each step, creating an irritating reminder of my unanticipated swim. Temper on a slow burn, I got to the car, loosened the reins of my magic, and ran my hand over the hood while slowly walking around it. I didn't have to be a driver to forge a connection with a vehicle—there just had to be a reason, and today, I had one. *Besides, Zev's cleanup crew shouldn't make a trip out here for nothing, right?*

Magic was a funny thing. Not only was it will-based—meaning the more stubborn a person was, the better mage they made—it relied on skill and instinct, not logic. However, it came in a few flavors, with the Arcane Families cultivating their bloodlines to capitalize on their specific magic types.

The big three fell under Elemental, Mystic, and Divine. The majority of the Arcane mages could link their magic to the elements of fire, water, earth, and air. Then there was the next group, who were all about psychic-based abilities. That was where I stood as a Transporter and Prism. It also made me a dual mage, and I wasn't the only one. Zev held that honor, as well, playing in both classifications as an animal mage and a combat mage. The last group was very small and belonged to those who gained their abilities from their chosen deities. I'd only met a couple, and each run-in made me very happy to be a Mystic mage, even one as rare as a Prism.

However, being a Prism wouldn't help alleviate my irritation with the Shed Twins, but being a Transporter? Oh yeah, that was going to come in real handy.

I decided to work out my frustration on their mode of transportation and circled the vehicle, keeping one hand in constant contact, first with the roof then the trunk as my magic locked on to the car. It washed over the engine, tasting fairly fresh oil, slightly dirty transmission fluid, a decent electrical charge in the battery, and the dull ache that came from an overabundance of miles. The tires were in fair shape but could use a rest, and the brakes were getting close to life. All were the familiar signs of a well-used but decently maintained rental.

I took my time getting to know the sedan and found my opening—a weakness in the timing chain. A slow grin curved my lips as I paused on the passenger side of the hood and considered my options. I could add a little pressure to the weak point of the chain so the dastardly duo would find themselves stranded on the lonely road to Vegas, or I could ensure it broke when they went to start it up, crippling the suck-squeeze-bang-blow process needed for a healthy engine start.

Choices, choices, choices.

It wasn't compassion for the two idiots in the shed that had me flexing my magic, torquing the tension on the chain until it snapped, ensuring they wouldn't be driving anywhere anytime soon. It was because severely damaging a car, which would happen if they were doing seventy-plus when the chain snapped, didn't sit well with me. Better the car be stuck here, in the middle of nowhere, where it would take time, money, and luck to get back up and running.

Magic pushed, and the chain snapped. I gave the sedan's hood a sympathetic pat. "Sorry, but it's better this way."

The Shed Twins could get lucky and find a mechanic to replace the timing chain, but it would cost them quite a few pretty pennies, and it wouldn't be a fast fix. In fact, it would cost them time, lots of time. Time I could use to put distance between us. Even if they abandoned the car, they would be stuck here until either a ride showed up or they risked pissing off fate by stealing one. It was up to them which way to roll.

Satisfied we wouldn't have to try shaking our shadows again, I headed back to the Gullwing, where Zev waited with passenger door up. When I got close, he asked, "We good?"

"We're good," I promised as I opened my door and got behind the wheel. I toed off my boots and, with some judicious wriggling around, pulled them out from underfoot and set them back behind the seats with our bags. Then I pulled the door down and got back to work.

EIGHT

IT WAS after two o'clock when we hit the clogged streets of Las Vegas and started inching our way along Las Vegas Boulevard. Despite being stuck in a box made up of a tour bus, two taxis, a small RV, and a purple Lamborghini Huracán Sterrato, we still managed to gain two car lengths after sitting at a light while swarms of humanity spilled through the intersection as they darted between hotels. Since we weren't in danger of moving anytime soon, I grabbed my phone, pulled up the number Toby had given me, and sent a text confirming we were close. The delivery address was smack-dab in the middle of a very large golf course, but to get there required running the gauntlet of the tourist-choked strip.

Zev was drumming his fingers against the ledge of his door, wearing an aura of impatience. "This is nuts."

"This is nothing." I handed him my phone. "In a couple of months, when summer officially sets in, you'll be lucky to get through this area in under an hour."

"Like I said, this is nuts," he groused. He checked my phone. "According to this, you want the next right."

In front of us, a truck with a huge billboard touting the

latest show was making its way through the intersection when a yellow taxi cut in front of it. The truck's brakes squealed as driver punched his horn, and the surrounding drivers picked up the call, adding to the wall of noise. The wave of pedestrians didn't slow, but heads turned, and a few of the more inebriated walkers added their voices to the din.

Welcome to Vegas.

The light turned, and traffic surged forward, forcing those on foot to rush to the safety of the sidewalks. We moved along the current, and I caught a break. I snuck between a motorcycle and a Jeep just in time to make the upcoming right that would get me off this amusement ride. Zev continued to play GPS as we made our way to the delivery point. The directions took us behind one of the casinos and down a back road. I knew we were close to the end only because a wrought-iron fence followed us on the left and guarded a high block wall determined to keep the masses from spoiling the greenery on the other side. The road ended at a gate complete with security.

The guard, wearing a gray suit and sunglasses, stepped out of his hut as I came to a stop.

"Need your license," I warned Zev as I reached back to dig mine out of my bag. When I had it, I rolled down the window.

Zev shifted in his seat, pulled out his wallet, and handed over his license.

I took it and waited until the guard closed in before greeting him with "Afternoon."

"Good afternoon." He returned my polite smile, his head angled so I caught sight of his earpiece. "May I help you?"

"Yes, My name is Rory Costas. This is Zev Aslanov." I handed over both our IDs. "We're with Wilson Custom Rides in Phoenix. I believe we're expected?" At least, I hoped so, because I didn't have a name to share since the new owner was still incognito.

"One moment." The guard went back to the hut, his hand coming up to his ear, and he spoke in a low tone I wasn't able to make out. He obviously got the reassurance he needed, because we didn't have to wait long before he was back. "Ms. Costas, Mr. Aslanov, please proceed up the drive and take the second left to the pavilion. You'll be directed to the members' garage." He handed back the licenses as the gate ahead started to roll back.

I handed off both licenses to Zev as I thanked the guard.

He inclined his head. "Of course."

I waited until the guard stepped back to put the car in gear, but I didn't move until the gate was fully opened. I followed his directions up the winding drive, and at the indicated left, I waited for a golf cart to putter across the entrance before rolling forward into the shaded members-only garage. To the left, a ramp disappeared at a downward slope, indicating there were multiple levels beyond the two we could see. To the right was a smaller parking lot roped off with an actual velvet rope strung up between black posts and a sign that read Members Only.

I rolled closer, and we were met with a young twenty-something in a collared shirt, pressed shorts, and a too-white-to-be-natural smile. "Hello, Ms. Costas. If you wouldn't mind parking in number six?" He motioned to the right. "It'll be the third spot in."

I left my window down while I all but coasted into the parking spot as a valet closed the distance between their podium and us. Once we were in place, I rolled up my window, released the restraint ward, and half turned in my seat. "Can you grab our stuff while I get this handed off?"

"Yep." Zev opened his door and kicked out a leg as the door rose above him.

I opened my door, pushing it up and helping it rise, when the valet's hand came out. I got out of the car and was met with another professional smile in a face closer to my age. "Ma'am."

"Thanks."

"Can I assist with your bags?"

I motioned to Zev, who was on the other side, dragging out one of our bags. "He's got it."

The valet stepped back. "Of course."

I scanned the small parking lot, hoping to spot whomever I was supposed to meet. No such luck. Besides the valets and an older couple making their way to the glass doors that guarded the hallowed halls of the country club, we were the only ones in the lot. Those doors slid open, disgorging a rush of air that caused the couple's clothes to flutter and a soft clamor of activity to spill out. The male half of the couple was letting his female companion step in first, when he pulled up short and moved aside to let two men pass by.

The duo beelined in our direction, so I moved out of the driver's-side door and around the car's hood to join Zev. The one in front was dressed in pressed slacks and an open-collar shirt. He was the picture of casual yet professional, but I had no doubt it was all very tailored. Right down to the... I double-checked his choice of footwear... *Are those loafers?*

Yes. Yes, they were, complete with that silly leather tassel. I managed to cover my irreverent snort by clearing my throat. I bet ten to one that this was our new owner.

Sure enough, he stopped in front of us and offered me his hand. "Ms. Costas, Mr. Aslanov, welcome."

I took it and murmured, "Hello, Mr....?"

He cocked his head. His brow furrowed, then it cleared. "Right, yes, the anonymity clause." His smile was there and gone. "Virgil." He let me go and held out his hand to Zev. "Virgil Hathaway." He released Zev's grip and rubbed his hands together. The afternoon sunlight glinted off the thick ring wrapped around his right pinky. His attention homed in on the car behind us, and his features took on a covetous gleam. "Did you have any issues?" Without waiting for an answer, he strode toward the car.

Based on his eagerness to get to the car, I briefly considered not answering since I wasn't sure he would hear it anyway. Instead, I went with "Nothing I couldn't handle." As he went to pass me, I put my hand on his arm. "Mr. Hathaway."

He stopped and half turned toward me with a puzzled frown. "Yes?"

I let him go and reminded him gently, "We need to verify ownership before I allow you to examine the car."

"Right, right." He rubbed his neck, his gaze lingering on the car before reluctantly returning to me. "Toby mentioned he was going to have it keyed to me as a precaution."

"That's my understanding, yes." It was one of those items Toby had run through with me that morning. Because of the contentious circumstances surrounding the car, he had hedged his bets with a verification ward. "If you have the owner's token, we can verify first then move on to the official paperwork."

"Of course." He twisted the chunky ring off his pinky and held it out. "Here, where do you need it?"

"If you take the driver's seat, I'll be happy to show you."

As Virgil went to the driver's side, I crossed over to the passenger side, brushing up against Zev. He caught my wrist, bringing me to a halt. Virgil's companion shot us a look, but we both ignored it.

Zev asked, "You good?"

"I'm good," I said. "You want to schedule a pickup? We should be done in about thirty minutes."

He dipped his chin in acknowledgement then with my bag in hand, his over his shoulder, he moved a few feet away to a nearby bench. He dumped both bags onto the seat then leaned a hip against the back as he went to his phone to get us a ride to the Four Seasons.

I slid into the passenger seat. "Okay, Mr. Hathaway, let's get you settled in."

✶✶✶✶✶✶✶✶✶✶✶✶✶✶✶✶✶✶✶✶✶✶✶✶✶

Twenty-five minutes later, I added my signature under Virgil's on our final-delivery certificate then handed the pen to Virgil's companion, Oscar, who happened to be our notary. He did his thing, which included adding an embossed seal set with his magical signature, then it was done. My once-in-a-lifetime ride was now the highly coveted possession of one Virgil Hathaway, and my bank account would soon collect a hefty deposit. *Win-win.*

"Mr. Hathaway"—I held out my hand one last time—"I hope you enjoy her."

His smile gained a proprietorial edge. "Oh, I intend to."

Between his tone and that look, I was a bit skeeved out. If the car had been an actual breathing woman, I would've worried about her safety being left alone with him. As it was, I was pretty sure the car was safe from harm. In fact, Virgil struck me as one of those collectors that would put that beauty in his showroom and she'd never see the road again, which was a waste.

Poor girl.

With a hefty dose of professionalism, I kept my distaste to myself. Luckily, our business was all but done, so I was about to take my leave when Oscar turned to Virgil and said, "Ellie wanted me to extend our apologies at not being able to join you and Julie at Dante's tonight."

Virgil waved away his apologies. "Honestly, it's for the best. Juls woke up with a sore throat and fever, so we would've had to cancel tonight anyway."

"Well, I hope the tickets don't go to waste."

Virgil turned to me. "I don't suppose you and your friend

would be interested in seeing the show *Beautiful Nightmare,* would you?"

I bit back my automatic yes to free tickets and forced a casual "I'm afraid I'm not familiar with that show. Is it new?"

Virgil nodded. "Just opened—what?" He looked to Oscar. "Two, three weeks ago?"

"Closer to three," Oscar said then smiled at me. "It's got a bit of everything—comedy, magic, and dance, if you like that kind of thing."

"I'm always up for good entertainment."

"Then this should be right up your alley, Ms. Costas," Virgil chimed in. "It's gotten spectacular reviews so far. Normally, I'd exchange these, but my schedule is too tight for an alternate night right now."

My polite reluctance was fading fast. "Are you sure?"

"Very. In fact, I insist you take them. Consider it an apology for whatever it was you 'handled' on the way in."

Ignoring the edge of condescension he couldn't quite erase, I gave in. "In that case, we'd love to accept. Thank you."

"Wonderful." His attention drifted back to the car. "I'll leave a message at the box office, letting them know you'll be picking up the tickets."

Easily recognizing the dismissal, I thanked him once again, shook hands with both men, then headed over to the valet bench where Zev was waiting.

He saw me coming, got to his feet, and picked up our bags. He held mine out when I was close enough to grab it. "Ready?"

"More than." I took my bag and slung it over my shoulder. "So, about that show tonight."

"We can check out what's playing, see if we can find the one you wanted, and get our tickets when we get to the suite."

"No need. We just scored a free pair."

He looked behind me, presumably while Virgil was still drooling over his newest collectable. "Really?" His attention came back to me. "Which one?"

"*Beautiful Nightmare* over at Dante's."

"Sounds interesting."

"Should be, according to the reviews."

He didn't comment, just raised a brow.

"Did I mention the 'free' part?"

"Free is good," he agreed.

I looked around. "Where's our ride?"

"Waiting back at the guard shack."

"Seriously?"

"Yep." He popped the *P*. "Rideshares are not allowed beyond the gate."

Oh, for the love of all that's holy. "Great," I grumbled as I started to walk away.

He kept pace with me. "If you don't want to walk it, we can hit up the valet, see if we can hitch a ride on one of their carts."

I considered his suggestion. "How long has the driver been waiting?"

His shoulders rose and fell in a negligent shrug. "About five minutes."

I looked back and saw that our earlier greeters were nowhere to be found, and it was anyone's guess when they would be back. Not inclined to wait around when I had two perfectly good feet, I heaved a sigh. "We'll walk it. It's probably faster than begging for a ride."

"And saves us a tip," he added in a dry voice.

I grinned as we set out together. "If you're that hard up, you can always write it off as a business expense."

"Too much work." He grinned as he caught my free hand in his. "Besides, haven't you heard—actual cash money is obsolete."

The last made me laugh as we followed the sidewalk

away from the clubhouse and back down to the guard shack. The guard stepped out of his little office and watched as we climbed into our ride. It made me wonder if he thought we would rush him then take over the damn country club. Before I could test my theory, I was settling into the back seat with Zev squeezing in next to me. Our driver, an older gent who gave off grandfather vibes, made pleasant conversation as he worked his way over to the Four Seasons.

I couldn't help but grin when Zev added a generous tip to our bill.

We waved off the bellman and stepped inside the expansive marble-floored reception area with soaring ceilings pierced by skylights and impressive chandeliers. Despite the elegant atmosphere, the crowd was the typical eclectic mix of Vegas tourists. Guest fashions rode the scale from T-shirts and Bermuda shorts paired with socks and sandals, to flowy linen pants and airy button-down shirts with leather sandals and manicured toes. We got to check-in and gave our names. Once they saw Sabella's on the reservation, we were all but hand delivered to the suite.

We stepped off the elevator and followed our attendant to the double door set off to the right. She touched the key card to the knob, triggering a security ward. The resulting flare of magic danced over me, and the hairs on my arms rose in response. I rubbed them back into place as she opened the door, stepped inside to hold it wide, and motioned us in. *"Siate i benvenuti, signora e signore."*

Since Italian wasn't my forte, I stuck with "Thank you," while Zev murmured, *"Grazie,"* as we passed her and stopped in the entryway of a stunning suite. It wasn't until our attendant had closed the door behind her, leaving us alone, that I breathed out. "Holy shit, Zev, look at this place."

There was a lot to take in. When Sabella indicated she was renting a two-bedroom suite, I'd figured we would have two bedrooms with en suite bathrooms, a living room, and because it was Sabella we were talking about, a kitchen and maybe dining room. I did not expect to be staying in an honest-to-goodness, fully furnished, two-thousand-square-foot apartment that included a balcony with a to-die-for view of the strip.

Ah, to be old Arcane money.

I shrugged off my bag and set in on the tiled floor next to a long glossy entryway table then crossed the plush carpet, ignoring the baby grand piano to my left and the leather sectional in the sunken living room to my right. Instead, I went straight to the floor-to-ceiling windows that opened on to the balcony, slid them open, and stepped outside.

We weren't the top floor, but we were close, and this far up, the light breeze that teased those below turned into a playful shove by a moody teenager. Since I didn't want to eat my hair, I turned into it so I could watch the ebb and flow of the figures meandering the sidewalks below. I had my arms braced as I leaned against the railing when Zev came up and caught me between him and the railing, his hands just outside my arms. I relaxed into him as he rubbed his chin against the top of my head, and we both continued to watch the world pass by.

Long, peaceful minutes ticked by before he said, "So, this is all ours for the night?"

"Mm-hmm."

His arms moved from the railing to curl around my hips, drawing me into him as he bent his head closer. I arched my neck, giving him access. The brush of his beard sent a wave of anticipatory goosebumps over my skin. He nuzzled my neck and woke a slow-burning hunger. It stretched awake, igniting a simmering mix of need and desire. Closing my eyes, I sank into him, releasing the railing to grip his wrists as his clever fingers found their way beneath my shirt to stroke tantalizingly along my ribs before teasingly dipping lower.

"Zev." Part protest, part encouragement, his name came out on a soft groan.

He murmured something I couldn't catch as my hunger rose to a roar, drowning me in want. My awareness narrowed to my body's rising demands for more. I wanted to reach back and hold him tight to me, even though I could feel every inch of him against me. But I was held captive by the fear that if I let go, I would be swept away and get lost in the storm.

Somehow, he got one hand free and cupped my chin, angling me so he could take my mouth in a toe-curling kiss. Anchored by the tangle of tongues and sweeping caresses, I finally gave in and turned toward him. Desperate to touch his skin, I tugged his shirt out of his jeans with one hand while the other freed his hair from his tie so I could hold on tightly. My urgency flipped a switch, and suddenly, we were stumbling back into the suite to indulge in our own version of sin.

NINE

AFTER SPENDING a relaxing afternoon testing the various horizontal surfaces in the suite's living room and bedroom, Zev and I cleaned up and made a run to one of the many shops to upgrade our clothing for the evening's activities. It took four stops before I found a sleek but simple deep-purple dress that I could wear without the annoying addition of stockings, pair with wedge heels, and that would still fit in with the posh crowd without breaking the bank. The wedge heels were the most important component what with the miles of walking required to get anywhere in Vegas. Annoyingly, Zev managed to find a black button-down with an embroidered diamond pattern that rode from shoulder to waist in a narrow strip that elevated his jeans from casual to sophisticated in the second store. He made use of his downtime while I hunted for my outfit by making our dinner reservation and checking in with his mysterious backup.

I only even knew about the check-ins because when I stepped out of the dressing room in the fourth store with the eighth outfit of the afternoon in search of his opinion, he barely looked up from his phone before decreeing it was "fine." Since shopping had worn the edge off my mellow from my earlier exercise, I muttered under my breath about him and his phone then stomped back to the dressing room. I had tossed the top onto the little bench and was in the process of unzipping the skirt when he gave a warning knock before invading the dressing room.

"Zev, you can't be in here," I snapped.

He slid the lock in place, moved toward me, caught my hips, and drew me close. "You've looked good in everything you've tried, but, babe, if you seriously don't get this figured out, I might be tempted to take you to the show in a bathrobe."

He wasn't the only frustrated one. Unlike Lena, who loved to troll clothing stores, I typically only went when necessary. The fact that I'd already been at this for over an hour was driving even me nuts. It was my turn to begrudgingly use the F-word. "Fine."

He pressed a kiss against my forehead then pulled back. "I was checking on the Shed Twins."

I leaned into him, hands on his chest. "And?"

"And they'd managed to get out of the shed and bail by the time the team got there."

"They find them stranded on the side of the road anywhere?"

He shook his head. "No sign of the car at the restaurant or anywhere on the highway between there and Vegas."

"Well, damn." *So much for sabotaging their ride.*

"That about covers it." His gaze flicked to the last two dresses hanging behind me. "Pick one or the other, and let's call it good, yeah?"

"Yeah."

He swiftly pressed his lips against mine before leaving me to my choices. Once I zipped up the purple one, I decided number nine was the winner, got dressed, took it to the counter, and made my decision final. With our purchases in hand, we headed back to the suite, transformed into our glitzier versions, and returned to our night on the town.

The show was scheduled for nine, so we lingered over dinner, enjoying our culinary delights. I splurged and took the seafood route, while Zev stuck to the tried-and-true surf and turf. Afterward, we wound our way toward Dante's, a newer casino and hotel that hadn't been there the last time I'd visited. Vegas was always in a state of upgrade, be it shows, shops, hotels, or casinos. Whatever it was, if it could be made bigger, brighter, and more exciting, they would do it. Every building lining the Vegas Strip was a testament to egos determined to push the envelope, and most of those egos belonged to the big-money investors.

Dante was no exception. There was no mistaking the fact the infamous poet and his Roman traveling companion had been the inspiration. My recollection of the poem was a little foggy, but I was pretty sure Dante wasn't a young, moody, rock-star figure, and Virgil wasn't a femme fatale with a wolf for a pet. Regardless, the hotel managed to get the theme's point across. The registration area sported a heavy forest motif, while staff dressed in crimson manned the desks. Just beyond the large check-in hall was the actual casino floor. The words *La Vòglia* were arched above the opening, where a low-hanging haze of smoke, real and probably fake, trickled out. To assist with the illusion of stepping into hell, red-tinged lighting illuminated a maze of slot machines and tables. Mesmerized patrons clustered around their game of choice as cocktail waitresses in corsets, tight miniskirts, and torn wings served drinks.

I tried sounding out La Vòglia under my breath in an attempt to figure out the pronunciation. Zev, obviously catching my lame attempts, leaned in close and said into my ear, "It's *la-voy-ya.*"

I looked at the word then back to him and raised my eyebrows.

Fluent in my nonverbal speak, he added, "It means 'craving' or 'want.'"

I took in the near-catatonic state of those held in thrall by the glittering lights, flashing screens, and chiming bells. "That fits, I guess."

We left the poor souls behind and stuck to the wide walkways that cut through the casino. We wandered the halls lined with craft shops toward the show's theater. It took us a bit to make it to the box office because I kept getting sidetracked by the various offerings on display. There was a professed Key offering charms guaranteed to increase luck at the tables or slots, an Illusion mage who offered temporary makeovers, and a scattered handful of Mystic-based mages offering everything from tarot readings to crystal healings.

As we were passing a brightly lit window, I made Zev stop. "I'll just be a minute."

He took in the window display then shot me a look. "You planning on getting inked?"

His cautious tone made me grin, but instead of answering, I headed in. I wasn't surprised when he trailed in after me. The walls of the shop were covered with various works of tattoo art that looked down at an impressive collection of inks and a variety of tools. There were two people inside; neither one paid Zev and me much attention. One sat at the counter working on a sketchpad, and the other was perusing the shelves.

I stopped in front of the heavily tattooed guy at counter. "Hi."

His hand stilled, and he managed to move just his eyes as he looked up from his drawing. "Hey."

"Do you carry Nobi ink?"

He set down his pencil and sat back as he swept his gaze over me, clearly trying to figure out why I was asking about top-of-the-line tattoo ink. "We do, but we only keep certain colors on hand." His *Why?* was left unspoken.

Undaunted by his wary tone, I dug a little deeper. "How much lead time do you need on orders?"

"Depends on the colors."

I nabbed a card from the little holder on the counter. "Got a ballpark?"

"Two to four weeks." He looked to the card, then to Zev, then back to me. "You do know you need to be a licensed artist to order, right?"

"Yep." I held the card back over my shoulder in a silent request to Zev to hold it for me. "But it's not for me." Zev took the card while I kept talking. "My friend has a shop in Tempe. He's been trying to get his hands on a couple of specific Nobi inks, but he's not having much luck."

The young man's wariness disappeared, replaced by interest. "Which shop?"

"Etched Chaos."

His grin of recognition wiped away any lingering traces of his previous skepticism. "Solid shop. Great roster of artists."

"You've been?"

"Yeah, lived in the Valley about five years back." He held out his right arm, turning it slowly as he pointed out the sinuous dragon created of rainbow of scales that coiled from wrist to elbow. "Had Umber do this one for me."

I rose on my toes and leaned in to get a better look. As always, Umber's particular flair came through in vivid detail. "That's gorgeous."

"Yeah, his work is the shit."

"It so is," I agreed.

He held out his hand. "Jay."

I shook it. "Rory." My left calf gave a twinge of protest at my prolonged position, so I dropped back down.

Jay's attention went to Zev then settled back on me. "You know Umber?"

"For years," I said. "Lately, he's been on a tear trying to get his hands on Mystic Alien—something about retention rates—but every place he's checked has been out of stock with no idea when it will be in."

The guy shook his head. "Not a surprise. That's a bitch to get your hands on because it's meant for Yantra work."

"Yantra?" Zev asked as he moved to my side to lean a hand against the counter while his other was a warm weight at the base of my spine.

"Yeah, high-dollar artwork where you infuse the ink with a cast, say, like, protection or an energy boost," Jay explained. "Umber's one of a handful of artists that can do that kind of thing." There was no missing his admiration of my friend. "If he's having trouble getting his hands on it, I'm not sure how much luck we'll have."

A little bummed but not overly so since it had been a spur-of-the-moment decision to come in, I asked, "So should I bother having him contact you?"

"Sure, he might as well. I don't mind make some calls and seeing what hits back?"

"Cool, how about I leave you his contact information?"

"That works."

A few minutes later, Zev and I were walking back out, hand in hand. We made it past three more stalls before my wandering eye was caught again, but Zev nudged me on with a reminder that we were going to be late. I sighed but turned away. If I was lucky, the vendor would still be around after the show. We got to the theater and joined the line of people waiting to get in. While we waited for our line to move, I leaned into Zev, who stood at my back, and indulged in a bit of people watching. Here in Vegas, that activity was a show all on its own where anyone and everyone could be found in the crowd.

There were singles set to mingle, couples out for a night of entertainment, families dazzled by the lights and sights of Sin City, and world-weary locals just catching a good show. I was on the edge of zoning out when a man standing over near the bar at the edge of the crowd caught my attention. He had his arm around a stylish brunette and was staring directly at us. I looked around to confirm what or who it was he was so fascinated by, and when I turned back, I had no doubt we were his focus because his hard gaze was aimed at me. His unnerving intensity dimmed my happy haze.

What the hell is his problem?

I straightened and tugged on Zev's arm. "Zev, do you—"

At some unseen signal, the crowd surged forward, and the rest of my question was drowned out by the excited voices of patrons eager to charge into the theater.

Zev held fast against the tide of bodies and leaned down, his lips brushing my ear as he asked, "What's wrong?"

I turned my face into him so he could hear me above the din. "We're being watched."

His previously relaxed demeanor went wired. He drew back, a frown darkening his face as his gaze swept around us. When he couldn't identify the threat, he dipped back to me. "Who?"

I turned back to point out where Mr. Angry and his companion had been, but they were gone. I used Zev's arm to keep me steady as I rose onto my tiptoes to scan the crowd. Nothing. They were gone. I dropped back down and shook my head. "Never mind. They're gone."

He curled his arm around my waist, did another scan, then nudged me forward so we moved with the others. "Let me know if you spot them."

I nodded.

We made our way to the ticket counter, where we somehow ended up behind a clearly inebriated couple on their honeymoon, or so their matching shirts claimed. The first five minutes of their interaction with the ticketing agent were comical, but my amusement waned as the minutes continued to tick by. Finally, the new Mr. and Mrs. stumbled away, tickets in hand. Then it was our turn, and we stepped up to the window.

The woman behind the plexiglass offered a professional but empty smile. "Good evening. May I have your name?"

I moved in front of Zev and took the lead. "Rory Costas and Zev Aslanov."

The agent's fingers flew over her keyboard. "I see you'll be guests for Mr. Hathaway's box tonight." When she looked up from her screen, warmth had infused her polite mask. "Your seats are in Balcony Three and include complimentary drinks and snacks." She slid a narrow brochure through the opening. "You're welcome to order here or later, whichever you prefer."

"I think we'll order later, thank you." I pick up the glossy menu and handed it off to Zev.

"Wonderful." She added two tickets to the counter. "Please don't hesitate to let us know if you need anything. Enjoy your show."

I took our tickets then Zev's hand, and we rejoined the tide of people heading in. We made our way through the crowd, giving the four-deep bar a pass, then up to second floor, where it wasn't so crowded. At the top of the stairs, an usher stood guard over a set of double doors. After checking our tickets, he held one open and let us in. I stepped over the threshold and was immediately forced to endure an invisible grope session as magic clutched at me, only to slide away when my Prism slapped it back. When the noise of the crowd outside turned off like a switch being thrown, I realized it was a muffling ward. I shook off my reaction and rubbed my arms in attempt to wipe away the annoying sensation.

Zev caught my movement. "You okay?"

I nodded. "Wasn't expecting the ward."

We moved down the hall and passed evenly spaced doors with numbers tucked discreetly on the walls next to them. Unlike the level below, this space had a hushed calm that was a welcome respite from the deafening din of voices and laughter. Plus, the air was cooler with no crushing crowd milling about, and it didn't carry the taint of smoke that made my throat itch. It was like its own little, exclusive world.

A girl could get used to this.

We found our box, stepped inside, and got hit with the unadulterated view. We were just to the right of center stage, which put us high enough to feel close to the action but not so high we needed binoculars to watch the show. There were four seats that resembled throne-like easy chairs, partnered with convenient side tables for drinks. There would be no brushing shoulders with our neighbors or worrying about someone's ass hitting our drinks here. Nope, it was like sitting in a living room.

Nice!

We settled into our seats, and I amused myself by leaning forward, my elbows on the edge of the low balcony as I watched those below. Zev wasn't as interested. Instead, he stretched out his legs and played with my hair. I pointed out a few of the more interesting patrons as we waited for the show to start. An usher had knocked once, asking if we needed anything as he set up a selection of snacks on a narrow counter along the back of the box.

"Ohh, fancy," I murmured to Zev.

Finished with the arrangement, the usher came back, took our drink order, then slipped away. About ten minutes later, he came back with our glasses. I touched my cup, which was glass, not plastic, to Zev's and said, "To free show tickets."

He grinned. "To free show tickets." He sipped his beer.

I brought my glass up and sipped at the bright bite of something tropical and rum before plucking the plastic stick piercing a couple of cherries and chunks of pineapple out of the icy mixture. Enjoying my fresh fruit, I checked the time and saw we had another ten minutes before curtain. Zev and I were talking about nothing important when there was a knock on the suite door. Whoever it was didn't wait for an answer before pushing in.

I turned without getting up, thinking only the usher would be so blunt as to barge in, but Zev got to his feet and rounded the seats, partially blocking my view.

"Virgil, I want to…" The voice stopped abruptly, and the man it belonged to pulled up short, just shy of colliding with Zev. "I'm sorry." Clearly flustered, he backed to the door, ducked his head outside, probably to check the number, then said, "I thought this was Virgil Hathaway's box."

Despite his explanation, something about him set my instincts quivering. Unfortunately, Zev's back was broad enough that I couldn't really see much of our uninvited guest.

I wasn't sure what message Zev's instincts had received, but his posture and voice remained coolly polite. "It is. Mr. Hathaway had another commitment tonight and passed along his tickets."

"Well, then," the man murmured then leaned to the side to peer around Zev. "My apologies to you and your…"

I sucked in a breath as he came into view. It was Mr. Angry. He was wearing a gracious smile now, no sign of his earlier temper anywhere in sight.

"Companion on interrupting your evening." His gaze turned diamond hard and equally sharp before he straightened. He clearly didn't believe it was just the two of us, because his gaze darted around as if Virgil were hiding in a corner or something.

Zev shifted a few inches to his left, and I caught sight of an attractive brunette wearing an irritated pout. "Damon." She put a red-tipped finger on his arm to regain his attention. "We should get to our seats." Her tone was somewhere between husky and whiny.

"Of course." Damon held out his hand to Zev. "Again, my apologies for barging in. I'll just catch up with Virgil later."

Zev switched his beer so he could shake Damon's hand. "No harm done."

I caught Damon's smile, and something about it made me wary, but he was turning and ushering his date out into the hall before I could pinpoint what it was. He pulled the door closed behind him. Unsettled, I stared at the closed door until Zev came back and retook his seat.

"You okay?"

I managed a stunned headshake as I untwisted until I was once again facing forward. "That was him."

Zev glared at the door, then his head swiveled back to me. "The guy who was staring?"

"Yeah."

Before Zev could comment, the lights signaled that showtime was imminent. He caught my hand, brought it to his lips, pressed a kiss to my palm, then set it against his thigh. "Nothing we can do about it now. Let's enjoy the show."

The trickle of unease Damon's presence had caused lingered, but Zev was right. Short of Damon doing something obvious—like attacking us outright—there was nothing to support my disquiet. Maybe I was still off balance from our earlier encounter with the Shed Twins, or maybe I was just overly paranoid. Regardless, there was no obvious threat to address.

I sucked in a deep breath, blew it out, and forced my body to ease back. The lights dropped low, bathing the theater in heavy shadows, and the crowd went quiet. A clap of thunder preceded a startling column of flame bursting from center stage as music thundered through the air. I let go of my worry and sat back, ready to get lost in someone's else's drama for the night.

TEN

THREE HOURS LATER, Zev and I made our return trip through the wide hall, but this time, every third shop or so was closed up tight. The few that remained opened were clearly winding down for the evening. Foot traffic wasn't as dense, but it was still going strong with late-night revelers making the most of their trip to Sin City. Drunken hollers and raucous laughter, mainly from those who couldn't have walked a straight line if they tried, clashed with the muffled bass beat from a nearby bar and the background rings and dings of the casino-floor machines.

The more sober wanderers veered out of their way and gave serious side-eye to the offenders while a few steely faced guards gazed over the mass of humanity. Luckily, I had Zev, who kept me tucked in at his side with an arm around my waist. I returned the favor, enjoying that he was my own personal forcefield against the stupidity of others.

Walking along in our bubble and riding the lingering wave of the fantastic show, I took a bit to realize Zev wasn't feeling the same. The arm around my waist squeezed, and his normally smooth stride hitched, giving me his weight for a moment before he straightened.

I tightened my hold on his waist, slowed our pace, and looked at him. Alarm skittered through me when I realized his normally olive-toned skin was pale and there was a drop of sweat at his temple. "Zev, are you okay?"

He stared down at me, his gaze a little hazy, then he did a long, slow blink. When his lashes rose, his dark eyes held a familiar awareness. He used his free hand to swipe at his temple, wiping away the telltale bead of moisture. "Yeah, just a little dizzy."

"You want to sit somewhere for a minute?" I looked around, trying to see if there was somewhere we could do just that.

"No, I'm good. Let's get to the room."

I didn't waste time arguing. We made our way back to the hotel, and by the time we hit the elevator, worry dominated my thoughts. I got us inside and pressed the button for our floor. Zev was leaning against the back wall, head down, gripping the railing so tightly that his knuckles pressed white against his skin as the door closed behind us.

The elevator slid up with a repetitive ding as I cupped his jaw and brought it up until I could catch his eyes. They were clouded and confused, and my worry redlined. He tried to pull his face away from me, but I held on.

"Talk to me." Without waiting for a response, I pressed the back of my hand to his brow. It was clammy but not overly heated. "What's going on?"

"Don't feel good."

Yeah, that's obvious.

The elevator came to a stop as the automated voice announced our floor. I slid my arm around Zev and tugged. "Come on. Let's get into the room."

At first, he didn't budge, but then he reluctantly let go of the railing and dropped his arm around my shoulders. I staggered a bit under his weight but managed to get the two of us off the elevator and down the hall. At the door, I had a moment of panic because I didn't have the key card, but he had enough presence of mind to fumble for it in his pocket.

We got inside, stumbled through the entryway, and almost took a header when I tried to get him down to the couch at the same time he seemed to lose his coordination. With some muttered oaths on my part, groans and grunts on his, he landed on the couch and collapsed back. He had one foot on the floor and threw his arm over his eyes.

Feeling useless, I sat on the edge of the couch and caught his free hand in mine. "What can I do?"

"Water," he mumbled.

I didn't need to be asked twice. I gave his hand a squeeze then headed to the kitchen. On my way there, I kicked off my shoes. The tile was cool under my feet. I came back with a chilled bottle of water from the fridge and retook my seat. "Here."

He didn't move his arm from his eyes, but his free hand rose, searching for the bottle. I guided it to the bottle, alarmed to see the tremor in his fingers as they closed around the plastic. Before I could get into it with him, he dropped his other arm to brace against the couch and struggled to sit up. I did my best to help, going so far as to cover his hand with mine as he brought the water up to drink. "I don't like this, Zev. I think I need to call a doctor."

"I'll be fine," he argued. "It's just my stomach, probably something I ate." He took a drink, paused, then took another before handing the bottle back.

I wasn't so sure, but for now, I didn't argue. If things didn't change quickly, that would be another story. I leaned over and stretched to set the water on the side table, then he gave a sudden jerk, followed by a guttural groan. His movements were so harsh as he curled around me like a constricting snake, his knee nailing my hip hard enough to leave a bruise.

Panic took over. "Zev!" One hand went to his head, which

was pressing into my gut, and the other went around his shoulders, holding him tightly.

His body jerked again. "Gonna hurl," he groaned.

I made a mad dash to the kitchen, chased by Zev's groans. I threw open cabinet doors until I found a bowl that held a bunch of snacks. I dumped them all on the counter and snagged the thin hand towel before racing back. I barely got the bowl under Zev's face in time.

Kneeling on the floor, all I could do was hold his hair back as he heaved. It felt like forever before the painful sounds stopped and he held out his hand. I gave him the hand towel to clean up, then he finally fell back, his face pale and coated in a layer of sweat, his eyes closed.

"How are you doing?" It was an inane but necessary question. If it really was a case of his dinner not agreeing with him, getting rid of it should help. If it was something else, then I didn't give a shit if he didn't like it, I was calling in a doctor. Better yet, if there was a healing mage on staff, they could haul ass up here.

"I think that's it for now," he mumbled, but he gripped the hand towel like a much-needed teddy bear.

I watched him for a long moment, and when I decided he was telling the truth, I picked up the bowl to head to the kitchen. Worry and agitation swirled in my head, so it wasn't until I was close to the sink that I realized something else was adding to my chaotic reaction. I shifted my grip on the bowl, realizing my palms felt scorched, as if they'd been pressed up against a hot pan.

"What the hell?" I muttered under my breath as I set the bowl in the sink.

As soon as I stopped touching the bowl, the ached eased off. After a quick mental sweep, I realized my Prism had locked into place at some point, shielding my hands from whatever swirled within the bowl. I stared at the nauseating mess and did my best not to add to the contents. Among the expected regurgitated mess were heart-stopping traces of blood.

I braced my hands on the edge of the sink as I stared down in horror, my pulse racing with dread. Without really thinking about it, I reached for my magic and eased back on the barrier I instinctively kept between me and the magical plane until my sight shifted. A flurry of colorful ribbons and threads ignited before me.

I sucked in a sharp breath and swore softly, "Godsdammit!"

Zev wasn't sick—he was cursed.

In the sink, the bowl was wrapped in a web of ugly yellow with flecks of black that appeared to move. My stomach roiled, and I slowly backed away, never taking my eyes off what sat in the sink. A hysterical part of me was prepared for it to grow fangs and attack. Not that it would. Even though I was seeing a visual representation of active magic, it had been set on Zev, and this mess was the resulting echo of its chaotic intent.

I knew what, or better yet, whom, I needed. I tore my gaze away, trying to remember where I had left my phone. I spotted it on the sofa table just behind the couch. I dashed over, picked it up, and hit Lena's contact. It rang twice.

"Rory? Hey!" my roommate's cherry voice greeted.

"Zev's been hexed," I blurted out, my voice sounding hollow and cold instead of on the edge of a meltdown.

Lena was all business. "Where are you?"

"Vegas, Four Seasons, in Sabella's suite."

"Tell me."

"Zev and I went to a show, but on the way back, he started not feeling well. We barely got back to the suite before he collapsed on the couch. He just finished throwing up. He's clammy, barely conscious, and in pain." I knew that last part because Zev was curling into himself on the couch in front of me, and I could hear his soft, pained groans. My grip tightened on my phone, and I whispered, "Lena, he's in a lot of pain."

"Don't freak on me, Rory. I need you."

Easier said than done. Put me in the direct line of a magical attack or behind the wheel doing over a hundred on surface streets, and it was nothing but ice in my veins. Stuck watching Zev being taken down by something I couldn't stop, and it was panic city.

Without giving me a chance to respond, Lena got straight to the point. "Can you tell what kind of hex it is?"

"No." I ran a shaky hand through my hair and turned to face the sink. "I only found it is because my Prism picked up on its presence when I went to empty the bowl."

"FaceTime me," she demanded.

I fumbled with my phone as I followed directions. She came on screen, her auburn hair bundled into a messy knot, her eyes sharp, her tone unshakable, and her expression keen but blank. "You said you noticed the hex in the bowl?"

I swallowed hard. "Yeah, I was getting ready to rinse it out, realized my Prism was reacting to something, so I checked things out." I didn't need to explain what all went into "checking things out," because she knew about my unique quirk of seeing magical echoes.

She raised a brow. "And?"

"And whatever he purged is webbed with a gross yellow with black flecks. When I look at it, it appears to be moving."

Her green eyes narrowed. "Sounds like a plague curse of some kind."

"Can you stop it?"

She didn't answer. Instead, she said, "Take me to the bowl first. Let's see if there's any clue as to what base was used."

Zev started to gag.

"Oh shit!" Like Pavlov's dog, I started to the kitchen to grab the damn bowl. Somehow, I didn't lose hold of my phone. Gods only knew what kind of visual roller-coaster ride my dash to the sink caused Lena. I all but threw my phone on the counter then reached one hand to the bowl and the other to the faucet.

"Rory, stop!" Lena called sharply, pulling me up short. "I need to see the contents first before you dump them."

"Right," I muttered. I forced myself to still and did my best not to listen to Zev. I reclaimed my phone and aimed the screen at the bowl, absently noting my hand wasn't exactly steady.

"A little closer," Lena directed.

I angled it closer. "There?"

"Yeah." She went silent, and the seconds stretched. Finally, she said, "I'm not seeing anything."

"Can I dump it now?"

"Yeah, but carefully. Let me know if anything's in it that shouldn't be."

I set the phone on the counter so I could turn on the faucet and dump the bowl. "You mean like blood?" My question came out a tad shrill.

"Traces, Rory. Those are just traces," she reassured me.

I did as she asked, carefully emptying the contents, but didn't see anything unexpected. I did a quick rinse then carried both the bowl and my phone as I beat feet back to Zev. I got the bowl back in position with nary a second to spare. Zev dragged it close and hunched over it. The noises he made were painful to hear.

Somewhere in the distance, I heard Lena talking, but it wasn't penetrating. Unable to do anything other than watch, I released the cresting wave of alarm with a continuous stream of hissed curses. When he finally collapsed back, face pale to the edge of gray and covered in a layer of sweat, I realized Lena was calling my name.

I snatched up my phone from the floor and snapped, "What?"

"Two things," she shot back, voice hard, face even harder. "Are you listening to me?"

"Yes."

"First, you're going to have a visitor. His name is…" She looked beyond her screen, and I heard a male voice say something. She came back. "Grayson, he's a Key with the Guild. Let him in." I opened my mouth to remind her of the Council's edict about me using Guild resources, but she lifted a hand and cut me off. "Requested by the Cordova Family, not you."

Since that other voice likely belonged to Evan, one of the best electro mages in the Arcane Guild, I didn't bother asking stupid questions and just rolled with it, keeping us on track. "Second?"

"Second, we're going to try a down-and-dirty nullification spell to hold things in check until Grayson gets there."

Okay, that would work. Anything was better than sitting around doing nothing.

"You need snake dust, red string, and sage."

Right. Phone in hand, I shoved to my feet, repeated the three items under my breath, and headed for the kitchen. I started ransacking the cabinets and drawers. I found red string wrapped around a rolled-up menu for a Thai restaurant, but that was it. I slammed the last kitchen cabinet and dragged my hand through my hair as frustration rode my ass. "Dammit!"

"Rory, are you listening to me?"

I startled and lifted my phone that I had all but forgotten about. "I'm here."

"Call down to the front desk."

Confused, I frowned. "For?"

"Sage and snake dust." When I blinked at her, she explained, "Standard first-aid items. Most hotels keep a supply on hand."

I went to the phone on the entryway table, hit the button for the speaker so Lena could hear both sides of the conversation, then hit zero. It buzzed twice, then a chirpy voice said, "This is Letty. How may I help you?"

I reached for my nonexistent patience. "Letty, do you have snake dust and sage on hand?"

She barely paused. "We do, Ms. Costas. We also have a purification packet on hand."

"A purification packet?" I repeated.

"Yes, it comes with…" I didn't hear the rest because Lena was demanding, "Get that!"

I jumped in when Letty paused. "I'll take one of those, the snake dust, and the sage."

"Of course, we'll send that right up."

"Thank you."

I spent the next few minutes pacing from the door to Zev and back. I could hear Lena talking, but since it was muffled and clearly to someone else, I concentrated on keeping my shit together. When the knock came, I rushed the door and yanked it open so fast, the bellman on the other side simply blinked.

Too wound up to care about being polite, I grabbed the small, wrapped box and accompanying bag out of his hands. "Thank you." Then I slammed the door shut and rushed back to Zev. I dumped the phone, the box, and the bag on the floor.

"Get the string, Rory," Lena said.

Leaving everything behind, I got up, ran to the kitchen, snagged the string I had left on the counter, and brought it back to my collection. Everything in one place, I asked Lena, "Okay, now what?"

"Let's see what we've got to work with."

We had the tin of snake dust and the bundle of sage. Once I emptied out the box, I added a shallow wooden plate that could double as a bowl if needed, a corked bottle of blessed water, a lighter, labeled incense, a miniature blade, a container of salt, a collection of crystal beads, and four small candles in white, black, red, and blue. All in all, it was quite the haul.

Lena went to work. "First up, do a basic protection circle."

She waited while I shoved the coffee and side tables out of the way and used most of the salt to line a rough, tight circle around the couch. Once I had the candles and crystals in place, I stayed clear of the salt and reclaimed the phone. "Done."

"Next, we're going to make a basic red bracelet," Lena said. "Here's what I need you to do…"

Minutes later, with a basic protection circle in place and sage smoke wreathing Zev's prone body, I carefully dragged the red ribbon through a thin layer of snake dust until it was coated. Then I sucked in a deep breath and forced my hand to hold steady as I threaded the ribbon through the four crystal beads identified by Lena. Holding the two ends of the ribbon so the beads wouldn't slide off, I managed to tie the makeshift bracelet onto Zev's left wrist.

I sat back on my heels as tremors ran through me. "Done."

"Good." Lena's tone had gentled. "Grayson should be there any minute, Rory."

Frustrated by my inability to do anything more, I fisted my hands in my lap. "Tell me he's going to be okay." The demand came out rough.

"He's going to be okay," Lena dutifully replied.

I watched Zev's chest rise and fall, and with nothing left to do but wait, I could feel the tears waiting to escape. I held them back with some deep breaths. My mind wasn't so easily distracted. It battered me with guilt. If I had been paying attention, I could have kept him protected. One the advantages of a Prism was the ability to expand my protective shield to others in the face of offensive magic. But this… this had snuck in when I wasn't looking, giving me no shot to keep Zev safe, and I was fucking furious. The minute Zev was clear, I was going on the hunt, and I knew just who I was starting with…

Damon.

ELEVEN

LENA STAYED on the phone with me as I waited for this Grayson to show up. She tried to offer words of comfort, but they were nothing more than an annoying buzz in my ear. I had to sit there while Zev endured another episode of trying to turn his stomach inside out, but with nothing left to give, all he could do was dry heave. Unfortunately, it didn't stop him from adding more crimson streaks in the bowl. My temper shifted from raging to ice-cold, burying my revealing tremors and threatening tears under a glacial barrier.

When the knock came, I rose from my knees like a runner erupting from the start line, jumped the salt line, raced through the suite, hit the door, and yanked it open without checking. I barely gave the man with a backpack on the other side a glance before I grabbed his arm and dragged him across the suite and to the couch where Zev lay.

When we stood over him, I turned to the Guild Key and demanded, "Fix him."

Instead of doing what I ordered, the man stepped over the salt line, shrugged off his backpack, dropped it to the floor, and sank into a crouch next to it.

"Grayson," Lena called from the phone I'd left on the floor where I had been sitting. "Thank you for coming so quickly."

"You caught me at a good time," he said as he studied Zev. Without looking at me, he asked, "How long has he been like this?"

I bent down, grabbed my phone, and checked the time. A few mental calculations later, even I was surprised by my answer since it felt much longer. "Forty, forty-five minutes."

Grayson rested his arms on his knees, his attention centered on Zev. "What do we know?"

I opened my mouth, but Lena got there first. "They were coming back from a show when Zev started showing signs of contamination. Rory got him up to the room. He collapsed and was violently ill. When Rory called me, I had her do a basic protection bracket and cleansing cast using hotel first-aid supplies."

While she talked, Grayson lifted Zev's left arm, his thumb brushing just below the red bracelet. He set Zev's arm down, and when Lena was done, he turned his head to look up at me. "Solid job." He shifted from crouch to kneeling with one knee on the floor. "What made you think he was hexed?"

Stymied by whom the question was directed toward, I took a breath, held on to the calm aura that surrounded Grayson, and kept it simple. "When he threw up, there was blood. It didn't look right."

"I'm thinking a plague hex," Lena added.

The dark-haired Key nodded. "Sounds about right." He raised his hands, palms down, and held them at the crown of Zev's head without touching. Under his hands, Zev let out another painful groan, but neither of us reacted. Instead, Grayson asked, "Can you walk me through your evening while I do a check?"

The air took on the heavy weight of magic and pressed against me even as relief started to seep through me, leaving my legs shaky. The sensation of Grayson's active magic didn't hurt, but it wasn't comfortable either. I ignored it as I took him through every moment from when we left the room until we returned, sharing Zev's initial assumption of food poisoning. During my explanation, I noted the tight space by the armrest between the couch and the circle's salt line. Deciding it would work, I sank to my knees and leaned against the armrest, taking care not to touch Zev. The last thing I wanted to do was interfere with Grayson's exam.

Grayson continued to work with an unwavering focus, running his hands along Zev's prone body. Zev flailed a couple of times, but for the most part, he was completely out of it. Since I had a highly skilled Key as my best friend, I knew what Grayson was doing. As Lena had once explained it, Keys looked at a mage's magical signature and used signs of damage to determine exposure to hexes. Considering how varied and unique each person's magic could be, I'd asked her how on earth a Key would even begin to guess at what didn't belong. She'd given me a visual—each magical signature was like a tailored coat, specific to the mage and their abilities. When a Key examined it, they were looking for snags in the fabric, missing stitches, or buttons, rips, tears, anything that shouldn't belong. Of course, it was a hell of a lot more complicated than that, but I got the general idea.

When I finished my abbreviated recap to Grayson, I fell quiet, waiting for him to finish. The Key continued his exam, pausing for a long, tense filled moments over Zev's stomach before slowly inching downward. He shot me a look as a frown creased the calm mask and added deep lines along his mouth and brow.

I gripped the cushioned armrest and dug my nails in so I wouldn't reach out and clutch at Zev. "What?"

"Rory," Lena softly warned from the phone, clearly picking up on the vibe in the room, even though she wasn't physically there.

Knowing that snapping at her or Grayson would get me

nowhere, I locked down my questions and grimly held on to my nonexistent patience.

Grayson shook his head and went back to his examination.

My decision paid off when a minute or so later, Grayson finally sat back and looked at me. "It's good you called when you did. He's ingested a modified bane hex."

It wasn't easy holding his gaze, not when magic burned in the depths, adding an unearthly light to his brown eyes, but I managed. "Explain."

"Bane hexes are designed to mimic illnesses but with much more fatal consequences."

Fatal? With one that one word, my breath stalled, and I could feel the blood rush out of my head.

Unaware of the blow he'd dealt me, he turned away and started to dig through his bag. "The good news here is that you recognized something was wrong straight-up. That means we have a chance to get ahead of it." He pulled out an object wrapped in black material and tied off with a green string and set it on the floor. "Interestingly enough, it—" He shot me a glance, and whatever he saw on my face made him leave his bag, lean in, and grab my hand where it rested above Zev's head. He squeezed my fingers. "Rory, take a breath."

I sucked in air, and the world stopped spinning.

"Another." He waited until I followed directions then said, "You good?"

"Yeah." It came out croaky, so I cleared my throat and added a definitive nod. "Yeah, I'm good. What do you need me to do?"

He gave one last squeeze to my hand, let me go, and went back to his bag. "Right now, nothing, but once I start to work, you need to keep him as calm as possible. First up, I'm reinforcing your circle." He pulled out chalk, a clear container of salt, a small hand mirror, and two bundles of what appeared to be dried sticks. "Then we'll get to work on purging the hex out of his system."

That doesn't sound good. Unsettled, I reached out and stroked my fingers over Zev's hair as Grayson kept talking.

"The good news is I've seen this particular hex before." He set a black zippered bag next to his other items.

That made me pause and look up. "Where?"

"Had a client who crossed the wrong loan shark." He picked up the chalk and started a rune on the floor.

"And your client is now…?"

His wry smile was there then gone as he continued to draw the symbols necessary to bolster the circle. "Just fine, and never misses a monthly installment on his payment to me."

Okay, that's good. "What about the loan shark?"

"Got a two-year sentence, a hefty fine, and an additional eighteen-month ban on accessing Arcane materials." He finished the complex design, connected it to the circle, and sat back. "He also had to give up his supplier. Turned out to be a midlevel Key who liked to spend their recreational time in a lab. Came up with some seriously nasty hexes and sold them on the down-low."

Just what we needed in this mix, a Franken-Key. Leave it to a mad scientist with curse-crafting abilities to turn something nasty into something beyond nasty. "Is he still around?"

"The supplier?"

I nodded.

"They're a her, not a he," Grayson said. "And nope, last I heard, she had hightailed it to Mexico with a trail of pissed-off customers on her ass."

That meant getting answers from the supplier was a no-go. "How sure are you that this hex is one of her creations?"

"Rory." Lena made my name an admonishment as it drifted through the air, a reminder she was still listening.

I looked toward my phone lying on the ground, part of me

wishing it was her getting ready to take on the hex, not some guy I didn't know. "It's Zev, Lena."

She didn't need more than those three words to understand the weight they carried. "I know," she said softly. "But I wouldn't have called Grayson in if I didn't trust him to deal with this."

Instead of taking offense, Grayson cut in. "Rory." He waited until he had my attention. "I know it's her." He didn't wait for my response but cupped a white crystal in his palm, murmured under his breath, then touched it to the rune. Magic surged, and I could all but hear it snap into place as he kicked up the protection level. He looked up as he brushed off his hands and gave me a reassuring grin. "The anchoring rune of the hex is marked with her signature."

Let's hear it for narcissistic personalities. "So you can reverse it?"

He shot me a look I couldn't interpret as he untied the green string on the bundle in black. "Can't reverse it. Hence the 'purge' part of the equation." He flipped open the black cloth to reveal a thick crystal in various shades that ran from deep, heart's-blood red to gold-lit amber.

"How will you make sure you got all of it?" I wasn't keen on the inability-to-reverse-it part of this situation. Magic could be as sneaky as shit. If even the tiniest bit was left behind, Zev could end up right back here—or worse.

Grayson shifted until he was sitting cross-legged on the floor, his position making him the nucleus of his interlocking runes. He held the thick crystal between his palms as he held my gaze. "I'm not sure how your man is doing it, but somehow, he's managing to hold the hex back from taking root."

I looked back down at Zev's pale face, taking in the deepening lines of pain and the dampness at his hairline. I knew how—he was a stubborn son of a bitch. Right now, I clung to that fact. "You're sure?"

"Very."

His answer made me look up, where his intensely seriously gaze held mine. There was something he wasn't saying or something he hadn't shared. A rock settled in my gut, and I swallowed back the nerves and asked, "How?"

"Because he's still breathing."

Yep, that would be it. My body jerked as if hit, but before I could regather my composure, Grayson closed his eyes and started to chant under his breath. Magic swelled around us, taking up space, and a silent wind, weighted with power, began to swirl through the circle. It picked up speed as the magic deepened, the pressure of it heavy enough to make my bones ache.

My Prism woke with a roar, and I fought it back. I had no idea if it would interfere with Grayson's spell. Since I was unwilling to risk it, I was left with no other choice than to endure. Holding it in check was like trying to hold back an avalanche with a tennis racket, and equally frustrating, but this was for Zev, so I kept at it.

Power coiled around the Key like a red cloak of warning. I closed my eyes as my hair whipped across my face, but even with my eyes closed, Grayson's reddish-gold glow colored the inside of my lids. His voice deepened, taking on a sonorous toll, like a deep bell. Its echoes rippled through the circle, hitting the edges and sweeping back toward the center.

The magic responded, following the rise and fall of the vocal tide. It was like being caught in ball filled with sloshing water. There was nowhere for the growing momentum of the waves to escape. Instead they grew and grew, drowning everything else out.

I lowered my head between my hands, where they clutched the couch's armrest and kept me from collapsing into a huddled ball. To combat the press of power, I focused on forcing air in and out of my lungs.

The ache of magic deepened, and my Prism really, really

didn't like it. My fight with my Prism neared a tipping point. One I wasn't sure I could win. I gritted my teeth, dug my fingers into the armrest so hard they were going numb, and shook under the magical onslaught. Just when I worried I would snap, Grayson fell quiet. The wind disappeared, and the battering ram of magic stepped back.

Arms shaking, I flexed my fingers, lifted my head, and pried my eyes open, then I quickly narrowed them against the fiery glow. It took a few seconds to comprehend what I was seeing. Grayson, eyes awash in magic, wore an aura of fire that matched the flickering walls of flames that had replaced the salt lines of protection circle.

That wasn't the only thing burning. The symbols he'd added danced and flickered, covering the color spectrum from yellow to red. All of it created an unearthly burning circle. But the most jaw-dropping thing was the thick red crystal that hovered midair at chest height in front of Grayson. Holding it aloft were lines of amber and crimson that stretched through the runes then out to Zev, wrapping him in an ethereal cocoon while starbursts of gold glittered like hyperactive fireflies around his midsection.

I sat there, stunned. I'd never seen anything like it, but then again, I'd never witnessed a Key working a plague spell.

Grayson moved his hands in a complex pattern, and some of the markings moved in sync, twisting and reshaping into a more complex rune. He waved it toward Zev, where it settled in the air just above Zev's stomach and stilled. Grayson reached down to the black zippered bag at his side, where it lay open, revealing a padded interior lined with a double row of vials. Without taking his gaze from Zev, he trailed his fingers over the vials until he came to one with a red top. I could have sworn that vial gave off a spark, but whatever it was that made it different from the others was known only to Grayson.

He plucked it out, thumbed off the top, and finally looked to me. "Can you lift his head? He needs to drink this."

Holding that power-filled gaze was hard, but I managed. Somehow. I nodded then leaned over the armrest to awkwardly get my hands under Zev so his head and shoulders were high enough for him drink without choking.

Once I had him in position, Grayson pressed the vial to Zev's lips and demanded, "Drink."

For the first time, Zev's lashes fluttered, and from my uncomfortable position above and behind him, I could see his eyes open. Not much but enough. He stiffened and tried to jerk away from the vial, but I held firm.

I leaned in, put my lips to his ear, and urged, "Zev, please, drink."

This time, when his lashes lifted, his dark, hazy gaze met mine. "Please," I whispered.

The tight muscles along his shoulders and neck softened. His gaze left mine, going to Grayson, then his lips parted. Grayson tipped the vial, keeping the pour slow so Zev had time to swallow. My arms strained under the awkward hold, but I held firm until the vial was empty. At Grayson's urging, I lowered Zev back to the couch.

Grayson set aside the used vial then turned his attention to the rune hovering above Zev's gut. He murmured something low that I couldn't catch, and a startling white flame sprang to life between his palms. He twisted his wrist, and the flame split into three cords. He continued to chant as he directed the magic into a braided cord. Once it was plaited, he threaded one end through the hovering rune, anchoring it. Then he cupped his hands around the free end and brought it close to the swirling fireflies dancing around Zev's stomach.

He turned flame-filled eyes my way. "Get ready. This is going to be rough."

Warned, I braced, and it was good I did. The minute Grayson connected the braided power, linking the rune and the fireflies, Zev let out a guttural yell and tried to fold in half in an attempt to escape whatever was happening. I scrambled to my feet because I had no leverage on my knees. I got my hands on his shoulders and put all my weight into holding them against the couch. I had no idea what Grayson did next, but Zev's hands rose to push me off.

The next few minutes became a blur as I dodged Zev's hands while trying to keep him contained as he flailed about. The pained noises he made went from gut-wrenching to heartbreaking, leaving me feeling raw. By the time his struggles had waned, I was breathing hard, and the side of my face ached where he had caught me unawares with his fist. Hot tears pooled in my eyes, but they were more about frustration than pain. Somehow, through our brief but intense struggles, I'd managed to come around the couch and was now all but lying on top of his chest, my hands locked on his wrists as I tried to keep him pinned.

Zev's head turned back and forth, hair plastered to his head by sweat, his face screwed up in agony. Low moans escaped from his locked jaw. All I could was hold on and whisper empty reassurances in a thick voice as magic roared around us. Time lost meaning, my world narrowing to containing Zev. Only when he finally went limp and his restless movements stilled did I notice that the eye-searing flames had dulled, then they flickered into nothing while the press of magic slowly seeped away.

Grayson was leaning heavily against the couch, but his attention was pinned on the hovering, rotating ball of angry red above Zev's stomach. It appeared to be eroding an even denser ball of shadow. Inside that opaque ball, flecks of ugly yellow snapped and sparked as Grayson's magic coiled tighter and tighter, compressing the mass. Finally, the red flames squeezed down, and the last of the shadows thinned to nothing. Grayson murmured something I couldn't make out under his breath, and the red ball slowly died away, taking the weight of magic with it.

"Tell me you're done." My demand came out rough.

Grayson's gaze met mine, no longer filled with flames but no less intense in his drawn and sweaty face. "We're done." He twisted until his ass was on the floor and his back was to the couch. He rested his arms on his bent knees and hung his head.

"Did you get it all?"

"He's clear," Grayson confirmed without looking up.

I sucked in a shuddering breath and slowly uncurled my fingers from Zev's wrists, absently noting the deep red marks left behind. I cupped Zev's jaw between my palms. Thankfully, his breathing had calmed, along with his heartbeat.

Relieved, I dropped my forehead against his until my hair fell around us and hid the tears that finally escaped. I could hear Lena and Grayson talking, but their conversation didn't really penetrate because my entire focus was the man under me. "Zev, baby, can you wake up for me?"

His brow furrowed as he frowned, and a soft, barely-there groan drifted from his lips. But what I needed to happen didn't, and his eyes remained closed.

"Zev, come on. Wake up for me." I kept up my whispered pleas until finally, fucking finally, his long lashes fluttered then lifted. I got my lips to curve into a shaky smile that was no less steady than my voice when I said, "Hey, you, welcome back."

TWELVE

I CLOSED the hotel suite's door behind Grayson then stood there a moment, forehead and palms pressed against the hard surface. My chest shuddered as I sucked in air then blew it out, doing my best to rid myself of the ugly mix of fear-drenched anxiety and mind-sharpening adrenaline.

While indulging in a momentary pity party, I silently offered thanks to whoever was watching over Zev and me for granting me great friends with serious connections. I had enough self-awareness to recognize that Lena's rock-solid support was the only reason panic hadn't reduced me to a state of something less substantial than Jell-O. Not only had she stayed on the line throughout the whole ordeal, but her no-nonsense, no-questions approach kept my ass in line. Hell, she hadn't hung up until Grayson had assured her Zev was in the clear and I wasn't channeling my inner berserker.

Grayson hadn't been far behind in taking his leave either. He had packed up his stuff as Zev gradually returned to the here and now. The entire time the Key was packing, he was also laying out orders. "He'll feel like crap for a bit, so make sure he takes it easy. No food, only water for the next three hours."

He pulled out a vial with a white top from his black case and handed it to me. "Have him drink this then same deal—no food, only water for two more hours. If he feels up to it after that, have him try something bland before hitting up an all-you-can-eat buffet. He should be close to normal by late morning. As for the red bracelet, leave it on until it falls off. Once it does, *you* burn it. Don't let him touch it."

Before I could demand details on that strange request, he was gone, leaving me with my neurotic breakdown and a groggy but thankfully conscious Zev half-reclined on the couch.

A muffled grunt from the living room had me snapping up straight and spinning around, only to see Zev struggling with an uncharacteristic awkwardness to his feet.

Of all the stupid, dumbass—

Anger zipped through me and fused my emotional cracks with steel as I shoved off the door and stalked back to the couch. "Sit your ass back down, Zev!"

Of course, he ignored me. "I'm fine." He managed to get to his feet by using the couch's armrest as a crutch, but that was as far as he could get. He stood there, swaying.

Fearing he was about to take a header, I picked up speed and snapped, "You are so far from fine, it's not even in your rearview!"

I got to him just as he tried to take his first ill-advised step. We collided as he all but fell into me, knocking me back a step. I hissed a couple of choice words as my knees almost buckled under his weight. Then it became a tangle of limbs as he tried to stand, and I did my best to ensure he didn't end up kissing the floor. It was an awkward battle involving a lot of cursing, a few insults, and some underhanded moves (on my part). In the end, I won, further proof that he was not fucking fine.

He flopped back on the couch, his face sweaty and pale,

but his eyes and voice were heated with a mix of frustration and embarrassment. "Dammit, Rory."

I stood between his sprawled legs, hands on my hips, breathing heavily as I held his glare with mine. "Don't 'dammit' me, Zev. You heard Grayson. You need to take it easy."

"I wasn't planning on running a marathon, Rory." He dragged an unsteady hand through his sweat-dampened hair and grimaced. "I just want to take a shower."

Empathy rolled through me, clearing a path for logic to traipse through my brain. We were both exhausted, and our tempers were on edge. Mine because I hated the helplessness that came from being forced to watch Zev endure something I couldn't fix. Not to mention the niggles of guilt that somehow this mess was tied to my reason for being here. Arrogant, maybe, but unfortunately, it could just as easily be true. As for Zev's pain-in-the-ass attitude, he wasn't the type to handle being less than badass, and no matter how much he wished differently, he was in no shape to take on a gnat.

Since sarcasm would only exacerbate things, I softened my tone. "Give me a minute to get the water going so it's ready for you, then we can make the trek to the bathroom."

He gave me a brooding glare before giving in. "Fine."

I opened my mouth to remind him to stay put, but when his face darkened in warning, I shook my head, turned on my heel, and headed to the bathroom. I hit one of the bedrooms and headed to the en suite. Safely out of Zev's line of sight, I blew out a long breath and felt my shoulders slump as some of the night's tension rode out the exhale. The bathroom's tile was cool under my bare feet as I went to the walk-in shower and started the water so it could heat up. I turned away and winced when I caught a glimpse of myself in the mirror.

Damn, Zev isn't the only one who needs a shower.

I left the exhausted-looking woman with wild hair behind

and went back to the living room and Zev. Thankfully, he hadn't made a break for it, something I wouldn't put past him. Instead, his head was resting against the back of the couch, his eyes closed, one arm on the armrest, one at his side, his legs sprawled. Not wanting to startle him, I touched his hand as I came around to stand in front of him, and his lashes rose and fell over the deep, velvet brown of his eyes.

I waited for them to rise and stay up before asking, "Ready?"

His answer was to push up out of the couch with slow, unsteady movements. Once he was up on his feet, I tucked myself under his arm, and we headed to the bathroom. Inside, steam was starting to curl around the edges of the mirror. Zev stripped down while I stayed close, setting out towels and keeping an eye on him. Normally, in this setting of a luxury shower in a swanky suite, I would be all about taking advantage of having all that was Zev at my disposal, but after they night we'd had, I was more worried about how to haul him out of the shower should he collapse. Once he was inside the shower, I chanced leaving him to grab his lounging pants and a T-shirt from his bag.

Since prepping towels and clean change of clothes didn't take me long, I leaned back against the bathroom counter and waited for him to finish. Between the steady sound and the steamy warmth of the falling water, it didn't take long for everything to catch up with me as I stared unseeingly at my bare feet against the pale tile. The bright polish on my toes was mesmerizing. So much so, it took a moment before the fact Zev had called my name penetrated. When it did, I looked up and said, "Sorry, what?"

He stood there, gloriously naked and wet, his hair swept back. "Come here."

"I'll take a shower later." If I took one now, there was a chance I would be done for the night.

"Rory, you're all but asleep on your feet. Get in here, shower, then we'll both crawl into bed."

I gave a fleeting thought to the mess that we left in the living room, then I thought, *Fuck it. It'll still be there in the morning.* Besides, Sabella wasn't coming in until early afternoon, and there was always hotel housekeeping if I got desperate.

I stepped into the oversized shower with Zev. The water felt so good, I was tempted to never leave. Instead, I washed off, with just a few minor detours to wash Zev's back and other parts, then we were both out, toweling off. I debated drying my hair as Zev pulled on his pants commando style. When he handed me his T-shirt, I followed his example and put it on. Then I let Zev lead me to bed. We had pulled back the sheets, and I was about to crawl in when I realized my phone was in the living room. With an aggrieved sigh, I reversed direction.

About to lie down, Zev stopped and asked, "Where are you going?"

I didn't stop walking as I answered. "Living room. I need my phone."

His "Why?" followed me.

Instead of resorting to yelling back and forth, I trudged to the living room, found my phone on the entry table, grabbed it and the vial Grayson left, and headed back. When I hit the doorway to the bedroom, I clued him in, holding up the vial and wiggling it. "Have to set an alarm."

He grimaced as I set it on the table next to his bed. "Hope to gods it goes down better than the first go-around."

Me too. I waited as he lay back, winced, sat up, shoved some pillows behind his back, and lay back again. When he appeared somewhat settled, I reached out and stroked my fingers through his hair. He closed his eyes, some of the lines around his eyes and mouth easing. It helped, seeing that, and a little more anxiety slipped away. "You want some water?"

He murmured, "Sure."

I leaned in, pressed my lips against his forehead, and went to straighten, only to stop when he caught my hip and held me in place. His gaze held mine as I braced a hand on his chest and one on the mattress next to him. I wasn't sure what he was searching for, but I let him look. He must have found it, because he gave my hip a squeeze then let me go.

I shuffled back to the kitchen and nabbed two bottles of chilled water. I turned off all but a soft light in the kitchen part before I headed back to the room. Partway back, I stopped, reversed course, hit the front door, activated the security wards, then retraced my steps back to the room. Zev hadn't moved, so I set the water on the table next to him as quietly as I could.

Without opening his eyes, he asked, "All good?"

"Yep." I skirted the bed and headed to the opposite side, where I set my water on the side table then climbed up beside him. Zev hadn't hogged all the pillows, so I arranged the two on my side then settled in, facing away from him. My head barely touched the pillows before an arm curled around my hips and tugged me back into a solid wall of heat. I sank into him, finding comfort in having him where he belonged.

I threaded my fingers with his and closed my eyes. "Night, babe. Love you."

I felt his lips hit the back of my head, then came his rumbled "Love you too."

The last little bit of tension inched away, and I fell into sleep.

The alarm went off close to four, and somehow, I wrangled a grumpy Zev into downing Grayson's vial. It didn't take him long to fall back to sleep, but that same state eluded me. After lying there, blinking into the darkness while my mind spun in endless, frustrating circles, I finally gave up and snuck out of bed.

I spent the next hour or so cleaning up from the previous night's activities, then I called Lena. It was Friday morning, so I knew she would be up early to get to work. I caught her between donning makeup and drinking coffee. It was too damn early to be up, but here I was, stirring creamer into my coffee and talking with Lena on my phone.

"So, what's Grayson's story?"

"Met him on a case up in Santa Fe," she answered readily enough. "There was a supposed La Llorona abduction, and the local authorities requested Guild assistance."

The Arcane Guild was a collection of magical contracted experts—mercenaries—who demanded top dollar for their services. Case in point, Lena being called into New Mexico to assist on a case. That request was easy enough since Guild employees underwent extensive training that landed them at the top of their particular mage classifications. Of course, that training cost quite a few pretty pennies, of which the Guild always got their cut first. Still, for Guild members, there was no shortage of job opportunities, because someone somewhere always had a mess that needed to be cleaned up.

"La Llorona abduction?" It sounded familiar, but I was having trouble placing it. I leaned back against the counter and sipped my coffee.

"Spirit of a scorned woman who hunts kids."

That did not sound fair at all. "Why kids and not the one who did her wrong?" *Say, the partner that did her dirty?*

"Well…" Lena's voice faded a bit then came back. "According to legend, Llorona, who tends to prefer the name Maria, found out about her less-than-faithful spouse and accidentally killed her two kids in a maddened fit of grief. When she realized what she'd done, she drowned herself in a fit of remorse, but her spirit is trapped here on earth eternally searching for her children. Problem is they're long gone, so to ease that guilt, she'll go after whatever ones she can find, which tends to be offspring of parents who can't keep it in their pants."

I wasn't sure that sounded much better. "Again, not exactly fair. The kiddos didn't do shit."

"I agree, but in this particular case, it wasn't a vengeful spirit so much as a really pissed-off soon-to-be-ex who happened to be a Tracer."

Now it made sense. "Let me guess—your necromancer decided to torment their ex by having a ghost mimic La Llorona."

"Mm-hmm." There was some rustling on the phone, then Lena's voice was back. "Not just any ghost, a previous girlfriend of said ex. The Tracer not only coerced the spirit to their bidding; they ensured it by reinforcing it with a nasty hex. By the time we got the Tracer into custody, the hex had warped into a seriously lethal binding. The spirit took a ride on the dark side, and it took both Grayson and me a shitload of rune work to get it untangled."

Considering Lena was a superstar in her own right, adding Grayson to that equation equaled serious firepower.

"The thing is," Lena continued, "I could've handled it, except that the hex was linked to a latent hex."

Latent hexes were harder than hell to spot because... well, they were latent. They were cast in such a way as to spring to nasty, ugly life when a specific trigger exploded into action. "So what? Grayson's a Static Key?" It was a distinction I'd only recently learned about.

Keys were the epitome of magical code-breakers, and their specialties could run the gamut from mages who could decrypt curses set in cyber-codes to those like Lena and Grayson who could reverse engineer complex, multilevel spell work. Because hexes and curses could be crafted from active and dormant casts, Keys were split into two groups— Static Keys or Agile Keys. Lena was an Agile Key, able to manipulate active casts with unparalleled finesse. If Grayson was a Static Key, his specialty would be in latent hexes.

"Dual Key, actually," Lena said.

Wow, talk about getting the most bang for your buck. I didn't want to think about what his hourly rate was. "Well, damn."

"Exactly," she said. "Which is why I called him in. Luckily for us, he was nearby and available."

And I was eternally grateful that was the case, but... "Tell me you aren't going to get flack for this."

"I'm not going to get flack for this," she dutifully repeated. "And neither are you. This was not a request made through the Guild. This was a personal request from a friend. You're clear from any pushback from the Council."

Because, let's not forget, the Council still had my ass planted in a damn corner in the naughty chair. "Next time you talk with him, tell him I owe him one." *Or maybe three, depending on his going rate.*

"Will do. Hang on a sec."

The sound of a bean grinder filled the line, and I waited it out.

She came back. "Okay, done. By the way, you need to order more coffee."

"Got it."

"So, when's Sabella getting in?"

I'd spent part of my early morning checking emails, one of which had included Sabella's flight information. "Her flight gets in at one twenty, and I've got to head out to pick up the car around lunch."

"Zev going with?" The sound of the fridge door opening and something heavy landing on a counter accompanied her question.

"Don't know." Even though I wasn't keen about leaving him on his own, which was silly considering the suite was warded and he was out of the woods, I also didn't want him to ignore Grayson's order to take it easy. Unfortunately, I had a feeling it would be a discussion I wouldn't win.

On the other end of the line, I heard liquid glugging followed by the *tink* of metal against ceramic as she prepped her own dose of caffeine, then she asked, "You have any idea of what happened?"

I listened to her put something back in the fridge and slam the door shut. "Got some suspicions but nothing concrete."

"Talk to me."

In an effort to ensure I wasn't blinded by my own biases, I spent the next ten minutes doing just that. I ran through the sequence of events from the night before. "I don't know who this Damon is or what his deal is, but my gut says he's behind it."

She asked, "You have anything other than a first name for this guy?"

I shook my head then remembered she couldn't see me. "No, but I have an idea of how to find out." The admission came out reluctantly, because if I followed through with this, I was skirting a very, very thin line on the Council's decree restricting me from accessing Guild resources.

Knowing me as well as she did, Lena had no trouble hearing what I wasn't saying. "Let me talk to him."

Once again, my shit was leaking into my best friend's life. After the last time, I'd sworn to do better. Yet here I was again. "Lena, I'm not sure—"

"Stop, Rory. This has nothing to do with the Guild. Evan doesn't need them to do what he does. This is a friend doing a favor for another friend, nothing more."

It was more than that. She knew it, and I knew it. But since I needed Evan's skills to get the skinny on this Damon guy, the urge to continue the argument faded quickly. "He needs to be careful."

"Please," she scoffed. "Cyberspace is my man's bitch, babe."

My lips quirked. "Make sure his bitch doesn't bite him in the ass."

"Whatever." She blew off my concern with a well-earned assurance of Evan's electronic hunting skills. "Did you catch the name of Damon's arm candy?"

"Nope."

"Notice anything unique? Scars? Tattoos? Interesting jewelry?"

"Nothing that sticks out." Then before I could rethink, I added, "But maybe see if there's a Damon with ties to Virgil Hathaway."

"Who's that?"

The faint connections swirling through my mind bumped into each other. "The new owner of the Gullwing."

"Wait. Back up. What's he got to do with this?"

Then I realized I'd left a very important part out of the conversation. I reversed course and took her through Toby's explanation of the anonymous competitor then followed that up with a recap of the showdown with the Shed Twins. "I might be way off base with all of this, but it's the only thing I can think of that would lead to something like this."

"Over a car? Seriously?" Lena sounded stunned.

"It's a hell of a car," I pointed out.

"If you say so," she answered, not sounding convinced. "I'll have him add it to his search, see what comes up, and let you know."

"Thank you." Those two words didn't convey how deeply I was feeling their meaning.

"No thanks needed, Rory. You'd do the same for me."

That was the goddess's honest truth. "I would, but still, thanks."

Her voice softened. "Always." Then it went back to normal. "Since I've got places to go and people to see, I'm going to let you go. You call me if anything changes."

It wasn't a question, but I still said, "I'll call."

She disconnected, and movement at the edge of my awareness snagged my attention. Zev was leaning against the wall where the hall met the kitchen, hair mussed, eyes heavy with the waning stages of sleep, watching me. I set down my coffee and moved into his space.

"Hey, you." I carefully brushed my fingers along his jaw. "How are you feeling?"

His gaze drifted over my face with a disconcerting intensity before it shifted to his hand, where he was tucking some of my hair behind my ear. "Better." His voice was hoarse as if his throat were raw, then his gaze came back to mine. "It doesn't feel like some animal is trying to claw its way out of my gut."

I dropped my gaze and let my lashes drift down to hide my wince. "Well, that's something, I guess." I settled my hands on his waist and gave a gentle nudge. "You should be in bed."

"Woke up, you were gone. Went looking." He trailed a finger from my ear down to my jaw then tipped my head up. "Heard you talking."

"Lena," I murmured. "I couldn't sleep, so I cleaned up and figured I'd call her back before she left for work." Determined to get him back where he belonged, I wrapped my arm around his hips and steered him back to the bedroom. "Come on, hot stuff, let's get you tucked in."

He held firm, refusing to move. "Tucked in? What am I? Three?"

There was a hint of offense in his tone, so I tilted my head, pressed my palm against his chest, and teased, "Only if I have to bribe you into following the doctor's orders."

He dropped his arm around my shoulders, leaned in, and brushed his nose against mine with a heart-tugging sweetness before straightening. "What kind of bribe are we talking about?"

My grin spread at the hint of provocativeness in his

banter. Not because of what it offered but because it meant he was on the road to recovery. "How about I promise to kiss it better?"

His answering smile was a bit rueful. "Not sure I can take that much goodness."

"Alternate offer." I led him back down the hall. "How about one kiss now, and we'll have a follow-up later?"

"Deal."

THIRTEEN

ZEV FELL BACK TO SLEEP, and I managed to catch another hour or so before I was back up. This time, I was extra careful to let him sleep even though I spent a good amount of time just watching him do it. I was relieved to see that even though faint circles still remained under his eyes, his overall color was back to normal. The lines around his eyes and mouth had eased, and his breathing was slow and steady. When my last fragments of anxiety were soothed away, I got up, grabbed my phone, and headed to the living room to start my day.

Just because we were in Vegas didn't mean I wasn't on the clock. I went through emails and pulled up Sabella's flight so I could track it. She was already in the air, and so far, it looked like she would be on time. I also had a message from the car rental company explaining they would be calling me in a couple more hours to confirm Sabella's reservation. By the time they did, I was on my fourth cup of coffee, and while my nerves were far from steady, I was definitely wired.

Hyped on caffeine, I may have gotten a little demanding with the reservation clerk, but with no idea who Damon's target was—me, Zev, or both—there was no way I wasn't taking every available precaution when picking up my great-aunt. That included upgrading her rental with the company's highest security package, which meant the luxury four-door sedan would be tricked out with multifaceted defensive wards.

As much as I appreciated the added security, it didn't alleviate all my concerns. I would have to deal with those lingering worries directly, including that Zev insisted on coming with me to pick up Sabella. Continuing the conversation that had started when he was in the shower, I asked the stubborn jackass, who was currently pulling on a shirt as I finished braiding my hair, "Do you really think that's wise?"

"I'm fine, Rory." Despite being muffled by his shirt, the exasperation in his voice was noticeable. His head popped through the collar as he tugged the material into place. He raked a hand through his damp hair then stepped in close until his body was pressed against mine.

I shot him a dark look then went back to braiding my hair. "Grayson said you were to take it easy."

Being busy tying off my hair left me wide-open when his hands hit the bathroom counter to create a flesh-and-bone cage. In the mirror, his gaze caught and held mine with a warmth he shared only with me, but it did jack all to ease his steely edge of determination. "I'm coming with you."

"Fine." It came out snappy, mainly because I knew arguing would get me nowhere.

He pressed his lips against the back of my neck, and goosebumps ran up and down my spine, loosening it enough that I sank back into him. He rested his chin on my shoulder. "I really am okay. I wouldn't lie about that."

"I know." And I did, but memories of him writhing on the floor with bloodstained lips weren't easily ignored. I toyed with the frayed edges of the red bracelet still wrapped around his wrist.

He stayed quiet, letting me brood for another minute or so, then he turned his hand over and caught my fingers with his. "Come on. Let's go find you something to put in your stomach besides coffee."

He went to step back, but I tightened my hold on his wrist, keeping him in place.

"What?" he asked.

I searched his face, looking for some sign I might have missed, because the man I knew wouldn't be this... calm about things. "Why aren't you more upset?"

He didn't pretend to misunderstand. "Two reasons. One, it's not good if both of us are letting our tempers lead the way."

Okay, valid point. "And two?"

"And two..." His voice hardened as the predator I knew and loved prowled out from behind the mature mask. "I'm waiting for Evan to confirm our target."

Reassured by his pitiless response, the claws that had gripped my chest since the minute he'd gone down finally eased up. "Got it." I squeezed his wrist then let him go. "Right, so, food. What do you feel like?"

It took another twenty minutes before we decided to bypass room service or the heavier offerings of the hotel restaurants. Instead, we decided to catch a rideshare to the car rental place. Sabella was coming in on a private charter and landing at North Las Vegas Airport. The smaller venue offered an escape from the hectic maze of McCarran's much busier terminals, but it meant an extra twenty-minute drive for me to pick up the car from the rental agency. After asking our driver to make a pitstop at a drive-through, we downed our egg-and-biscuit combos on the way.

The agency's service was quick and efficient, but it still took us close to forty minutes to sign the paperwork, verify coverage, and review the vehicle and its warding before I was able to finally get behind the wheel. While Zev clicked his seat belt into place, I checked the status of Sabella's flight.

The pilot must have caught a tailwind or whatever, because the plane was now arriving fifteen minutes early. A check of the time confirmed I had enough time to get back to the smaller airport with time to spare. We hit a couple of spots that tested my schedule, but Zev and I were sitting on the blue couches in the waiting area of the terminal when Sabella came into view on the arm of a bemused pilot.

I shook my head as I got to my feet, Zev rising next to me. It was always amusing to watch my great-aunt's impact on mere mortals. All it took was a smile or frown to cast those orbiting around her to either dazzling heights or plummeting into the pit of despondency. Granted, I wasn't immune. Even now, after knowing our familial connection, I stepped warily, because she was a force to be reckoned with.

Despite our shared genetics, she was not only taller and curvier than me, but her hair was a mix of golds and browns, making it appear a lighter, more golden version of mine. Currently, a pair of sunglasses was perched on top. She carried herself with an innate grace few could match. There were one or two fine lines on her aristocratic face, and if a guess had to be made on her age, most would put her in her early fifties. They would be under by about ten years. Power followed in her wake as she moved through the small airport with an innate grace born from being the head of one of the original twenty-seven Arcane Families and a woman used to being in charge.

She caught sight of us, and a smile broke over her face. She said something to the pilot, who dipped his head in acknowledgment but couldn't hide the color along his cheeks. She patted his arm, let him go, and started toward us.

We met her halfway. She caught me up in a hug and murmured, "*Cattivella*. I'm so glad to see you."

The first time she'd used the diminutive, I had to ask its

meaning. When she shared it meant "troublemaker," all I could do was laugh. Even now, it still made me smile. "*Zia* Sabella. Nice to see you haven't lost your charming touch." I aimed a knowing look to the young pilot, who watched her walk toward us.

She didn't bother looking back, but her husky laugh was unmistakable. When she was close enough not be overheard, she said, "He's a lovely young man, but *young* is the key word." She turned to Zev and leaned in to exchange air-kisses. "Zev, *caro*, I'm so glad you could come for the weekend."

"Thanks for the invite." He straightened and looked around. "Where are your bags?"

She waved a long-fingered hand in the air. "They'll be delivered to the hotel."

"In that case…" He offered her his arm.

She gave another low laugh and accepted his offer as I took up a position on her other side, keeping her securely between us. As we headed for the exit, I asked, "So, how was your trip?"

Her amusement dimmed, and her nose wrinkled in irritation. "It was tedious in some parts, better in others."

Hmm, sounds like there's a story in there. "And your friends?"

"Good, good. They're getting ready to head over to France to visit to sit with their grandbabies while their parents attend a business conference." The exit doors slid open, and she pulled her sunglasses down to hold back the morning light. "How's the suite?"

I did the same with mine as we stepped outside. "It's nice."

Our conversation stayed light as we got to the car. When Zev held Sabella back while I checked on the security wards, she took it in another direction. "Why do I get the impression that something has happened?"

My great-aunt was no one's fool. Not that I didn't expect her to pick up on the undercurrents, but I wasn't about to discuss things in the open.

"It was an interesting evening," I said as I pulled open the back door for her to get in.

She moved into the space between us, gripping the edge of the door in one hand while she kept hold of Zev's in the other. "You'll share?"

My dark lenses met hers, and I gave a tiny nod. "In the car, though."

She studied me for a long moment, then, with a slight headshake, she slid into the back seat. Zev stepped back, and I closed the door. He caught my hand as I went to get into the driver's seat, and I looked back over my shoulder, my eyebrows raised in silent question.

He kept his voice low, probably so it wouldn't carry. "All of it?"

Realizing he was asking how much I planned to reveal, I said, "Yeah, all of it."

It was no use keeping anything from Sabella. Not only had I tried that in the past with less-than-stellar results, but she knew more about the subversive maneuvering that swam under the surface of the Arcane society than anyone I knew. If Evan failed to get us a name, I was betting she would put the pieces together and find one.

Without argument, Zev let me go so we could both get in the car. As soon as we cleared the airport and traffic eased up, Sabella started in. "What happened that has you so vigilant?"

I flexed my fingers on the steering wheel and breathed away the tension so I could keep my calm as I filled her in on all that had happened, with Zev interjecting here and there. Even though I tried to read her reactions through the rearview mirror, she didn't give me much to work with. Her head was turned to the window, giving me her profile as she listened.

I went through my meeting with Tony, how we'd picked up the Gullwing, and our subsequent shadows before our little altercation with the roadside restaurant. "After Zev put the Shed Twins in time-out, we made it to town and handed off the keys to Virgil Hathaway."

"These Shed Twins," Sabella said, her voice keen. "Where are they now?"

"We don't know," Zev answered.

"Hmm." Instead of pursing that, she switched lanes. "Virgil Hathaway? As in the middle son of Winston Hathaway?"

Something in her voice made me want to check her expression in the rearview mirror, but I didn't dare take my attention from navigating from the far-left lane to the upcoming exit. "Didn't ask for his family's lineage, but unless there are two of them hanging out on the Strip with money to burn, I'll go with yes?"

She then proceeded to educate us on who the loafer-wearing, slightly sleazy car aficionado truly was. "If he's one and the same, his family is behind the conglomerate Regal Enterprises."

Zev twisted in his seat so he could look at Sabella. "Aren't they one of the bigger players in the North American entertainment industry?"

"Entertainment?" I asked, thinking of the show from the night before. "As in, like, last night's show?"

"No, more like the burlesque type," Zev said.

"Don't be shy, Zev," Sabella chided. "Regal Entertainment was born and bred in Vegas. They started out in the early days with a string of strip clubs, and over time, they've rebranded into a chain of top-dollar, high-end clubs and burlesque shows that span the US and Canada. Last year, they snagged quite a feather in their cap when one of the entertainment arms of the Moretti Family signed a merger which will allow Hathaway to expand into Europe within the year."

That would explain how Virgil could afford the Gullwing.

I caught Zev's frown. "The Morettis are one of the European originals. How did Hathaway get their signature on a merger?"

Amusement and a hint of approval wove through Sabella's voice when she said, "Because Moretti the Younger, who has no qualms about expanding questionable ventures, managed to convince the board of directors that Moretti the Senior is borderline senile."

I asked, "Is he really?"

"Is he really what?"

"Senile? Or was it an opportunity for Moretti the Younger to take the wheel?"

She patted my shoulder. "You're too young to be so cynical."

I blew out a puff of air. "Please, if you're willing to use shareholders to force out your parent, I'm thinking compassion is the smallest component of consideration." Not to mention the older Arcane Families were beyond ruthless when it came to power.

"In this case, Moretti Senior is definitely losing it, but not to the extreme extent his son portrayed." The leather whispered a groan as she sat back. "However, the younger Moretti is not only keen on utilizing new innovations to grow the family fortunes, but he's willing to take the risks for the associated payoffs."

Zev straightened in his seat, his tone drier than the desert around us. "And clubs and shows are going to start raking in the cash?"

A light laugh came from the back seat. "No, but overhauling Moretti's outdated dinner clubs with Hathaway's more risqué touch will do double duty by offsetting the accumulated debt that particular business arm has accrued while expanding Moretti's waning reputation with the younger generations."

"So a win-win, then." I hit the turn signal and began gliding through traffic to catch the upcoming exit ramp.

"Perhaps, perhaps not." She didn't elaborate, and after a moment, she circled back around to our original conversation. "Did you find out who it was that wanted Virgil's toy?"

I slid in between a Jeep and a trundling van that was held together with duct tape and got off the freeway. Stopped at the light, I exchanged a look with Zev before I answered, "We think so."

"What kind of answer is that?"

Before I could take umbrage at her exasperated question, Zev took over. "We only have a first name, and that's because it's the only person we can think who had access to me to lay a hex."

An electric awareness surged through the car, wiping out whatever easygoing vibe remained, and Sabella's question carried a sharp edge. "Hex?" Before either of us could answer, she added, "As you appear to be okay and Rory's not rampaging through the Strip, I'm assuming you've disabled it."

"I'm good," Zev said at the same time as I said, "I had Lena call in reinforcements."

Sabella ignored Zev and homed in on my response. "Who did she send?"

"Grayson, no last name." At least not one I could remember, if Lena had even shared it. Things were kind of a blur, but I didn't think she had. "He's a dual-level Key with the Guild."

"Does the Council—"

"No." I cut her off before she could finish, trying my best not to be irritated. "Lena made a personal request to a friend."

"Good." She paused. "A dual-level Key? How close was it?"

Too fucking close. "Close enough."

"But I'm fine now." Zev left no room for debate in his statement. Then he lifted his arm high enough so Sabella could see the red bracelet on his wrist. "This is all that's left."

"Be sure you don't touch it when it falls off," she advised.

Hearing that warning for the second time, this time around not when I was freaking out over whether or not Zev would survive, I finally asked, "What happens if he does?"

"It's a basic talisman that focuses protective magic on its wearer," she said. "If that same wearer touches it once it completes its job, they negate its work."

"Seriously? That's all it takes to mess it up?"

"It's a magical construct. Whether its potency is fueled by power or belief is up for debate, but it's wise to err on the side of caution."

I didn't mind being careful, especially if kept Zev from harm. "Guess it's good that I've already promised to be the one that burns it," I said, unsurprised that she knew what that bit of thread meant.

"Who got close enough to poison you?" Even though there was a hint of anger in her question, it also carried bits of disbelief.

I understood both. Considering his position as the Cordova Family's Arbiter, Zev wasn't one to be off guard. Hell, he was normally the one in position to take others off guard. "Damon."

"Damon?" she repeated as if that would help her pin down a face.

"Heard anything about a Damon being connected to Virgil?" When she didn't answer straight-out and instead made a noncommittal hum, I pushed. "Sabella?"

"I think I've heard the name somewhere, but I'm having trouble placing it. Perhaps I can ask around."

I wasn't sure if I wanted her asking around. Bad enough Zev and I were being targeted. If this really was about the damn car and Virgil, I wanted to keep Sabella clear. I went to warn her off, when Zev spoke up.

"Or we can wait and see if Evan can get us his last name."

"Which won't be until he's not on the Guild's clock," I added before she could ask. "I already warned Lena that her even asking him was skating a thin line, but she wouldn't back down."

"Of course she wouldn't, dear, and you'd be silly to even think she would," Sabella chided. "I'm surprised he hasn't sent you a name yet."

"It's only been a few hours. Plus, it's Friday, and he's at work. I'm not expecting anything until later." Since the Guild closed down at five, we still had hours to go. "So, what's on the agenda for today?"

"I thought I'd stop by a couple of shops this afternoon then finish up with a lovely dinner at this little place I know."

I exchanged a quick look with Zev, who said, "Sounds like a date."

"*Che buono,*" she said in a pleased little murmur. "It'll be a lovely evening."

FOURTEEN

ONCE WE GOT BACK to the hotel, I bullied Zev into lying down while we waited for Sabella's luggage to arrive. He managed to start a half-assed argument before Sabella and I teamed up and badgered him into our way of thinking. Only when he got our promise to stick to the two-stops-only shopping itinerary did he retreat to the bedroom, glaring and grumbling the entire time.

I waited until the door closed with a soft snick before I turned to my great-aunt. "Thank you."

Seated in the corner of the plush sectional, she waved her glass of ice and sparkling water in the air as if to wipe away my words. "You do realize he'll probably track us down within an hour after we leave, don't you?"

"I'm aware." I slouched a little deeper into the couch cushion until I could rest my head against the back, stretched my legs out, then crossed them at the ankles. Zev's identity centered around protecting those he considered his, so he would be uncomfortable having to take an hour or two to recover from almost dying. "But he really does need to rest."

She studied me for a moment, and whatever she saw had her asking quietly, "How close was it, really?"

Since she was family and Zev meant something to both of us, I was brutally honest. "According to Grayson, it was a modified bane hex, and if Lena hadn't called him in when she did, Zev wouldn't have made it."

Something dark and untamed flickered and glowed in her hazel eyes, like an incoming thunderstorm, before her lashes drifted down, and she studied her glass. When she returned her gaze to mine, her eyes were more green than hazel, a dangerous sign. "This Grayson, was he able to identify who crafted the hex?"

"A midlevel, black-market Key that ghosted to Mexico to escape her upset customers."

"Does this Key have a name?" she asked with a studied indifference that didn't fool me in the least.

It's nice to know where I inherited my need for vengeance from. "Didn't get one."

"Mmm." That soft hum was her only response before she took a sip of her water, but I had a feeling Grayson would be getting a follow-up call.

I waited until she lowered her glass before saying, "You'll call me when you find out."

She didn't answer, simply held my gaze a moment before changing the subject. "I got a call from Christina the other day."

I managed not to wince as she homed in on the one conversational switch I wasn't sure I was ready to make. "How's the Councilwoman doing?"

"As well as can be expected." She paused, probably expecting me to ask, but when I didn't, she continued "Your contract is scheduled to come under review next week."

It was my turn for a noncommittal hum.

Her eyes narrowed. "What is this?" She emphasized "this" by circling her glass in the air.

I laced my fingers over my gut and stared at my boots. I

had no idea how she would take my decision, so I tried to circle around it. "This is me playing it cool."

Her inelegant snort took me by surprise, and I looked over to see her shaking her head. "Bullshit," she said once she caught my eye. "Tell me what's going on in that head of yours."

It sucked how much the orphaned girl raised by the state still lived in me, because my desire not to disappoint her was twisting me up. But I wasn't that little girl anymore, and while Sabella might not agree with my decision, she wouldn't throw away her last connection to her dead twin's daughter. At least, I hoped she wouldn't. "I'm not sure I want to renew the Council's contract."

Instead of the expected reproach, I got a slow, sharp smile. "Good."

Taken aback, I blinked. "Um, what?"

"I said, 'Good.'" She sat back, crossing one tailored linen leg over the other.

Totally confused now, I sputtered, "But aren't you… like… I don't know… upset that I'd even consider turning it down?"

"Not in the least." And there was no trace of lie in her voice. "In fact, it shows how intelligent you are that you would."

Okay, what the hell? Thrown, I shot her a frown. "But you've always said how important it was to cultivate connections—"

"And power," she pointed out. "Yes, it is. However, what has been, and always will be, more important is whether you choose to be a tool others use—"

"Or the threat they'll think twice about pulling." I finished the familiar refrain. Why I hadn't remembered that little nugget was beyond me. Maybe because I'd been so wrapped up in my own head for too damn long, making this decision much more difficult than it truly was. The knots in my gut started to unravel, evidence I'd been more wound up than I realized about this impending conversation.

She lifted her glass in a silent toast. "Exactly." She lowered the glass back to the armrest. "I'm not surprised you want to distance yourself from the Council. Others will view your refusal of exclusivity to the Council as proof of your neutrality."

"*If* I choose not to re-up the contract, it doesn't mean I won't still consider jobs from them."

"Of course not, but you've shared many times that your intentions have always been to remain independent of what you call 'Family drama.' However, I have to admit you were starting to worry me recently with how far you would be willing to go to stay clear."

"Worry you?"

"Mm-hmm." She studied me with a frown. "Even though you've done your best not to share, I'm not unaware of the financial toll you've taken with the withdrawal of the Council's contract." She tapped a polished nail against her glass as she watched me. "For curiosity's sake, how close did you come to taking that job down in Green Valley, the one with the art dealer?"

Well, shit. How does she know these things? Heat rose under my cheeks, but in a small victory, I managed not squirm. "Does it matter?"

The dealer had approached me about delivering an art piece to a customer in Mexico. Like any good Transporter, I'd requested a copy of the piece's provenance, an official record of ownership I would need when dealing with the authorities while crossing the border. The dealer hemmed and hawed then offered a five-figure bonus on top of an already-expensive bill, but I held firm on my request. He reluctantly promised he would have the paperwork to me in twenty-four hours.

After his awkward avoidance dance, I decided to do a

little more digging into the dealer while I waited for the documents. I had to go down a few less-than-legit rabbit holes, but I finally ran down a couple of whispers of not-so-legal sales. Now, admittedly, there had been a time when those whispers wouldn't have given me pause, but that time had passed. I'd learned a few hard lessons about the difference between riding the line between black and white and charging blithely right over it. Therefore, when he called me back to say he had the paperwork in hand, and after some serious internal debate between ethics and practicality, I politely declined the job, citing unexpected scheduling conflicts. He hadn't taken it well, but losing a potential client was much more preferable than spending time in a Mexican jail cell, no matter how tempting the eventual paycheck.

Granted, my choice had been touch and go. I held my aunt's gaze. "I didn't take it."

"I'm aware, but that wasn't my question." She pinned me in place, a shrewd light in her eyes. "How close, Rory?"

I dropped my head back, glared at the ceiling, and admitted reluctantly, "Too fucking close, okay? But I wasn't about to risk my business or my reputation, no matter how dicey things were getting with money being so tight."

"And therein lies my concern."

Not following, I stopped glaring at the ceiling and shifted my gaze back to her. "About what?"

She avoided my gaze by keeping hers on the glass in her hand as she swirled the liquid inside. "When our relationship became public, it renewed attention from sources I'd foolishly thought long dormant."

This did not sound good, but it was an unexpected opening. "Hence the reason you've been out of sorts?"

She looked startled, as if surprised. "Out of sorts?"

Now it was my turn to take the conversation down uninvited roads. "Something's been eating at you for the last few months. Any chance you want to share?"

Her lips thinned.

"I haven't pushed because I figured when you were ready, you'd talk, but…"

"But?" she prompted reluctantly.

"But you've stayed tight-lipped."

"And perhaps there was good reason for that."

"Perhaps there was." I took care to keep my tone neutral as I sat up and braced my arms on my knees. "But you keep pushing about my business decisions, which should not impact you in any way, and it makes me wonder why."

"Do you know that one of the first things considered when planning a hostile takeover is identifying your target's potential weak points?" she asked without looking away from me. "Most often those weaknesses revolve around finances, or lack thereof."

Her nonanswer set my mind spinning. I dropped my gaze to the floor between my feet as, like a series of rapid-fire snapshots, the pieces fell into place. "The job, it was a setup."

"Yes, it was," she confirmed. "A smaller, subtler play in a much larger game."

I looked up. "The larger game being the reason behind your extended visit back east and your son's recent issues overseas."

She inclined her head. "I won't go into detail, as it no longer matters."

And that could be because whoever was foolish enough to threaten Sabella and her family's holdings was dead, bankrupt, or both.

"But suffice to say, you were considered an access point. Something I was not notified about until well after the fact." Something she did not sound at all happy about.

I tilted my head and offered cautiously, "Should I apologize?"

"For?"

I shrugged. "Hell if I know, but I feel like…" I honestly

had not the first clue how I felt about this. Bits and pieces of conversations and reactions filtered through my head like a kaleidoscope, and the picture shifted again. This time, I knew exactly how I felt. "No, nope, nuh-uh. I take it back. Forget I even asked. There's not one damn thing I need to apologize for." Anger fueled by frustration warmed my words. I clasped my hands and pressed my fingers into my knuckles so tightly, it turned them bloodless. "How high is the possibility that the attack on Zev is tied to whatever it is you had to do to resolve your 'issues'?"

"Truthfully?" She gave a very Gallic shrug. "It could swing either way."

I ground my teeth and fought for patience. Sabella's position was such that she rarely, if ever, had to justify her actions. Hell, I'd watched the Council tippy-toe around her more than once, and that was one group of scary-ass mages. But even though I'd railed against her claiming me as hers before grudgingly giving in and acknowledging our relationship, a part of me felt betrayed. I didn't need years of therapy to understand why that deep-seated insecurity would always sprout such dark thoughts.

Didn't I deserve to be warned that someone I loved might be a target? Hell, that I might be a target?

If I blurted out those questions, all I would get in return was a haughty look complete with brush-off, so I swallowed down my temper. "Why?"

"Are you asking why it could swing either way?"

No, but I would go with that. For now. I gave a sharp nod.

There was a spark of amusement or satisfaction—I wasn't sure which—there and gone before she regained her impassive façade. "First, because I'm still working to uncover not only the who but also the reasons behind the why."

That brought my anger to an abrupt halt and replaced it with a return of my earlier tendrils of uneasiness.

"Second," she continued in an ominous tone, unaware or

uncaring that I was starting to freak out, "as our particular Family's history has proven, when it comes to such conflicts, nothing and no one is off-limits."

I felt my face pale as my heart thudded hard and fast in my ears. "Are you saying this goes back to that?"

"That" being the string of assassinations whose victims included both my parents, my maternal grandmother, who happened to be Sabella's twin, and even as far back my great-grandfather, the twins' father. My parents had tried desperately to escape their fates, even changing their names, but in the end, they couldn't get far-enough away.

Even Sabella was too late. She'd finally tracked down my mom, only to discover she'd been dead for two years. I'd already become a ward of the state. Fueled by grief and darker things, my great-aunt had taken her vengeance and left me to make my way with the Arcane Guild, thinking it was safer for me to be an orphan than connected in any way to her. I'd asked her once if the decision had been more self-serving than selfless. Her answer? "Both."

"I thought you took care of things?" *Read, "wiped out entire lineages to avenge the Giordano deaths."*

"Things were finished." Frustration flashed through her face, tightening her lips and narrowing her eyes. "But it seems that the saying that nothing is certain except death and taxes is all too real."

"Meaning you missed someone." And if all of this conjecture was true, me and mine were going to pay for it. *Shitshitshit. Zev wasn't the only person I counted as mine.*

I shot to my feet and dug out my phone. "Dammit, I need to warn to Lena."

Sabella set down her glass and rose with me. She caught my wrist and gave it a tug, stopping me from hitting Lena's number. "No, you don't."

"I'm not leaving her in the wind," I all but snarled.

Her grip tightened enough to send a flare of pain up to

my elbow. "I'm not asking you to, Rory. Take a breath and listen to me." She waited for me to angrily suck in air and blow it out, but she didn't let me go. "What are you going to tell Lena to watch for?" Her gaze was sharp and hard, almost as hard as her voice. "Who should she watch for? Hmm?"

"I don't know," I snapped. "Anyone or anything suspicious."

"She's a highly rated Guild Key," Sabella said, pointing out the obvious. "She already does that. What else can you tell her?"

I ground my teeth in frustration. I didn't have an answer.

She gave my wrist a shake then let it go. "If I had specifics to share, I would, but I don't."

I clutched my phone. "What do you have?"

"Not much." She ran a hand over her hip, a nervous tell it had taken me months to pick up on. "Just an itch at the back of my neck and a gut feeling."

"There has to be something more than that." I blanked the screen on my phone, put it back in my pocket, then folded my arms over my chest.

She paced a couple steps away. "I wish there was, but I have nothing solid, just bits and pieces."

"And what are those bits and pieces?"

"Whispers started some time ago that have grown in strength and undermined the board's confidence in our business dealings. It was Xanto who noticed it first. He tried his best to do damage control, but when he realized his patch job wasn't holding, he called me in."

I recognized the name of her oldest son, the one who ran the extensive Giordano business holdings. "The first time you flew back to Italy after you offered me a job?"

"Yes, that was the beginning, at least, for us. Since then, we've uncovered a handful of other areas with similar issues, and we've been taking care of them one by one. But this last one was the worst, and had we not reacted as quickly as we did, we would've lost our foothold here in America."

"Has it been focused on just business?"

She shook her head. "I went home in November because someone tried to kidnap my grandbaby." She turned away to pace over to the balcony doors. "Xanto's wife, Anise, was able to intervene and keep little Isaiah safe, but the attempt left the family shaken."

I bet it did. To take on the Rossi Family spoke to a level of arrogance that was stupid, arrogant, or both. "Why didn't you tell me any of this?"

She stayed at the window, her attention focused outside. "What could you do?"

"I don't know, but something." Not to mention, it would've been nice to know.

She looked back over her shoulder. "I appreciate the thought, *cara*, but truthfully"—she turned back to the view—"Xanto and I considered it handled."

I walked over and joined her, leaning a shoulder against the heavy glass as I studied her profile. "And you have no idea who's behind this?"

"No."

"What about the idiot who tried to snatch Isaiah?"

Her lips curved up, but the small smile was full of cruel satisfaction. "He didn't survive Anise's displeasure." The momentary reveal of the iron-willed matriarch faded away. "We have people working other avenues, but unfortunately, such things require a more nuanced approach."

Translation: her Hunters were on the trail, but they were being sneaky about it so as not to piss off the other powerful Families when they finally brought their prey to ground. "So, what do we do here?"

"We go shopping?"

I blinked. That was not the answer I expected. "Are you nuts?"

She turned to me, linked her arm through mine, and drew me away from the window. "Not in the slightest. But I am willing to play the entitled matriarch who's arrogant enough to forego security because she believes she's solved her family's issues."

I look to the beautiful, devious woman I shared DNA with and couldn't help matching her smile. "You want to play bait?"

"Darling, don't you know? The most dangerous predators are the ones who know how to play prey."

FIFTEEN

"WHAT DO YOU THINK?" A couple hours later, Sabella was twisting this way and that to check out her outfit in the ornate mirror provided in the private changing room.

Since this was the third time she'd tried on the exact same blouse, I waved to the nearby metal rack. "Add it to the others." The "others" were two pairs of tailored slacks, a scarf skirt, three blouses in red, green, and deep purple that was close to black, and a copper-toned sheath that thumbed its nose at the all-too-common concept of little black dress. All were proof that unlike me, my aunt loved shopping.

She faced the mirror and struck a pose as she examined her reflection. "Hmm, I think I will."

I barely refrained from shouting, *Hallelujah!*

The shopping assistant who had latched on to Sabella the minute she swanned into the high-end designer store murmured with the appropriate amount of enthusiasm, "Wonderful. Would you like to see anything else?"

Please say no. Please say no. I sent the mental plea out into the universe in hopes someone would hear it and deign to answer.

"No, thank you." Sabella finally turned away from the

mirror and said the most beautiful thing. "This should be enough for now."

Oh, thank gods!

My phone vibrated with an incoming text. My pulse tripped with my hope that it was Evan. Instead, it was Zev: *Where are you?*

While Sabella changed back and concluded her business, I shot back a quick *In hell.*

"Is that Zev?"

I looked up to see my aunt back in her original outfit. "Yeah, he's wondering where we are."

She took a seat on a padded bench and slid her feet back into the sky-high heels she insisted on wearing. "Well, you can let him know we're heading back." She gave one elegantly shod heel a tug, then she got up and headed toward the door. "Did he make reservations like I asked?"

"Already done." I shoved my way out of the poufy chair I'd collapsed in when we hit this store forty minutes earlier. I followed her out of the changing room area. "We're on for a six-fifteen table."

"And it's what? Four now?"

I didn't need to check the time, because it was etched in my head. "Four forty, actually."

She paused, pursed her lips, then made one of those expressive hand waves she was so fond of. "We'll be fine."

It took another ten minutes to wrap things up. Thankfully, I didn't have to act the pack mule because this store, much like the previous one, was happy to send Sabella's purchases to her suite at the Four Seasons.

Normally, I would have no issue carrying her bags—I'd done it before—but from the moment we'd stepped out of the hotel lobby to wait for the valet to bring the sedan around, my neck had itched like it was covered in hives. The disquieting sensation was bad enough, and I seriously debated manhandling my aunt back to the room. I wouldn't have been the least bit successful, because Sabella was determined to play this game to its bitter end.

With no choice but to stay the course of playing bait, I kept my Prism locked and loaded, ready for anything, even though it was a low-level drain on my energy. Nothing I couldn't handle, especially after training for hours on end with Zev on how to utilize my magic both offensively and defensively. The latter much more instinctive than the former.

That was the thing with Prisms—as a rare class of mages who could not only withstand most magical attacks but turn them back on the caster, we were uniquely suited to play human shields for other mages. In the past, the wealthy Families had utilized our abilities to keep their bloodlines intact, but like it was with most finite resources, overuse had depleted the resource. The last few remaining Prisms had disappeared and gone underground once they saw the ugly writing on the wall. In order to avoid becoming extinct in truth, they'd become another fantastical tale in the Arcane's urban-legend compendium. Unfortunately, their decision had left those of us who came after—and I knew of only me—completely unaware of what it meant to be a Prism.

My introduction had come when I was a kid, after a pyromage tried to prove he was the king of the shelter and ended up with a face full of fire. That was the first time I heard the term *Prism*, and the source was a schizophrenic homeless man named Algin. Armed with an actual label, I tried to find more information, but the Arcane Families had done a hell of a job wiping the history books clear.

It wasn't until I hooked up with Zev and Sabella that I finally got my hands on an unchanged documentation of what being a Prism really meant. To say it was eye-opening was putting it mildly. My learning curve had been steep and was still rocky, but there had been enough to help me refine and hone the power that lay within me.

"Shall we?" Sabella's voice snapped my attention back to the present.

"After you."

I followed her out into the rush of humanity that filled the wide walkways. Vegas was a world of its own, where hotels were full-fledged entertainment centers and shopping malls that offered whatever a materialistic heart desired. Our first stop had been the north end of the strip, but now we were back in the thick of it at Cesar's Palace, a shopper's mecca and a freaking nightmare when trying to watch Sabella's back.

While a Prism's shield remained invisible to the naked eye, every time a passerby with even a drop of power at their disposal got close, it reacted, strengthening or easing back as needed. That was where the magical drain came in. I told Lena once it was like carrying a glass of water through a mob in a blacked-out room while trying not to spill the contents. It had taken months to figure how to ride the rise and fall of the Prism in action, and in this current environment, I was thrilled to have that training to fall back on.

Eventually, we made our way to the escalator, and that was about the time that annoying itch started again. This time, as we strolled past windows, I used the reflective surfaces to check our back trail. Not ideal, but it was better than being obvious about it. I kept close to Sabella, which made it easier to keep her contained inside my Prism. She wasn't unaware of what I was doing, but other than a beleaguered sigh, she didn't protest and adjusted her pace to fall in with mine.

It also helped that this part of the mall wasn't as populated. Nothing caught my attention until we started down the quieter walkway that led to the parking garage. It was a flash that could be easily missed in the busier main halls, but here, where the amount of foot traffic dropped drastically, it was hard to miss. A familiar, pissed-off face.

"Well, shit." I curled my hand around Sabella's elbow and upped our pace.

"What?"

"We've got company."

"Lovely."

Leave it to her to make it sound like we were about to sit down to a tea party. "No, actually, it's not."

"You know this is why we're here." She kept her voice low so her words stayed between us.

"Right, but I'd rather not face off against the Shed Twins in front of an audience that can double as collateral." This short hall to the parking garage was also less than ideal because there was only one exit—the sliding doors leading into the garage. No fire access doors or Maintenance Only doors where I could lure them out of the limelight.

"Who are we running from?"

"Blond on the left at eleven o'clock. Dark and murderous to the right at four."

"Abilities?"

"Left casting mage, can mess with your perception of reality. One to the right likes to use magical bullets and turn things into metal."

I barely caught her murmured, "Well, then," before power swelled from my aunt and lapped against my Prism. Her magic felt like super-sharp claws kneading my skin from the inside out. I gritted my teeth until it slowly retreated. It didn't disappear—oh, no, *that* would be a relief. Instead, it crouched at the edge of my awareness, waiting for its prey to wander closer. It made me remind her, "Dead mages can't give you answers."

Her light laugh was far from amused. "I'm aware."

We were close enough to the glass doors now that Sabella was able to pick them out of the reflection. "They're getting closer," she pointed out unhelpfully.

"I'm aware."

"Well, I hope you have a plan."

No, what I had was a half-assed idea, but even that was better than nothing.

We hit whatever invisible point necessary to trigger the doors. They whooshed open, and we got a face full of exhaust-ladened air. I nudged Sabella ahead of me as we rushed across the concrete and into the collection of parked vehicles. Overhead, the rumble of a passing truck vibrated through the concrete space, drowning out our passage.

My first priority was getting Sabella to safety, and the safest place I had for her was parked about five hundred feet from the entrance and half-hidden by a two-foot-thick dividing wall that blocked off the front and passenger side. It might be stupid to head for where we'd be, for all intents and purposes, cornered, but I would rather have those two walls at my back than nothing at all.

I waited for the echoes to fade before saying, "Head to the car."

She shot me a disgusted look. "I'm not about to sit in the back seat and watch while you have all the fun."

"Just get to the car. Please." I stayed behind her as we hurried across the pavement.

A faint squeal of tires and an approaching engine proceeded a dark SUV appearing at the far end of the garage as it came down the ramp from the level above. There was something about how it rolled past the first row then the second that caught my attention.

Shitshitshit.

Could the Shed Twins have brought in a third?

Maybe?

Just in case, I gave up all pretense of casualness and covered the last few feet at sprint, nearly knocking Sabella into the car. I slapped my palm on the emblem embedded in the center of the trunk. *"Sim sala bim!"*

The ward released with a snap, and the hidden

compartment concealed above the rear license plate popped open. I grabbed my backup weapon, a Glock 43X, then spun around, holding it down by my side, to check the status of both approaches. Using a flex of magical muscle, I brushed a metaphoric hand over the SUV and felt the inaudible click as I connected with the mechanics. I narrowed my focus and found my target, a shut-off valve for the fuel pump tucked behind an access panel, but I held back until I knew for certain the SUV was a threat.

In the meantime, I clocked the Shed Twins' approach.

Time to divide and conquer. "I'm calling the one on the right."

"I'll take the one to the left," she confirmed.

The SUV turned down our row.

"Rory." There was a hint of warning in her voice.

"I've got it."

Before I could shut down the SUV, another engine joined the echoing rumbles, this time with a stutter that indicated a timing issue. A well-used compact with muted music stuffed inside faded paint crashed the party and brought the approaching Shed Twins to a stop as it puttered its way between us and them as it searched and found an open spot on the row over.

The Shed Twins watched the new arrival park.

I watched the Shed Twins.

The SUV slowed to a crawl.

Sabella waited with the patience of a black widow spider, calm and cool in the center of her web.

Together, we all played statue while the compact's occupants shut down the music, locked up, and on a burst of laughter and conversation, headed in for a day of shopping while completely ignoring the weirdly still tableau in progress.

I used the reprieve bought by their distraction to trigger the SUV's emergency shut-off valve and tried not to grin when I heard the resulting sputter. For good measure, I engaged the auto locks so I wouldn't have to deal with uninvited guests.

One threat down. Two to go.

As soon as the two women disappeared inside, the Twins were back on the move. They stalked forward with a deliberateness that was probably meant to intimidate.

It failed. I fought rolling my eyes at their obviousness. *Did they learn that crap at Bad Guys 101?*

They separated as they got closer. My target, the darker-haired one, wore a scowl as he angled toward Sabella, likely because he considered her the less dangerous one, and put distance between him and his partner.

Idiot.

The blond half stayed the course, and his gaze clocked the gun at my side before rising to lock with mine. His lips curled into a sneering grin as he slowed to a stop, keeping a good distance between us. "Well, hello again, Ms. Costas."

I reinforced my Prism, which now covered both Sabella and me, meaning we were basically boxed in with the car. "You know, I didn't catch your name."

"Feel free to call me Mr. White."

I tilted my head toward his partner.

Heeding my silent question, he said, "Mr. Black."

Definitely a graduate of Bad Guys 101. "Well, Mr. White, Mr. Black, I see you finally made it to Vegas."

"A little later than planned, but all's well that ends well."

The air around us stilled, and the ambient noise fell silent, leaving behind an ominous weight. The hair on my arms started to rise, and power ebbed from Mr. Black's direction. Movement at the edge of my vision caught my attention, and I lifted my gun to chest height, the barrel aimed in Mr. Black's general direction.

"Ah-ah-ah," I heard Sabella say in a singsong tone.

"Young man, I would suggest you reconsider whatever it is you're thinking."

I didn't dare take my attention off the mage in front of me, but it was hard as hell not giving in to the urge to look over. It was time to get this show on the road. "What do you want?"

In true villain fashion, he answered with a question of his own. "Where's your friend?"

Done with the games, I curled my finger softly around the trigger and snapped out each word with soft but deadly demand. "What. Do. You. Want."

"Me?" he asked with obviously fake innocence as he lifted his hands, palms out. "Nothing much. I mean, I'd love some payback, but—"

His power whipped out with incredible speed as all pretense of civility went up in a puff of smoke.

I hardened my Prism even as a barrage of magical bullets rained down.

Sabella's familiar burn of amber fire swept past me to coil around Mr. White like a giant serpent. An answering flare of pale yellow met the green onslaught, and the two clashed, filling the air with Arcane energy.

There was no time to watch what happened next. I left Mr. White to Sabella and turned my attention to Mr. Black just as two thick ropes of gunmetal gray snaked out, one going for my legs, the other higher.

Instinct overrode logic, and I dove out of the way of the twisting vines, my finger squeezing the trigger even as I landed off-balance and stumbled back, my heart racing. The resulting echo of the gunshot left my ears ringing. I slammed my hip into the car with bruising force. I used my free hand to shove off the metal and reclaim my balance just as Mr. Black's ropes struck out for the second time.

This time, my brain kicked in with a vengeance. My Prism would hold back the worst of his attack, so no sense in wasting energy trying to play dodgeball. One rope went for my legs, the second for my arms. I shifted my Prism just as the coils made contact. They squeezed relentlessly even as I forced my shield to expand, creating a few inches of space between me and what I could now see were metallic ropes. With a grinding screech, the two magics collided, another storm of magical projectiles right on its heels.

I heard a male grunt from somewhere to my left, as if someone had taken a punch to the gut, but busy holding off the dual attack, I couldn't check on Sabella. I took comfort in the knowledge it would take more than a narcissistic bully to take her down.

The pressure increased until it felt like it was trying to move through cement. Mr. Black's face was contorted into a strained grimace, his eyes burning with rage, as he sent another wave of magic hurtling toward me. More metallic ropes joined the first two. They piled on slowly, wrapping me up like a mummy.

Then tiny barbs erupted like some grotesque version of goosebumps. Panic clawed at the back of my brain, but since I was more concerned about being squeezed out like that last bit of toothpaste, I ignored it. Instead, I channeled all my fury and frustration into my magic, carving out more inches between me and my metal bindings.

A snarled growl emerged from somewhere and made me bare my teeth in a feral grin. I gathered up my power, layered it with intent, then set it off like a bomb. A flash of brilliant light filled my vision, leaving me blind, but a pained howl filled my ears. Even better, the weight of magical cement and confining chains took a step back. Even though my vision was a hazy screen of gray interspersed with little white starbursts, I lifted my gun, aimed it at the man-shaped shadow near Mr. Black's position, and fired.

SIXTEEN

"MRS. ROSSI, PLEASE RECONSIDER."

Sabella patted the EMT's arm, playing up the grandmotherly persona to the hilt. "I appreciate your concern, my dear, but I promise you I'm perfectly fine. No need to pester the hospital staff."

Clearly recognizing there was no changing Sabella's mind, the young woman gave a soft sigh and continued repacking her bag. "Fine, but if anything should change, I'm advising you, on record, to get to a doctor."

Sabella's benevolent mask slipped enough for me to glimpse her impatience before she got it back in place, so I stepped in. "I'll keep an eye on her," I promised the EMT.

She looked between the two of us, clearly weighing my sincerity. "Good." She zipped up her bag and rose from her crouch in front of the open back-passenger door. "I'll go let the officer know you're available."

"Thanks." I didn't move from where I was leaning against the back-rear panel, while Sabella sat in the back passenger seat. Together, we watched the EMT make a beeline to one of the responding officers.

"I do hope they make this quick," Sabella said, her voice

low so it wouldn't carry. "Did you ask Zev to move out our reservation?"

"I did." And when I shared why, the dancing dots indicating a text in progress stayed on my screen for two whole minutes before finally disappearing. Unfortunately, there was no actual response associated, which didn't bode well.

"Good."

The EMT made her report and was now heading over to the ambulance that was partially blocking off the row. Her partner was crouched next to Mr. White, who was flat on the ground, eyes open but slightly wild, as the EMT held his hands, palms down, over Mr. White's torso. A yellowish glow covered the EMT's hands almost to his elbows as he worked a casting. At least I was far enough away to escape the magical spillover. Standing next to them was another officer, feet spread, one hand clasping his wrist, his face impassive as he watched the EMT work.

"What'd you do?" I asked my aunt without taking my attention off of Mr. White.

"Nothing permanent," she answered. "I'm sure the on-staff med mages will get him back on his feet in no time."

Even as she answered, I caught the jerky movement as Mr. White's left leg rose about two inches before dropping back to the cement.

"I'm fucking shot! I need a doctor!" The furious near shout came from Mr. Black, who was being escorted by another uniform, his arms bound behind him. Ignoring him, the officer opened the back door of one of the squad cars and manhandled Mr. Black around.

Over the top of the car, our eyes connected. Fury filled his gaze, and I wasn't sure how smug mine was. I was betting it was pretty fucking smug, though, especially when ruddy color filled his face and his lip curled in a snarl. The officer palmed the top of Mr. Black's head and stuffed him in the back seat.

"Nice shot," Sabella murmured, amusement clear.

"I was aiming higher." I managed to tag the idiot on his hip, not the shoulder I was aiming for, but then again, I was blind when I pulled the trigger.

"You may want to put more time in at the target range, then, dear."

My bitten off laugh didn't drown out the sound of a heavy car door being slammed. I turned to the SUV that did not have backup for the Shed Twins. In fact, it was an older couple from Minnesota hitting Vegas for the first time, and they were the reason Sabella and I were now facing a plethora of questions from the authorities.

They hadn't been stalking us; they'd been trying to find a parking space close to the entrance. When the older gent realized something was going down between us and the Shed Twins, he'd been reluctant to drive away, then after I shut down the engine and locked them inside, they'd ended up with a front-row seat to the whole show. His wife had called 911, and here we were. The SUV's engine came to life, and it reversed slowly.

The officer who'd be talking to the couple watched the SUV until it turned and left the garage, then he turned around and started our way.

"Incoming." I straightened from my lean then let out a pained hiss and wince as abused body parts protested. *If it's this bad now, tomorrow will be a bitch.*

The uniform got close, his face set to "professional concern," and said, "Mrs. Rossi, Ms. Costas, I'm Sergeant Collins. Thank you for waiting."

Sabella inclined her head. "Of course, Sergeant, but I do hope we can get this done fairly quickly, as I'm otherwise committed this evening."

Suitably warned, he got down to business. We were in the

midst of answering his questions when there was a pause in the surrounding hustle and bustle. I looked over my shoulder to see Zev stalking toward me like an impending thunderstorm. One brave uniform went to intercept, only to be stopped by a more grizzled responder who warned him off with a headshake.

Unable to look away, with a strange mix of relief and want, I watched him bear down. The relief, I totally understood, as seeing him at his intimidating best eased the lingering concerns I carried. The want part, which was both inconvenient and inappropriate at the moment, I chalked up to adrenaline letdown.

Or he's just a sexy motherfucker.

He stepped right into my space, crowding me. I didn't mind. In fact, it was all I could do not to close those last few inches and lean into him. His dark gaze swept over me then Sabella before he ground out, "Next time, I'm coming with."

For some reason, I found his grumpy-ass comment amusing and endearing.

Ye gods, who are you, woman?

Before I could question if interacting with the Shed Twins had caused brain damage, Sabella sighed and patted his arm. "We're fine, Zev."

His gaze came back to me, and an eyebrow drifted up in question.

"We're good," I confirmed.

"And you are?" the sergeant asked.

Zev's nostrils flared as he sucked in a deep breath, crossed his arms over his chest, then pivoted to stand next to me, feet set apart, his shoulder brushing mine as he pinned his attention to Sergeant Collins. "Zev Aslanov."

There was no flicker of recognition from the sergeant, but then again, unlike Sabella, the Cordova Family was a power in Phoenix, not on a larger scale. So intimidating reputation or not, Zev's hadn't quite made inroads on Sin City.

"He's with us," Sabella added.

Speculation pooled in the sergeant's eyes. I could see the assumptions come together for him—big guy with menacing aura at the beck and call of a legendary Arcane matriarch, creating the incorrect impression of the who and what that was Zev.

"I see," he said in a barely disguised undertone.

No, he doesn't, but as soon as he gets back and runs Zev's name, he will.

A heavy engine started, and we all turned to watch the ambulance pull away. I felt the moment Zev caught sight of Mr. Black in the patrol car. He stiffened and shot me a look. "Where's the other one?"

In return, I tilted my head toward the ambulance getting ready to exit the garage. "In there."

Zev's jaw flexed and his eyes flared, but Collins interrupted. "Do you know those two?"

Then it was Zev's turn to answer questions. By the time Collins handed over his business card, the ache in my body had set up shop in my head. I shut the back passenger door as Zev shook hands with Collins. Since the police had exchanged my gun for a claim ticket that I could use to reclaim my weapon at an unspecified later date, I closed the hidden compartment and reset the rental's ward before heading for the driver's-side door.

Zev got there first. "No." He flattened his hand against the doorjamb.

Stymied, I frowned up at him. "No what?"

"You are not driving."

Fuming, I glared at him and opened my mouth to argue. Before I could say a word, Zev caught my chin and pressed a hard kiss to my mouth. My body lit up like a sparkler at the simple touch, my mind emptying of anything but taste and touch. I grabbed on to his hips as my body swayed, and when he lifted his head, I was left in a bit of daze.

"Passenger seat." It was an order, pure and simple.

My glare made a comeback, and my fists hit my hips in a warning sign, but it was the shadow of unearned guilt that flitted through his dark eyes that left me biting my bottom lip and swallowing back my ire. I searched his face until what I was seeing clicked. Irrational though it was, the big dork was beating himself up for not coming along. If he held true to form, that meant this would be an argument I wouldn't win, so I gave in with a huffed "Fine."

•••••••••••••••••••••••••••

I followed Sabella into the suite. Behind me, Zev closed the door then threw the security lock for good measure. The tense silence that had accompanied our ride home and up the elevator settled in for an extended visit. I could feel Zev at my back, his frustration and anger breathing down my neck. The man was jonesing for an outlet. Too damn bad I wasn't.

Without looking at him, I held up a hand and warned, "Don't even think about starting in on me, Zev." I aimed for the couch while Sabella zeroed in on the kitchen. "We're fine. The idiots are behind bars, and no one's dead."

Cupboards opened and closed, ice clinked against glass, and liquid splashed.

Undaunted, Zev stalked me. "And why is that?"

I collapsed into the couch, a heartfelt groan escaping as the cushion cuddled my bruises. I rested my head against the back of the couch and closed my eyes, feeling tension ease back. I rubbed at my temple, hoping to nudge the ache back a bit. "Why is what?"

"Why weren't there body bags at the scene?" The couch shifted under his weight as he sat next to me.

I opened one eye. "Um, because murder is illegal?"

"Not murder if it's self-defense."

Wow, he just couldn't help himself, could he? "Are you serious right now?"

"Children…" Sabella used the warning tone familiar to children of all ages. Her heels clicked across the tile, then a glass with liquid and ice was held in front of my face. "Take it." She wiggled her wrist, making the contents slosh.

I sighed, opened both eyes, took the glass, and brought it up to my lips.

"These too." She held out two white tablets on her palm.

"Thanks." I shot the pain relievers and chased them down with water.

She turned to Zev and tapped his nose. "Leave her alone." His lip curled in a snarl, but she held her polished-tipped finger in his face and wiggled it warningly. "Uh-uh. Just take a breath and stop trying to start an argument because you're mad at yourself."

Despite his heavy scruff and goatee, there was no missing the flex of muscle in his jaw as he gritted his teeth and held Sabella's gaze. Just when I was considering dumping the water in my glass over his thick head, the tension drained out of his body. His shoulders slumped. He dropped his head, ran a hand over the back of his neck, and let out a soft curse.

Sabella awarded his concession with a soft brush of her hand over his bent head. "All's well that ends well." She headed back to the kitchen.

"It could've ended differently," he grumbled.

"Yeah, and it would've if you were there," I shot back. "Instead of being free tonight to make our reservation, we would be spending it behind bars and waiting for Mari to show up to bail your ass, and probably ours, out." *Okay, so maybe I am in the mood to argue.*

He shot me a dark look.

I met it without flinching. "Tell me I'm wrong."

Since he couldn't, he resorted to glaring harder.

"If you two don't stop, I'm putting you both in time-outs,"

Sabella snapped as she rejoined us. There was another glass in her hand, this one filled with amber.

Zev dialed back his frustration, the thunderclouds drifting out of his face, leaving behind traces of exhaustion and stress that plucked at my heart.

The last twenty-four hours had not been kind to him. Cutting him a break, I blew out a big breath and laid my aching head against his shoulder.

He shifted from his slouch to prop his legs on the coffee table. Then he lifted his arm and curled it over my shoulder, pulling me in until my head rested against his solid chest. His heart kept a steady beat under my ear. With each beat, a little more of my tension slipped away. I tucked my glass in close so I wouldn't spill it.

Sabella took a seat at the other end of the sectional, her gaze thoughtful as it took us in, and she sipped her drink. When she lowered her glass, she said, "As Rory was quick to point out, dead men can't talk, and as there are questions I'd like answers to, it's best they remain breathing."

"You aren't the only one with questions." Zev's voice rumbled under me.

"Going to be hard to ask them anything when they're behind bars," I said. "Not to mention that they won't exactly be motivated to share."

Sabella made a soft hum of agreement as she tapped her glass with her finger, the polished tip making a quiet, steady chime. "No, I wouldn't think so, since I'm sure they won't be detained for long."

I couldn't help but agree. "You think whoever they're working for is going to bail them out?"

"Bail them out, no." She gazed out in front of her, whatever thoughts she chased well-hidden. "Keep them from talking, definitely."

Zev shift his weight, and I looked up as he reached for his pocket to take out his phone and thumbed the screen. He found whoever he was looking for and brought up the message screen. He started typing.

"Who are you texting?"

"Locke," he answered as he kept up the thumb-typing. "He might have an in with someone local that can keep an eye on the two idiots. Maybe keep them alive until we can get someone in to talk to them."

There was one person who might be able to finagle their way into a jail cell. "Does that mean you're calling in Mari too?"

"No," Sabella cut in before Zev could answer. "Leave Mari be. She mentioned she'd be tied up this weekend."

Bright ideas done, I said, "I don't think Vegas PD is going to let us have a sit-down with them."

"I have no intention of imposing on the police in such a way. However, as Mari is unavailable, I'll have Val handle this little situation."

"Val?" Not a name I'd heard before, but then again, I didn't know all of my great-aunt's minions.

"Valentine Fontaine." She leaned forward to put her glass on the coffee table, and I lost her gaze. It remained averted as she sat back and crossed her legs.

A note in her voice made me shift to fully face her. "And this Valentine person is who, exactly?"

"He's Xanto's legal advisor," she said, brushing imaginary lint from her linen slacks, her tone deliberately casual. "He's in town for a couple of days. In fact, I was planning on inviting him to dinner tonight, before we were… delayed."

Was that… Oh my gods, it was.

The unflappable Arcane maven Sabella Rossi-Giordano was blushing!

I wasn't the only one who noticed, since Zev's amused chuckle accompanied my incredulous "Dinner?"

That earned me a scowl. "What is that"—she waved her

glass in the air—"in your voice?" A whisper of accent I rarely heard crept into her voice.

"Nothing." I grinned, enjoying the unusual sight of a flustered Sabella. "But now you've made me curious."

Her scowl deepened.

I ignored it and kept teasing. "Does Xanto know you've got the hots for his lawyer?"

"Rory Costas!" she admonished. "Behave."

I blinked innocently at her. "Where's the fun in that?"

Her scowl held for a moment longer then disappeared under a reluctant twitch of lips as she shook her head. "You're a pain in my ass."

"Ah, but you still love me."

"Of course I do."

The instantaneous but heartfelt declaration snuck under my guard and sucker punched me, leaving me emotionally winded.

Ignorant of the soft blow she'd landed, she kept talking. "I'll talk to Val before dinner, fill him in on the situation, see what he can find out."

"Between his interest and Locke's contacts, we might be able to keep the two breathing," Zev said. "Or at least make whoever is pulling their strings think twice before cutting loose ends."

I tucked away the gift Sabella had given me and focused on the here and now. I tilted my head back so I could see Zev's face. "You think if we point out how helpful we are in keeping them alive, they'll be inclined to cough up who hired them?"

"I'd say the odds are not in our favor," Sabella answered.

I dropped my head and met her gaze. "Yeah, that's what I'm afraid of."

SEVENTEEN

I MANAGED to sneak in a power nap before Sabella ushered us out of the suite for our dinner reservation. Though brief, it helped. When I woke, wrapped in Zev's arms, the ache in my head had downgraded to a negligible nuisance, and another shot of over-the-counter pain relievers smoothed out the bodily complaints as well. Since I hadn't packed for multiple daily clothing changes, I paired my jeans with one of my more dressier "work" tops for a casual-chic look. Thankfully, Vegas catered to the wild, weird, and fabulous, so showing up to a four-star restaurant in nice jeans and a fancy top didn't necessarily equal an automatic ejection at the door.

We caught a cab to the Sabella's restaurant of choice, and thanks to Vegas traffic, what should have been a five-minute ride ended up closer to fifteen. Our driver dropped us off at another valet station. Even though fall was in the air, it was a lovely evening—not too hot, not to cool, with the occasional breeze to keep things refreshing.

Our route took us through an outdoor collection of shops, restaurants, and venues that filled the space between hotels. The walkways were filled, but not quite to the extreme as those along the Strip. As we strolled through, we garnered quite a few curious looks—me in an eclectic mix-and-match, Sabella with her classic lines and jewel-toned silk and linen, and Zev rocking the bad-boy sexy vibe in shades of black, the red string bracelet still tied around his wrist the only pop of color. We had to make an interesting trio.

We found the wide courtyard that fronted the tucked-away, top-tier restaurant, Charisma Cuisine, and Sabella glided up to the maître d' who manned the reservations list. The tall brunette was top-to-toe elegant in her tailored sage blouse, cream-colored fitted skirt, and jade-green stilettos, but her smile was warm and real as we approached.

"Welcome back, Mrs. Giordano. Let me take you back to your table."

"Thank you, Chelsea." Sabella waited for Chelsea to join her, then the two of them led the way. "You look lovely tonight. How is your little one doing?"

They exchanged small talk, leaving Zev and me to follow. We followed the outer edge of the patio offering al fresco dining options then swept through the wide archway that led into the restaurant. Zev stayed at my side, his arm curled low so the warm weight of his palm rested against my hip, which was helpful since I was busy taking in the ambiance.

Diners of all ages filled the small two- and three-person tables. Some were clearly making this a night to remember in their tailored cuts, flowy skirts, and quiet, intimate conversations. Others were swept up in a sense of joie de vivre with bright laughter and their excited tones.

We passed a table of twentysomethings teasing and toasting one of their members. Based on their glitzy outfits, Charisma was just the first stop of many for the night. Next up was a wide-eyed woman who was busy soaking everything in then leaning into her partner, who was doing a better job of not gawking. Clearly, they were making the most of their Vegas experience and trying a taste of how the presumably other half lived. All in all, it was a people watchers' nirvana, and I loved it.

Chelsea's heels didn't make a sound as we made our way over the thick carpet of the dining room. Plush, curved couches complete with accent pillows served as bench seating for linen-draped black tables. There were padded high-back chairs for those who didn't want to recline and dine.

The indigo walls held abstract but tasteful artwork illuminated by the soft glow of chandeliers above and tabletop candles. Those same walls were broken up by alcoves that offered an illusion of privacy with more spacious seating. Just under the murmur of conversation was an accompanying melody of strings. Elegant and sophisticated, it still managed to feel welcoming, which boded well for the cuisine.

As Chelsea led us to one of the alcoves, a brush of power turned my head to the right, where two men sat at an intimate table tucked into the corner. Not sure why magic was part of the equation, I took a peek behind the metaphysical curtain that hung between reality and magic then giggled softly.

Zev pulled out my chair, waited for me to take a seat, then leaned in until his lips nearly touched my ear. "What are you giggling at?"

I angled my head so I could keep my answer between us. "Illusion mages, four o'clock."

He straightened, and I felt his lips hit the crown of my head as he checked out the table. He waited until he claimed his chair next to me before he said, "I'm guessing first date."

I pulled the linen napkin free of the heavy silverware. "I'm betting blind first date."

"Who are you two talking about?" Sabella asked once Chelsea left us.

"The two very-good-looking young men over in the corner." I waited for her to cast a casual glance in that direction before adding, "They're illusion mages, both of them, and trust me, they're putting their best faces forward." *Or what they think is their best face, considering all the chiseled angles and smoldering glances.*

"Ah, young love," she murmured.

"Not so sure love has much to do with it."

Our server slipped inside our alcove, took our drink orders, then slipped away. Zev scooted his chair close to mine then draped his arm over the high back, his fingers playing with my hair. I leaned against him, enjoying his touch, and noticed the extra place setting. "Isn't your Valentine joining us?"

Sabella paused in unfolding her linen napkin to shoot me a narrow-eyed glare. "He's not my anything."

The lady doth protest a bit too much. Biting my lower lip so it wouldn't give away my amusement, I lifted my glass to sip my water.

"However," she continued as she smoothed the napkin across her lap, "he'll be here shortly."

We continued with our idle chatter as the server returned with our beverages and inquired about appetizers. Sabella placed an order in fluent French, of which I recognized the phrase *l'amuse-bouche.* Satisfied we would get something to nibble on while waiting on the mysterious Val and our main course, I indulged in my proclivity of people watching. A burst of laughter came from the alcove off to the right. Something about it teased my awareness, but before I could bring it to light, I clocked Val's entrance.

"I do believe your guest has arrived," I murmured without taking my attention away from his approach.

Valentine Fortune fit his name. He wore a dark-gray casual suit with no tie, which matched the thick, wavy hair of white, silver, and gray that was undeniably attractive when paired with his light-tan skin. It was swept back from a heavy brow, angled nose, and chiseled jaw. He was tall, close to

Zev's six-two. He was solidly built, not bulky and not fat, but fit. He definitely took care of himself. As his gaze landed on Sabella, the aloof-patrician look melted away. A startling white smile took him from attractive to "holy silver fox." And I wasn't the only one watching him move toward us. He was trailing quite a few feminine, and even a couple male, sighs in his wake.

He got to Sabella, who had risen from her seat. "Sabella." His voice, which rode the edge of bass and baritone, turned my great-aunt's name into an evocative greeting. He took her hands in his and pulled her in to brush his lips over her cheek. "Thank you for inviting me to join you tonight."

When he pulled back, her face carried a hint of red, and there was a definite sparkle in her eyes. "I did promise you dinner, Val."

"That you did," he returned, his smile gaining a hint of roguishness. "And I had no intention of letting you wiggle your way out of that promise."

"Who said I'd try?" Even though her color deepened, she kept hold of Val's hand as she motioned with her other toward Zev and me. "Val, this is my niece, Rory, and her partner, Zev Aslanov."

I rose with Zev and shook hands as we all exchanged greetings. Eventually, we settled back around the table, and it was clear this was, for all intents and purposes, a double date, not a business dinner. Val repositioned his chair close to Sabella, who didn't even bat an eyelash at his move.

I wasn't quite sure how I felt about the whole situation. Amused, definitely, but also a little weirded out at witnessing my very sophisticated aunt flirting skillfully with an older, urbane version of a bad boy. Watching the two banter and how Sabella lit up in a way I'd never seen, it struck me that there was a lot left to learn about my aunt.

Our server made a return appearance, delivered our appetizer, and took Val's drink order.

Once the server disappeared, Sabella turned to Val. "Did you have any luck with my request, Val?"

"I reached out to the chief of police to ask, but unfortunately, the best he could do was get you and me in around nine."

"Any chance they'll make bail?" Zev asked.

"They could, but thanks to the added weight of the eyewitness account from a couple by the name of Addison, it won't be tonight," Val said. "It seems one of your assailants is under guard at the hospital." He looked to me. "Dare I ask how that happened?"

I tipped my head at my aunt. "Ask her. I was busy with the other idiot."

He turned and gave Sabella a look. "I should've recognized your handiwork."

"Yes, you should've, so why didn't you?" she asked archly as she picked up her drink.

"Because the Addisons happened to be Traditionalists, so to them, magic is magic is magic."

That was one way to describe how those who held little to no magical abilities would view an Arcane fight. Ask a Traditionalist to differentiate between a combat mage and a casting mage, and the only way they would hit the right answer was luck.

"Plus, there was the fact that both of your assailants are still breathing," Val drawled, but there was a hint of respect beneath the teasing note.

Zev barked out a laugh. "Yep, he definitely knows you."

Val's lips curled into a grin that was just this side of predatory as he brushed a hand over Sabella's shoulder. "Oh, I'm quite aware of just what Sabella is capable of."

She shot him a coy look over the rim of her glass. "Don't be too sure about that." She sipped her martini.

Humor softened the edges of his smile as he rested his arm along the back edge of her chair. "I'd like to point out that if you plan on asking either of them questions, I suggest you do so tomorrow morning."

Her eyebrows rose in question.

Val answered, "They're scheduled to go before a judge for their bail hearing at ten. I can get us access before the hearing."

Not about to let Sabella hog all the interrogational fun, I leaned into Zev. "Want to take the one at the hospital?"

He shrugged. "Sure." He looked at Val and Sabella. "If you two are good with taking the one behind bars, we'll swing by the hospital."

Val dipped his chin. "Works for me. Sabella?"

She gave a little hum and set down her glass. "I'll be ready at eight. Why don't you pick me up?"

Pleasure lit Val's face. "I'd be happy to."

Plans in place, our conversation shifted to less problematic topics as our dinners were served then enjoyed. Val was an interesting man who lived in California but traveled extensively for his clients. There didn't seem to be too many of said clients, but if they were all the stature of the Giordano Family, that made complete sense. Based on the names that dotted their shared stories, I guessed his dealings centered around two, if not three, Arcane Families, which meant he was quite the legal heavyweight. And yet despite the demands of his position, he'd carved out time to have dinner with Sabella.

Val and Sabella sitting in a tree…

I stuffed a thinly sliced fried potato topped with some kind of delightful cream, smoked salmon, and expensive fish eggs into my mouth and hoped my aunt missed my knowing grin.

Despite their vast array of shared acquaintances, Sabella and Val didn't leave Zev and me out of the conversation. Amusing anecdotes were shared, and the identities of those involved kept vague enough not to jeopardize client confidentiality.

After the main course, we were enjoying a brief respite before tackling the dessert menu, so I took advantage and made a break for the ladies' room.

I gave the bathroom attendant a quick smile as I passed the trio of women in little black dresses, sky-high heels, and stylish upsweeps, making use of the mirrors and sinks. I beelined for one of the frosted-glass doors that lined the wall. I shut myself inside, took care of business, then took my turn at the marble-basin sink. The trio was down to a duo, and I tuned out their chatter as I washed my hands.

One of the stall doors opened, and another woman joined me. Maybe a handful of years older than me, she had brown hair tastefully streaked with gold and looked as if she shopped at the same stores as Sabella. Our eyes met in the mirror, and we exchanged the polite upturn of lips.

When I was done, the attendant handed me a towel. Hands dry, I turned to leave, murmuring, "Excuse me," to the black-dress duo currently blocking the exit. That earned me a brief apology that barely put a hitch in their conversation as they slid to the side. I left the posh bathroom, shaking my head. The last place I would want to stand around and chat in was a damn bathroom, no matter how posh.

Servers were working the room, so I took a different route back to our table to avoid a collision. I noticed an older gent with a cane heading my way, so I stopped to give him room to pass and caught sight of a familiar face.

Virgil Hathaway was at a large table with an empty chair next to him and a mixed group of other couples laughing and chatting away. There was an older couple, the male half of which bore a striking resemblance to Virgil, and I guessed that was Winston Hathaway, his father. Oscar, the bodyguard-slash-right-hand-man, was there with an attractive dark-haired woman at his side, and rounding out the group was one more couple. The male sported silver at his temples, and his companion's matching silver-threaded chic bob was the epitome of classy.

I wonder…

I considered interrupting to see if I could get more information on the mysterious Damon, but before I could form an acceptable approach, Virgil's head turned my way, and his face lit up. For a disconcerting, what-the-hell-moment, I thought he was looking at me, but then a quiet "Excuse me" bumped me out of my head. It was the brunette from the bathroom.

Realizing I had blocked the path between tables, I shifted to the side. "So sorry."

She flashed a half smile and moved by me with a murmured "Thank you."

I gathered my wits and turned back to watch her make her way straight to Virgil, who was now standing. His attention shifted beyond the brunette and swept over me. For a moment, I thought I would get a pass, but then it came back, and recognition hit. "Ms. Costas!"

The brunette had made it to his side and had paused with her hand on her chair to look at whoever had caught Virgil's attention.

I returned his greeting with a nod and a slight smile, trying my best to be polite, but then he waved me over.

The brunette's gaze went from me then back to Virgil as a slight frown marred her expression. She said something, and Virgil curled his arm around her, tucking her close before responding. Whatever he said erased the frown lines, and the smile that came my way was open and friendly. Virgil got her settled into her chair and said something to the table at large, turning heads my way, then he was walking toward me.

Guess I am going over. I wove around the nearby diners and met him a few feet from his table. "Good evening, Mr. Hathaway."

"Ms. Costas, lovely to see you." His gaze went behind me then came back. "Are you here alone?"

"No, Zev and I are having dinner with friends." I made a vague motion toward the alcoves as his dining companions watched on. "Thank you again for the show tickets."

"Did you enjoy it?"

"We did." Figuring now was as good a time as any, I decided to give it a shot. "As a matter of fact, your f—"

"Virgil." It was amazing how much the deep voice could make the name sound like an order. We both turned to the table to find the elder Hathaway was eyeing us. "Why don't you introduce your friend, son?"

Virgil turned to me and lowered his voice. "Do you have a minute?"

"Of course."

I followed him to the table and endured the round of introductions. My guess about his father was proven correct, as I was introduced to Winston first, then his mother, Amanda. After that came the brunette, Virgil's significant other, Julie Wright, or Juls, followed by Oscar and his wife, Ellie. The last couple was a Beau and Carol Lennox, family friends.

"A pleasure," I said to the group at large and got the same in return.

"You're a Transporter; is that right?" Winston's sharp gaze was assessing as he wiped his mouth with a cloth napkin.

"Yes, sir."

He nodded and set the napkin aside. "How long have you been with Wilson's little shop?"

It was clear where Virgil got his insular attitude from, and I could feel my smile gain a cool edge. "I don't work for Wilson's Custom Rides," I corrected with painful courtesy. "I'm an independent contractor who specializes in secured Arcane deliveries. As Mr. Wilson required a top-tier Transporter due to the inherent challenges of your son's particularly delivery, he asked if I'd be interested in assisting."

His bushy eyebrows rose, and his mouth opened, but his wife covered his hand on the table and got there first. "Challenges?" She shot a worried look at her son. "What kind of challenges are you talking about?"

A hint of color rode Virgil's cheeks as he scratched behind his ear. "It's fine, Mom. There was a bit of a bidding war, and I was being cautious."

"Cautious?" She let go of her husband. "Over a car?"

"It's not just any car, Mandy," Beau said with practiced ease. Clearly, he was used to playing moderator. "My understanding is that particular car is highly coveted in certain circles, so it's no surprise someone might get a tad upset at losing out on owning it."

"Especially someone like Damon," Juls muttered, and my breath caught at the familiar name.

Winston's eyes narrowed, but before he could share whatever was working behind that disdainful expression, Virgil was hurriedly talking. "Yes, Damon. You know how much he hates to lose. Especially to me." There was an undeniable hint of smugness to that last bit.

"Oh, for heaven's sake, Virgil." His mother's worry disappeared under exasperation as his father tapped his thick fingers against the table. "Tell me you didn't deliberately goad the man with this purchase?"

Her son tried and failed to pull off the innocent look. "I wasn't goading anyone, Mom. I simply had a stronger offer than him."

"Rory." My name in Zev's voice was my only warning before his arm settled around my waist. "There you are. We were worried you got lost."

"I ran into Mr. Hathaway." I quickly introduced Zev to the table.

When I was done, Oscar asked, "Did you two enjoy the show last night?"

I exchanged a look with Zev then took the lead. "We did. It was wonderful. We appreciate the tickets." I looked to Julie. "I'm sorry you missed out."

"Virgil already got us another set of tickets." She waved off my apology. "Was it really as good as the reviews said?"

We spent a couple minutes discussing the show, and when I had the chance, I casually dropped in, "We did have a visitor to the box, but he didn't share his name. He was with a brunette who called him Damon and indicated he'd catch up with you later. He appeared agitated about something." *Nudge, nudge.*

Julie sighed. "Let me guess—he didn't bother to knock, but barged in?"

I nodded. "As I said, he seemed a bit upset."

"Or he was hoping to cause drama," she said.

"Juls." The soft admonishment came from Virgil's mother.

Julie sighed. "Please, Mandy, we all know Damon Innes is a drama king and doesn't do polite."

Zev's hand on my hip squeezed as we got a name for Mr. Angry, but his voice remained unruffled when he warned Virgil, "I don't know what the deal is with this Damon, but I will say you may want to be careful in your future interactions."

Virgil gave a raspberry like *pfft* that meant Zev's warning was falling on deaf ears.

But Oscar was a different story. "Oh, we most certainly will be." A hard-ass demeanor that did not bode well for Damon had replaced his relaxed manner.

But Oscar would have to wait his turn, because Zev and I were going to get to Damon first.

EIGHTEEN

THE NEXT MORNING, Zev and I changed course. Not only had we scored Damon's full name, but when we returned to the suite, I had an email from Evan. Lena's snuggle bunny managed to uncover some interesting tidbits about Damon Innes.

Like Virgil, he was the heir apparent to the family business, which was headquartered in San Diego. His job title contained the letters VP, and his office hours were flexible at best, nonexistent at worse. Most likely because him being in an office wasn't conducive to enhancing the company's bottom line, not with the buried reports that hinted at misappropriation of funds and a couple of harassment charges. All of that had been erased from the official records but not the social ones. It was amazing the amount of dirt that could be found out in the world of social media. Everyone had an opinion and wanted to share. But Evan hadn't stopped there.

Damon wasn't a Vegas local, but he did travel to Sin City often in the guise of doing business. Strangely enough, the company never seemed to put him up in one of their corporate suites. Instead, Evan discovered that Damon apparently spent an inordinate amount of time with a Darlene Hedgerow, a brunette who bore a striking resemblance to the one who'd been hanging on his arm at the theater. She also happened to own a home in the Vegas foothills. Evan added a warning that it would be a crapshoot on catching Damon with Darlene, especially since Vegas seemed to have more hotel rooms than homes.

"He may not even be there," I told Zev as I poured coffee into to-go cups.

"He might not," Zev agreed as he finished tying back his hair. "But Evan said there was a pending charge from late last night that corresponds to Darlene's place."

I finished securing lids on our java infusions. "So we check it out."

"We check it out," he said.

"Are we hitting the hospital first or Darlene's?" If our first stop was the hospital, we would be hitting the nurses' station at about eight, which, depending on the visiting hours, may or may not require a wait. However, if we were to go to Darlene's, chances were high we would be dragging her out of bed. Rude though it was, at least we wouldn't have to chase her down.

"Leave the hospital to me and Val." Sabella joined us, looking her typical regal best. She arrowed in on the coffee I was preparing. "Do you have another one of those?"

My answer was to set up a third cup and fill it with the last of our pot. "You sure you and Val will have enough time to cover both before the bail hearing?" I added in the cream-to-sugar ratio Sabella preferred then handed it over.

She took it with a murmur of thanks. "I'll message you if we run into any issues."

"That works." Zev leaned back against the counter next to me. "You're driving."

"Duh." I handed him his no-frills coffee. "When we get there, you get to be the one to wake up Sleeping Beauty."

His fingers brushed mine as he took it. "You really think she'll be sleeping at eight-something in the morning?"

I added cream to my cup and stirred. "Evan said she listed her occupation as 'artist,' but she gets hefty deposits into her account like clockwork." I secured my lid, lifted the cup, and blew across the tiny opening. "That sound like someone who's up at eight?" I sipped.

His lips twitched. "Probably not."

"Right." I moved around him and headed for the entryway. "You ready?"

"Yep."

I stopped next to my aunt and exchanged air kisses. No way did I want to leave with scarlet-red marks. "Watch your ass."

Her smile was all sorts of Cheshire. "Always."

I got to the narrow table by the door and grabbed my sunglasses and the rental keys. "Come on, Zev. Let's go play alarm clock."

•.

The address Evan had given us took us away from the Strip and farther into the Vegas foothills. The rental's GPS routed us toward Lake Las Vegas, where sprawling ranch homes on acre-sized lots were replaced by newer constructions tucked behind art-deco gates. Darlene's address was behind one such gate, but lucky for us, It was wide-open.

So much for security.

I followed the GPS directions through quiet streets as we drove by one- and two-story homes with just enough differences to tell them apart but not enough to make them unique. We made our last turn, and every instinct I possessed snapped to attention. My "Oh hell" collided with Zev's muttered "What the fuck?"

In front of the house that I was pretty sure belonged to

Darlene Hedgerow was a black-and-white SUV clearly marked with Vegas Police. An ambulance sat in the driveway, angled in such a way as to block in the sporty little Acura on the right side. A Dodge Charger kissed the SUV's bumper, and I could see the faint outline of a light bar in the back window, marking it as an unmarked vehicle, which meant we probably had a detective or someone similar on site.

"Do we stop?" I wanted to because I wanted to know what the hell was going on.

"No. Too many questions." Then Zev clocked the uniform standing near the open front door, watching us come closer. "Dammit, never mind. Find somewhere to park."

I found a spot a couple doors down that wouldn't block a driveway and pulled over. "How do we do this? They're going to be all over us, especially since we've got no connection to Darlene."

He undid his seatbelt. "We either lie our asses off…"

Which would make things a hundred times worse, especially since we didn't have home-field advantage here.

"Or we play it straight."

"I say play it straight." I shut off the engine and released my belt. "Let's get what information we can, then we can set either Evan or Val loose to get more." I really didn't want to get on the wrong side of the authorities or the local big-name Families. Besides, I'd been on a drama-free streak until I agreed to do this job, and lying would just tempt Fate into leading me into trouble.

We got out and closed our doors, the sound overly loud in the quiet neighborhood. I joined Zev on the sidewalk, and together, we headed toward Darlene's house.

The uniform came down the walkway. He met us at the end of the drive with his hands on his hips and his eyes hidden behind dark lenses. "Can I help you?"

Zev took the lead. "We're looking for a Ms. Darlene Hedgerow."

That caught the officer's attention, because although his expression didn't change, the air around him did. "And you are?"

"Zev Aslanov."

"Rory Costas," I added when the dark lenses turned my way.

"Can I see some ID?" He held out his hand.

Zev and I fished out our wallets and handed over our licenses.

"Thank you." The officer took his time studying them before handing them back. "Mr. Aslanov, Ms. Costas, how do you know Ms. Hedgerow?"

"We don't, actually," Zev said as he put his license back in his wallet. He tucked it in his back pocket then folded his arms over his chest. "We were actually looking for a mutual acquaintance. We were hoping he was here."

"And who is this acquaintance?"

"Damon Innes."

The officer's shoulders straightened, and he reached for the radio attached to his shoulder. "Would you mind giving me just a moment?" It was phrased as a question, but it was clearly a demand to sit tight.

"Of course," Zev said, but the officer was already moving away.

He didn't go far, just closer to the door so there was enough space between us that we could hear the rumble of his voice as he spoke into his radio but couldn't make out the actual words. We waited while he had a brief one-sided conversation. When he returned, his tone was carefully neutral. "Would you mind following me inside?"

We followed him toward the house. We had reached the porch when I heard another vehicle approach. I stopped and turned to watch another black SUV pull in. Instead of white letters indicating Vegas Police on the side, there were fluorescent green letters that spelled out ACRT.

That's not good. The fact that the Arcane Criminal Response Team was joining the party set off all kinds of alarm bells.

I turned back to Officer Not-So-Friendly, who had one foot inside. I could hear someone crying from inside the house. "What's going on?"

He pushed his sunglasses to the top of his head, revealing somber brown eyes with a heavy fringe of lashes, something that did not fit with the rest of the hard angles of his face. "Ms. Hedgerow and an unidentified male appear to have been victims of a home invasion."

Must have been one hell of a home invasion to call in the heavy hitters.

Behind us, car doors slammed. We all looked back to watch two ACRT agents, a male and female, approach. They watched us back. Both were in the standard uniform of black cargos and pale-green T-shirts.

The female agent wore a red backpack on one shoulder and an ACRT cap with her blond hair threaded in a loose ponytail through the back. "Morning, Ty, what do we have?"

"Evidence of a magical entry and remnants of something close to a containment ward."

"Was the door open when you got here?" the male agent asked as the two stopped at the edge of the porch. He was built along the lines of a small tank, with steel hair buzzed closed to his scalp, wide shoulders, and thick thighs. His black backpack was bulging.

Officer Ty shook his head. "Neighbor called it in. Said she was out walking her dog, saw the door was open, and came up to make sure the resident was okay. They weren't." The last bit came out a bit grim.

"She contaminate my scene?"

That came from the female agent with M. Hays displayed on the left side of her shirt. Her partner's showed K. Porter.

"She says she didn't touch either one of them," Officer Ty said.

"Mm-hmm, we'll see." It was clear Agent Hays was a glass-half-empty kind of woman.

"Considering we're having problems accessing the residents, I tend to believe her."

Hays's gaze sharpened, and she perked up. "Like that, is it?" When Ty nodded, she shrugged off her backpack and held it at her side. "Right, we'll check out the neighbor and get her cleared before we tackle the rest."

Zev and I moved off to the side while Officer Ty stepped back into the house, one hand holding the door wide so the two agents could enter. "That would be good. Vines is inside with her now."

"Copy that," Agent Porter said as he followed Hays inside.

Assumptions zipped through my mind about why exactly they would have problems getting to the residents. The one that stuck out was if ACRT was on scene, that mean active magic had been used during the commission of the crime. If that magic was still active and keeping them from accessing the bodies, then maybe, just maybe, they might find the assistance of a Prism helpful.

Taking advantage of Officer Ty being out of earshot, I sidled closer to Zev and turned away, ostensibly to gaze out at the street, where a couple of the nosier neighbors were inching their way into the know. With my back to the house, I kept my voice low and said, "If ACRT runs into trouble, we might have an in."

He bumped my shoulder.

Taking that as agreement, I turned back as Officer Ty pulled the front door almost closed and rejoined us on the porch. Before he could say anything, Zev spoke. "Officer, you mentioned Ms. Hedgerow was found with an unidentified male?"

"She was," Officer Ty confirmed.

Zev and I exchanged a look. I was pretty sure we were

both wondering the same thing—what were the odds that the unidentified male was Damon Innes?

Being the observant type, Officer Ty did not miss our visual exchange. "Do you know who he is?"

"Maybe," Zev said as he dug out his phone. He thumbed the screen until he found what he needed then turned it to face Officer Ty. "Is this the guy inside?"

Officer Ty took the phone and studied it carefully. When he looked up, his question was sharp. "Who is this?"

"That is Damon Innes," Zev said. "We were hoping Ms. Hedgerow would be able to tell us where we could find him."

Officer Ty handed the phone back. "Why are you looking for him?"

And that quick, we had our confirmation that Damon was the unidentified dead male.

Shit.

That meant our only shot of finding out what happened inside that house was convincing the authorities or, more importantly, ACRT, that we could help. I looked at Zev, and Zev looked at me. He cocked his head in question. I returned a small nod, then we filled Officer Ty in on our last couple of days.

I started with picking up the Gullwing and the client's concerns of potential interference during the delivery. Zev glossed over the confrontation with the Shed Twins, making it sound like a simple verbal dispute. We shared the run-in at the theater, followed by Zev being cursed and calling in a Guild Key for assistance.

That one got a raised brow, but Zev remained surprisingly forthright. He even shared our suspicion that Damon was behind the hex, which made Officer Ty's jaw tighten. Things didn't get any better when I finished up with yesterday's incident in the parking garage. In fact, by the time we were done, Officer Ty's jaw was so tight, I was afraid it would break.

"Do you have a report number for yesterday's incident?" The question was ground out even as he reached for his radio.

"No, I'm sorry, I don't," I said. "I'm sure it's in the paperwork back at our suite."

"Wait here." He stalked off the porch and into the yard, where he had another inaudible one-sided conversation with his radio.

"Are you sure it was wise to share all that?" I asked in a very low voice as we watched Officer Ty pace.

"Nothing we've done has crossed a line," Zev said just as softly. "Which means the minute he starts to connect names, especially Sabella's, he's going to know that this home invasion is now a Family matter. Once he accepts that, then I can offer my assistance."

"And you think he's really going to let you butt into this?" I couldn't see it. Zev's influence was a direct result of his connection to the Cordova Family, and the Cordovas didn't hold sway in Vegas.

"They will when this gets back to the chief of police, who, I'm betting, is currently playing host to—"

"Sabella and Val," I finished, finally catching on.

"Exactly."

And once my aunt got involved, she could insist on our involvement. I grimaced thinking of how that would go over with the officers and agents on scene. "They are not going to like that."

Zev shrugged. "Probably not, but I'm sure whoever's in charge understands the value of playing politics."

"Lovely." I loaded enough sarcasm into that one word to sink an elephant.

We both watched Officer Ty pace between two blooming bougainvillea that stood sentry on either side of a wide window. He came to a stop near the edge of the yard, as far from us as he could get. His back was stiff and his head bent, and he rubbed a hand over the back of his neck.

Yeah, he's not happy with whatever is coming over his radio.

It was another minute before his hand dropped to his side, his head lifted, and his shoulders rose and fell. He said something into his radio then stood there for a brief moment before turning to stalk back toward us.

We watched him come and waited.

He stopped in front of us, eyes hard, jaw harder, and a scowl darkening his face. "I need you two to wait out here." He waited for our nods before pivoting on a heel and storming inside.

"I hate it when you're right," I muttered to Zev.

He grinned.

About five minutes later, the door opened again. A gray-haired woman in an oversized pink T-shirt and gray joggers came out holding a football-sized furball to her chest. Her eyes were red, swollen, and a little dull as her gaze swept over us, and she was accompanied by another female who was about twenty years younger. Dressed in a polo shirt and tactical pants with a badge and holster clipped at her waist, the younger one helped the older one cross the porch and get down the cement steps.

"Gina, Officer Scott's going to escort you back to your place and wait until your daughter arrives, okay?"

"Thank you, Melanie." Gina's voice cracked a bit on the end as a sobbing sigh escaped. The dog in her arms gave a little yip and licked at her chin.

"You're very welcome," Melanie said as she passed off escorting service to Ty, who was obviously Officer Scott. "Daughter's incoming, should be here in about fifteen."

Ty nodded. "Come on, Gina. Let's get you and Mimi back home."

Melanie stood at the foot of the steps with her hands on her hips as Ty guided Gina through the pristine front yard and to the sidewalk before they crossed the street. She turned back, and her attention locked on to Zev and me with no trace of her earlier compassionate demeanor in sight. Instead, she was all business when she stopped in front of us. Her dark eyes were assessing as she tucked the black strands of her angled bob behind one ear then held out her hand. "Mr. Aslanov, Ms. Costas, I'm Lieutenant Encinas."

Zev shook first. "Zev."

Then it was my turn. "Rory."

"Right, Zev, Rory." Her hands went back to her hips as she studied us. "According to my chief, it's been suggested that you two might be able to assist with figuring out what went down inside."

"We're happy to help however we can, Lieutenant," Zev answered.

"Mm-hmm." She turned to look out over the yard, her gaze lingering on the gathered lookie-loos. I swore I heard her mutter, "Dammit," before she sighed, shook her head, and turned back to us with an insincere smile. "Let's take this inside."

We left the neighbors behind, and Lieutenant Encinas stopped us in the tiled entryway as she closed the door. "Got to be honest—I'm not real thrilled to have two civilians on my crime scene, but apparently the Giordano Family has insisted you two could be helpful, though I'm at a loss as to how."

Zev took the lead. "Until we know what it is you're dealing with, I'm not sure how to answer that, Lieutenant."

She crossed her arms over her chest. "Why don't we start with why my chief thinks you can help here? What is it you two do?"

"I'm an Arbiter for the Cordova Family in Phoenix."

Her body tightened as if taking a hit, and her gaze sharpened. "The Cordova Family? Are they involved?"

"We're allies of the Giordano Family." Zev had neatly sidestepped the answer.

It became clear Encinas was very familiar with the varied flavors that Family enforcers came in—investigators, trackers, personal security, and espionage—when she followed up with, "Hunter, Hound, Sentinel, or Scout?"

Zev, who had taken all those roles at one point or another since I'd known him, stuck with the one most familiar. "Hunter."

"What brought you to Vegas?"

"Not business, I can assure you," he drawled.

I wanted to roll my eyes at his answer. It was like he wanted to piss her off. "He's with me."

Not losing one bit of her irritation, her attention shifted to me. "Is that right?" There was a hefty amount of doubt in her voice.

I did my best not to take offense. "I got asked to make a last-minute run to Vegas, and since we had plans, we shifted them to here."

She turned to me. "And your role in this?"

"Transporter. For Mrs. Giordano."

Encinas eyed us both. Whatever she was thinking, she kept well hidden behind an impassive façade, but there was a press of magic that swept over me, raising every hair on my arm. My Prism didn't like it and snapped into place, taking the disconcerting sting of tiny bites along my nerve endings to an uncomfortable and annoying nibble. I had enough practice with fending off magical attacks to rein in my Prism's instinctive response to return her hit and, instead, shrug it off. She wasn't trying to take me out; she was simply trying to determine what kind of power I carried.

Good fucking luck, Lieutenant.

Zev, on the other hand, didn't like Encinas's method of asking. A deep-blue burst of miniature lightning erupted midair between the two.

Encinas winced and hastily etched a blocking ward before taking a step back, all without taking her gaze off Zev. "You're not just a Hunter." It came out a bit breathy from her near miss as she glared at him.

It was Zev's turn to fold his arms over his chest. "No, I'm not."

When he didn't offer anything more, she conceded, "Care to share?"

He took his time and finally said, "Animal mage."

Okay, maybe it wasn't just Zev that needed to have a pissing contest.

She turned dark eyes to me. "And you… I can't figure you out, but you're something more than a Transporter."

Interesting. "I'll share if you will," I said, because I really wanted to know how she'd figured us out.

Encinas lips curved, not with smugness but humor laced with apology. "I'm an Auralist."

It was my turn to react. "Oh wow, cool!"

That got a soft laugh.

But I didn't mind, because it was cool. As an aura reader, all Encinas had to do was catch a glimpse at a person's aura to know what kind of mage she was dealing with. The fact she couldn't fully read Zev and me probably meant something, but it wasn't something to worry about now. Still, it was a nifty power to have.

Keeping my promise, I said, "Prism."

Shock replaced Lieutenant Encinas's smile, her mouth dropped open, and she blinked. "No shit?"

Used to that particular reaction, I couldn't help but grin. "No shit."

Color rose under her skin and along her cheeks. "Sorry."

"No apology needed."

She continued to stare at me for a long moment, her mouth opening then closing only to reopen. Clearly, she wanted to say something but was trying to figure out how.

My humor dimmed, and I started to feel a bit uncomfortable. Needing to get this part over, I said, "Just ask."

She closed her eyes, pinched the bridge of her nose, and

blew out along breath. When she reopened her eyes and dropped her hand, she was back to her professional best. "A Prism?"

I gave a slow nod.

"Are you truly immune to magic?"

"For simplicity's sake, let's just say it's hard to hurt me magically." It was easier than getting into the ins and outs of the magic that lived in Prisms. Especially since that same magic drove other mages to basically hunt us into near extinction.

Some days, it sucks to be a mythical unicorn in the mage world.

She looked toward the entryway that headed deeper into the house. Whatever she was considering left her face grim with determination. She turned back to us. "Maybe having you help isn't such a bad idea after all." She didn't give either of us a chance to respond to that little gem. "Scott mentioned you're looking for Damon Innes."

We both nodded.

She looked at Zev. "You believe he hexed you. Is that correct?"

"Yes."

"What kind of hex?"

"A Bane hex," I answered.

Her brows rose, and she eyed Zev. "How'd you survive that?"

"Luck and a damn-good Key."

She didn't follow the expected route and press for Grayson's name. Instead, she switched gears. "And Darlene Hedgerow's part in this?"

I spoke up. "We think she was the woman with Mr. Innes at the theater. If she is, we were hoping she would know where to find him."

"Outside of your conversation at the show, did either of you have any direct interactions with Mr. Innes or Ms. Hedgerow?"

"No," Zev answered first.

"No," I echoed.

She looked back to the entryway, clearly weighing her options. It didn't take her long. She turned back to us, all business. "I've got two bodies in the other room. I need you to confirm if this is the couple you saw at the theater. I'm sure I don't have to remind you that whatever you see is part of an ongoing investigation and, as such, should not be shared with the public at large. Understood?"

"Understood," I said.

"Can we share with Mrs. Giordano and her lawyer?" Zev asked.

Her expression cooled just a touch, probably because no one liked playing politics. "As long as my chief gives the okay."

"Got it," Zev said.

"Don't touch anything and stay clear, unless ACRT says otherwise."

We nodded.

She led the way, and we followed.

NINETEEN

LIEUTENANT ENCINAS TOOK us through the archway, down a short hall, and through a set of double doors. We stepped into a massive bedroom, where a pair of EMTs stood at the ready with a stretcher and body bags. The room also held the ACRT team and their equipment, a full-size sofa, a bookcase, a four-poster bed with matching end tables and dressers, and chaise lounge tucked off to the side. The muted conversation of those on scene paused as we walked over the lush carpet and through a lingering haze of magic that hung on the air.

I wasn't sure anyone else could feel it, but to me, it was like walking through curtains of spiderwebs, and it left goosebumps running up and down my skin. The closer I got to the bed, the worse that feeling got until I stopped a good four feet away. Zev and Encinas continued around until they stood at the bed's foot, leaving the two ACRT agents standing on opposite sides. Everyone kept clear of the two thick lines of salt that ringed the bed.

Between them ran a series of runes and sigils laid out in what appeared to be colored ash or chalk; I wasn't sure which. Hell, I wasn't even sure I recognize most of them. Likely, they were customized by the ACRT team to fit their investigative needs.

But it was what was on the bed that held my attention. The duvet appeared to have been kicked aside at some point. Maybe when the two occupants had been otherwise occupied. They sure as shit weren't occupied now, though. Whatever had happened had caught them unawares.

The woman was sprawled on her stomach, the silk sheets barely covering her ass and leaving her back bare. She was partially hanging over the edge, her dark brown-hair obscuring her face. Her arm was dangling, fingertips brushing the carpet. It was hard to tell what had happened. If I didn't know she was dead, I would've assumed she was simply passed out.

The man was a different story. He was curled on his side, bare ass and back to the door, his legs drawn up like he was going to cannonball into the bed, but his back was a canvas of mottled blues, yellows, and purples as if he'd been beaten. One arm was extended toward the woman, the hand clutching the sheets. His other arm was hidden by his position, so I carefully stepped around the scattered bags and equipment until I could see his face. Then I wished I hadn't. The frozen, twisted features were marred by rusty stains of dried blood from his eyes, nose, ears, and mouth, but under the blood, I saw the familiar features of Damon Innes.

"Is this who you two saw at the theater?" Encinas asked.

I cleared my throat, trying to keep the nausea from rising. "Yeah," I croaked. I tore my gaze away from the macabre couple to find Encinas and the two ACRT agents watching me, but it was the small and steady red dot on Agent Porter's shoulder that clued me in that the scene was being recorded.

Great, just what we need, a permanent record of our involvement.

Since I wasn't keen on having my particular abilities recorded for posterity's sake, I moved what I hoped was far enough back to put me out of camera range. As Zev rounded the bed, I caught his hand, and when he stopped next to me, his eyes met mine. I slid mine to the side to indicate Porter's recording device.

Luckily, Zev was fluent in silent exchanges, and he was quick to clue in. He tugged free of my hold then crouched so he could see the bodies better. Without looking at Porter, he asked, "I'm assuming we're on record?"

"We are," Encinas confirmed.

He nodded. "Then, yes, that's Damon." He stayed in his crouch but pivoted toward the dead woman and reached out, only to stop short and look up at Agent Hays. "May I?"

"Let me." She used a glove-covered hand to move the brown hair aside.

Dried blood painted a grisly mask over the feminine features.

Zev angled his head as he studied her. "Rory, you have that photo of Darlene?"

I fumbled for my phone, grateful to have an excuse to stop looking at the bodies. I pulled up the picture that Evan had sent us, then I handed it over to Zev. He held up the screen, and a long tense moment passed before he said, "That's Darlene."

"You mind?" Encinas asked, holding her hand out for my phone.

Zev straightened, then, in order to avoid disturbing the salt circle, crossed behind me, his other hand settling against the base of my spine as he handed my phone over.

Encinas took it, studied the image, then handed it back to Zev. "Thank you."

Zev thumbed the screen, turning it black, and handed it back to me.

"Do you know what happened?" I shoved the phone into my back pocket.

"Not yet," Hays answered. She looked over the expanse of the bed to her partner. "Ready?"

He nodded.

She pulled out a small canvas bag from one of her vest's many pockets and sank into a crouch. She poured the bag's contents onto the floor, filling in the last couple of inches of the outer ring and closing the circle as she murmured under her breath. A ripple of power whispered over me, and the two salt lines gained a soft, barely-there glow.

Hays rose and looked around the room. "Right. I need everyone to step back at least two feet from the circle. We need to take a reading, and I don't want any interference."

The two EMTs who stood off to the side shifted nervously but didn't budge from their position on the far side of the room. Zev and I stepped back, and Lieutenant Encinas joined us, giving the ACRT agents the floor.

Agent Porter, who stood at the head of the bed, put one hand on the bedpost closest to him, extended his other arm, and held out his hand, palm down, over Damon's body. He closed his eyes and took a couple of deep breaths, like a swimmer preparing to dive. His lips moved, but there was no sound. Instead, a small orb flicked into being and hovered at the top of his head. Then in slow motion, the orb began to spill over him, until he was outlined in a shimmer of power from head to toe.

The air between his palm and Damon's head rippled like a heat wave, and that strange visual warp spread over Damon then crept over Darlene's body like an invisible tide. When it had swallowed both bodies, it was as if we were seeing them through a thin layer of rippling water. A faint wisp that could either be fog or mist started to rise from the corpses, slowly at first, then faster.

Uneasy, I inched back from the bed. There was no way to

pinpoint why, but what I did know was that I really, *really* didn't want to be near whatever was going down on that bed. And I wasn't the only one.

Next to me, Encinas also inched back, her face pale, her throat working as she looked away. On my other side, Zev shifted closer as if to step between me and whatever was happening. I grabbed the back of his shirt, holding him in place and keeping my line of sight open.

The strange mist turned opaque, its vague shape gaining depth and dimension as it churned and expanded. There was something creepy about it, and no one moved or spoke as Porter worked his magic. The air in the room cooled, and a chill ran over me. There was a shuffle of feet, and I looked over to see one of the EMTs grimace and rub at his arms. I had no idea what kind of mage Porter was, but based upon the situation, I was betting he was some flavor of necromancer. If this whole thing weren't being recorded, I might have risked taking a metaphysical peek to see if I could read his magical signature, but I was stuck with making assumptions.

Porter's magic filled the circle, and I could feel its echo brush up against my Prism. Thankfully, whatever he was doing wasn't fueled by aggression, so it didn't trigger the Prism's instinct to defend. I could just imagine how that would play out. Boomeranging Porter's corpse magic back to him would lead to a bunch of uncomfortable questions.

The seconds ticked by, stretching into a minute, then another, before the magic finally began to retreat. When it flickered out, Porter blew out a long breath, opened his eyes, and shook out his hand. The lines on his face were a little deeper, and his wide shoulders had gained a slight hunch. His voice was a bit rough when he said, "TOD matches body-temp readings. She went first; he followed."

Unaffected by her partner's show, Hays checked the bulky utilitarian watch on her wrist and frowned. "That puts her time of death between two fifteen and two thirty this morning, and his closer to three." She propped her fists on her hips, her gaze on Darlene and Damon. "Get anything else?"

"Nothing beyond the expected." He rotated his neck as if working out kinks. "However they were hit, they didn't know it until it was too late. From what I can glean, they were having a good time until she started feeling sick. He wasn't doing too hot either, and it got progressively worse."

Hays sighed. "Right, I'll notify the ME to send a call out for a corpse talker. Maybe they'll have more luck."

Her partner snorted. "Don't hold your breath. Last I heard, the waiting list for a top-tier Tracer was at least a month."

"A month?" she repeated. "What happened to what's his name? Adrian? Adan?"

"Aiden," Porter said. "Got an offer from a company back east that the Guild couldn't top."

"Make the call, Agent," Encinas said, breaking into story time. "Tell whoever's on call at the medical examiner's office to expedite the request. Maybe we can cut that month-long waiting time down. I've got no signs of a break-in, no weapons, magical or otherwise, to even get a starting point on how they were taken down."

"Copy that," Hays said. "Before we call it, I've got one more idea we can try. We can do a level-three Arcane scan, see if anything pops. If we're lucky, you'll get your starting point, if not…" She shrugged. "We're back to waiting on the ME's request."

I had no idea what all was involved with a level-three Arcane scan, but one of the EMTs asked, "You want us to clear out, then?"

Encinas looked to Hays. "You need the bodies, right?"

"Yep."

Encinas turned back to the EMTs. "You two mind waiting in the other room?"

The talkative EMT said, "Not a problem."

I swore the other one muttered, "I'm out," under his breath as the two headed for the door.

Once they were out of sight, Hays eyed Zev and me. "You two staying?"

Zev looked at me, and I shrugged. Staying wouldn't have been my first choice, but with Damon dead, we needed whatever answers we could get. I wasn't convinced Encinas would share those answers if she got them. Zev was clearly thinking along the same lines because he turned to the lieutenant and said, "We'd like to, if we can."

She thought it over and gave a nod before turning to Hays. "Let's do this."

The two ACRT agents didn't mess around and got to work. Before long, the runes ignited with a whoosh. A steady, muted mix of green-and-gold power was once again pulsed through the markings caught between the double ring of salt. Magic filled the room, adding a skin-ruffling chill and the faint scent of decay to the air before settling like a weight against my Prism.

Hays and Porter were focused on their casting, but Zev was slowly stalking the circle around the bed's edge and foot. I had no idea what he hoped to find, but Encinas didn't stop him. He moved behind Hays to come around to her other side. Then he came to an abrupt stop, his gaze on something I couldn't see.

"Did you see that?" Hays asked.

"Yeah," Zev confirmed.

"What is it?" Porter was staring at Darlene's body.

Zev sank to his heels, his attention never leaving Darlene. "I caught a flash but didn't get a good look." He put his hand against the floor and leaned in without breaching the circle.

Hays's expression turned grim as she looked at her partner. "We're going to have to flush out whatever that was."

A bead of sweat crept down Porter's temple. "Going to be tricky trapping it and keeping the rest of the scene intact. We're going to need another set of hands."

"How about mine?" Zev asked from where he was crouched.

The two ACRT agents exchange skeptical looks.

"If it helps," Encinas said. "He's a Hunter."

Porter eyed Zev then looked to Hays. "That would work."

"You'll have to be fast," Hays warned Zev.

He straightened and brushed his hand off against his thigh. "I can do fast." He studied the circle. "Can you rekey this so I can get in?"

"Give me a minute." Hays moved down the circle, stopped, then pulled a small bag from her pocket. She brought it up to her mouth to use her teeth to loosen the tie. Once it was open, she poured its contents into her hand and held her fist over the rune. Her lips moved as she released a trickle of dust or ash and retraced the markings on the floor. She added a spiral to the initial mark. When she was done, the magic lapping at my Prism slipped back, and the glow of power in the section in front of Zev dimmed.

"Okay." She brushed off her hand and turned to Zev. "On three, step inside the double ring and place your feet on either side of the Nyd marking to your left there. See it?"

A thin layer of blue danced over Zev's body and infused his dark eyes with an eerie glow. "I see it."

Hays continued her directions. "Once you're inside, be careful not to break any of the markings. If you do, we'll lose the whole scene, not to mention whatever is hiding from us. You can cross to the inner circle, but I would advise doing that only if necessary. You don't want to be exposed for too long, and I can't guarantee that whatever active magic is at play won't strike out. So long as you don't break any of the markings, the circle should hold."

Despite the dread pooling in my gut, I had to ask, "What happens if he does?"

She looked at me. "We're all screwed." She turned back to Zev. "I don't want to be screwed. Understood?"

"Understood."

"Right, then." She took a deep breath, raised her arms, spread them wide, and turned her palms in toward the bed. There was a shift in the room as if the air pressure changed as magic surged, then sparks erupted like a miniature firework. "One, two, three."

As the last *e* left Hays's mouth, Zev stepped over the line and through the narrow opening. The magic powering the circle whipped around him and struck the thin blue layer of his magic. Another, brighter, bigger flash erupted, and the weight against my Prism disappeared. Zev's hair whipped forward then back as if he were caught in a savage gust of wind, but once both of his feet were inside the double ring, the power swept back. Hays wove a sigil in the air, and the narrow opening she'd created disappeared. The green-gold band resumed its solid burning ring and locked Zev inside.

It made me nervous to see him essentially trapped, but there was nothing for me to do but watch the events unfold—and it didn't take long for that to happen. Hays and Porter worked the casting, their movements smooth and practiced. After a moment, I realized they were tightening the inner circle to basically flush out whatever had been scuttling around earlier.

Zev stood at the ready, his attention focused on what was happening. Even though the active magic was effectively confined by the circle, I could still feel the ebb and flow of its presence as the two agents worked. From the outside looking in, the three of them appeared to be just standing there for a long, tense minute. Then, at some unseen signal, they all moved.

Porter brought his arms in as if doing a butterfly press but with straight arms. The muscles in Hays's neck strained, and her body angled forward as if she were walking into a headwind. Her hands were up and trembling as if holding back an invisible foe. Zev had lunged forward, somehow managing to avoid the runes as he ended up half-on, half-off the bed. His knee landed on the mattress in the narrow space between Darlene and Damon as he reached for something I couldn't see. He barely caught himself on one hand, his torso just inches from Darlene's back, as magic erupted into a storm of green, gold, blue, and amber in a dizzying kaleidoscope.

While the visual barrage left me blinking little white dots from my vision, my Prism remained quiet. Clearly, Hays's circle was holding fast. I fisted my hands at my sides as I tried to slow my rapid breathing.

The last flashes of expended power faded as Zev carefully untangled himself from the bed and its occupants. Since he was forced to use only one hand, his movements were a bit awkward, but he finally got back to his feet. Only then were we able to see what he held.

Caught in his fist was what appeared to be a wriggling tube sock. It was hard to discern its coloring because it was fluctuating from a dull, dusty brown to an even-uglier drab yellow. "What the hell is that?"

Instead of answering, Zev sent cords of blue flame over the amorphous worm, wrapping it up into a magical cocoon. The minute the last cord settled into place, they ignited once more, and a high-pitched squeal that hit just on the upper range of my hearing erupted, repeating over and over in a desperate shriek.

I winced.

"This," Zev said once the shrieks finally died, "is what we call a hexed creation."

His magic pulled back to reveal something that looked like a monstrous cross between a scorpion and a lizard. It had a narrow body that squirmed like a centipede's and a long, segmented tail that ended in a nasty-looking, needle-thin point. The eyeless head moved like a snake's, weaving back and forth as a deep-red tongue darted in and out.

It squirmed in Zev's grasp as it whipped its stinger around, trying hard to stab Zev, but it couldn't seem to pierce that thin veil of blue that coated his hand and arm. "And I'm betting it's also why these two are dead."

TWENTY

IT TOOK SOME COORDINATION, plus me running out to the ACRT SUV to grab a containment cage, but we finally got the deadly hexed creation locked away. Agents Hays and Porter finished what they needed to do with the scene and eventually released the bodies.

The EMTs zipped Darlene and Damon into black bags covered in silver-embroidered runes. I recognized one as a standard "stay dead" sigil necromancers used to ensure a body stayed inert. It made me wonder how often EMTs had to deal with unexpected resurrections to make that a standard procedure.

I was standing on Darlene's porch with Zev and Lieutenant Encinas as the ambulance, with no siren but lights flashing, pulled away from the curb to head back to the medical examiner's office. The lookie-loos from earlier had disappeared back inside their homes, which was a small blessing. Agent Porter came out of the house with the containment cage in hand. We moved aside to let him through then watched him set it inside the ACRT vehicle.

"Will they be able to track down who created that thing?" Encinas asked Zev.

"Maybe, but I wouldn't hold my breath."

Hays joined us, pulling the door closed behind her and hitching her bag on her shoulder.

"Why's that?" the lieutenant asked.

"The fluctuation in color means it's degrading," Hays answered.

"Degrading?" That didn't sound good. "What? Is it going to go up in a puff of smoke or something?"

"Or something," Zev said. "These types of hexes are meant to stick around long enough to strike their intended target and infect them with the curse. Generally, the first strike carries the most magic, making it the most lethal bite. With each successive strike, the magic powering the hex becomes progressively weaker, resulting in a less effective impact and less corporal version of the creature."

"So it disappears," I said.

"It disappears," he confirmed.

"Which makes trapping one of these things beyond tricky," Hays added. She eyed Zev with what I hoped was professional interest. Otherwise, I would have to take offense on his behalf. "You've got serious skills to be able to nab that thing in its state, much less keep it off you."

Zev gave her one of his empty, polite smiles that he used to dodge unwanted attention. "I've had practice."

Modesty, thy name is avoidance.

Hays didn't take offense at his brush-off. Instead she offered him her hand. "Practice or skills, we appreciate the help in there."

"Glad I could help." He shook her hand.

Hays pulled her hand back, resettled her pack strap, and turned to Encinas. "We'll get our report submitted, but just so you know, if you hadn't called us in when you did, we'd all still be trying to figure out what the hell happened here. Porter and I found signs of two bites on the female vic and five on the male, which means the hex was on borrowed time.

We've got a call in to the office so we can do what we can before its gone, so I'll keep you posted if we find anything useful."

"Appreciate it," Encinas said. "Just make sure it doesn't get out of that cage during transport."

A grin slashed through Hays's serious expression. "Don't worry. Porter will keep it intact."

With that, she went to join her partner in their SUV, and we watched them drive away. My phone vibrated with an incoming text as Zev shared our contact information with Encinas. We said our goodbyes and headed back to the rental. Once inside, I read through the series of texts from Sabella as Zev got settled.

"What is it?" he asked.

"Sabella and Evan. As of twenty minutes ago, Sabella's on her way with Val to the hospital to tackle the other half of the Shed Twins, and Evan wants us to call." I handed over my phone then started up the car. I told the navigation system to route us back to the hotel. As it plotted our route, I told Zev, "Can you call Evan and put him on speakerphone? I haven't had a chance to connect my phone to the car yet."

"Sure."

The sound of the phone ringing filled the car as I made my way out of the neighborhood.

"Hey, Rory."

"Hey back. You've got me and Zev. What's up?"

"Hey, Zev." Evan didn't wait for a response but kept talking. "Were you able to track down Damon?"

I risked sharing a look with Zev before turning back to my driving. "Yeah, why?"

"Well, you know how much I hate leaving loose ends?"

More like his need for answers bordered on obsessive-compulsive, not that I was complaining. "Yeah…"

"Well, I found two accounts he's done his best to hide."

"Like financial accounts?"

"That's one. The other appears to be a virtual drive."

"So it could hold anything," Zev said.

"Yep, and whatever it is, he's got it locked down with some serious encryption."

I hit the blinker and waited for a compact to zip by before switching lanes. "Can you break it?"

"I can, but it will take time."

"How long?" Zev asked before I could.

"Best guess? Eight, maybe ten hours, tops." Evan paused. "Any chance of asking him politely about it?"

I gave a derisive snort. "Considering he's on his way to the medical examiner's office, I'm going to say no. Though, even if he was still breathing, I don't think he'd be eager to share."

Evan let out a low whistle. "Right, guess I know how I'm spending my Saturday, then."

I winced, knowing my request meant interrupting Lena's quality time with her snuggle bunny, because now that Evan had a challenge, he wouldn't let it go until he beat it. "Tell Lena I owe her."

"Why her? I'm the one doing the work," he complained.

"Because she's better at holding a grudge."

"You've got a point," he conceded. "I'm definitely throwing your ass under the bus."

"I'll figure out a way to pay her back."

"Oh, don't worry. She'll be more than happy to give you a list of options."

Wasn't that the truth, but then again, I would happily take it. Without Evan's help, we would be at the mercy of the police, and they weren't going to share shit with Zev and me.

"Send us whatever you can, when you can," Zev said. "And Fields?"

"Yeah?"

"If things get dire with Lena, I've got connections with a spa up in Sedona and can call in a favor."

Evan didn't even hesitate. "I'm going to take you up on that."

Zev grinned. "I'll make a call."

"Right, time to play! Later." He disconnected.

Zev dumped my phone in the cup holder in the console between us then settled back in his seat and rubbed his eyes. The unusual sign of fatigue worried me, especially since he was still coming back from his own fight with a hex.

"You doing okay?" I asked softly.

"I'm good. Just a headache. Could probably do with some food if you're up for it."

Since it was closing in on lunch, I could get on board. "How about we head back to the hotel? You can stretch out for a few, and I'll see what's available for lunch?"

He reached over and squeezed my thigh. "That works." He left his hand where it was, the warm weight of it comforting as I navigated through traffic to find my spot on the freeway.

I covered his hand with mine and held on as I drove one-handed. "A connection, huh?" I teased and caught his grin out of the corner of my eye.

"Don't worry, babe. They owe me more than one favor."

My lips curved. "Good."

✶✶✶✶✶✶✶✶✶✶✶✶✶✶✶✶✶✶✶✶✶✶✶✶

We got back to the hotel, dropped the rental off with the valet, then made our way through the glass doors to the expansive lobby only to walk into organized chaos. Our timing was for shit, because clearly it was close to checkout.

The long reservation counters were filled, and lines radiated from each station. We wove our way through piles of suitcases and mounds of duffle bags while trying not to bump the milling bodies. It was like being caught in a human-size version of a pinball game, complete with the loud clangs and dings coming from the adjoining casino floor.

By the time we hit the elevators that went up to the private suites, my tolerance for having my personal space invaded was close to nil, and my neck itched like crazy. The fourth time I stopped to look around, Zev pulled me in close and asked, "What's wrong?"

We stood there, the only still things in a river of bodies, which earned us a couple of dirty looks and a few comments I chose to ignore. "I don't know." I looked around without a clue as to why I was so jumpy. Finally, I grabbed his hand and started moving again. "I think I'm just peopled out."

"Yeah, I get that."

Together, we hustled to the elevator. In some sort of minor miracle, we caught an empty one. Zev keyed the access ward then hit the button for our floor. The doors slid closed, and I slumped against the back wall with a relieved sigh. "Please tell me you can hold off on lunch until that mess disappears."

He chuckled as he leaned against the sidewall and folded his arms over his chest. "There's always room service."

I gave his suggestion serious consideration, but… "I'm not sure my stomach's up for something that heavy."

"Yeah, mine either."

I took in his slumped shoulders. "Let's get you off your feet and get some painkillers in you to get ahead of that headache. Then I'll brave the horde for a lighter option."

The soft ding heralded our arrival, and the doors slid open. Zev waited for me to exit first. As I passed him, he bent down and said, "There are other options for getting rid of a headache."

I stepped clear of the doors, and when he joined me, I pressed in close, my palms against his chest. I tilted my head back as he bent his forward. I pushed up to my toes and pressed a soft kiss to his lips. When I was done, I said, "You are such a guy."

Despite his exhaustion and pain, his grin still conveyed a serious amount of wicked heat. "Is that a complaint?"

"Nope." I patted his chest. "But I don't want you passing out on me right in the middle of the good stuff."

That earned a laugh as he turned, curled an arm around my waist, and started toward the suite. "The good stuff, eh?"

My smile was all kinds of satisfied as I murmured, "The very good stuff."

⁘⁘⁘⁘⁘⁘⁘⁘⁘⁘⁘⁘⁘⁘⁘⁘⁘⁘

Forty-five happy minutes later, I left Zev dozing in the suite and headed down in search of food. Thankfully, the earlier crowd had thinned to below mosh-pit levels, so I wasn't feeling quite so claustrophobic as I wove around clusters of gawking tourists and dodged oblivious huddles of inebriated partygoers milling the wide walkways.

I felt my shoulders inch down from my ears as I left the heavy scents and ear-numbing din of the casino floor behind for the interconnected passages that linked the hotels along the strip. There was something to be said for not having to brave the heat to get from one attraction to another.

Unfortunately, that same convenience played havoc with my sense of direction. Normally, my internal GPS was spot-on, but the seemingly endless stretch of walkways fooled me into making a wrong turn.

Grumbling under my breath, I stepped off the moving walkway and moved off to the side, out of the flow of foot traffic. I used my phone to reorient myself then course corrected. I did that little hop-skip transition off the moving walkway and headed for the double door leading outside. I had crossed with the mass of bodies at the traffic light when that paranoid itch from earlier made a comeback. I looked around, but nothing stuck out. I shrugged it off as a by-product of being stuck in a crowd and made my way into a plaza ringed with storefronts.

I found the highly rated bistro Zev and I had agreed on. It offered neither delivery nor indoor dining, hence my decision to hoof it. Based upon the fact that there were three lines, each at least five people deep, I was not the only one trying to avoid the overpriced, sit-down dining options that rampaged through Sin City.

I got to the counter and gave my order to a young man with bright eyes, dark hair, and a golden glow, who called it back to the kitchen with the flowing cadence of the islands. Payment made, I wandered over to a two-person table arranged around the dancing fountain to wait.

To pass the time, I pulled up my emails, occasionally batting away a gnat or fly. That was a drawback about sitting outside when the outside temps were bearable—those that flew and buzzed their way through life considered it prime airtime.

A quick scan of emails showed a couple of job requests that could hold until Monday and one from Mari. Seeing her name spiked my anxiety. This had to be about my probationary period. I worried my lip and considered putting off opening it.

"Suck it up, Rory," I muttered under my breath and clicked it open. I read Mari's succinct message informing me we had an appointment with the Arcane Council in a week. There was no way to escape my looming decision, not when it was laid out in black-and-white. This was it, my time to ride or die. There was no more stalling, no more time to ponder the what-ifs. I had to pick a path. Go left and forge my own way; go right and be led by someone, or something, I could never fully trust.

I knew what my decision was, what it had been for the last few weeks—I was no one's tool. The weight of indecision that had been riding my ass disappeared, but it left behind a low-level anxiety. After a little emotional poking and prodding, I recognized it for what it was—a nervous excitement about what lay ahead—the unknown. I closed Mari's message without responding then started clearing out unwanted offers for car insurance, sales on things I never wanted in the first place, and a few weird-looking ones that I knew better than to even open.

I was setting up a reminder in my calendar to follow up on a request from a university research department when my order was called. I got up, shoved my phone into my back pocket, and headed over to the counter. I grabbed the plastic bag holding our food then added in napkins and utensils from the mobile station sitting nearby. I turned to head back only to pull up short when an older man stood in front of me, a woman at his side.

"Ms. Costas, I thought that was you."

It took me a second to place their faces. "Mr. and Mrs. Lennox, right? Friends of the Hathaways."

He smiled. "Please, call me Beau."

"Beau." I turned to his wife, who was juggling a couple of shopping bags.

"Carol," she offered, returning my smile and offering her hand as well. "Lovely to see you again, Ms. Costas."

I took it, squeezed, and let her go. "You, as well, and you can call me Rory. I don't mind."

For some reason, that made Beau laugh. Behind me someone murmured, "Excuse me," as they tried to get to the condiment station.

Beau brushed my arm as he waved toward a shaded spot off to the side. "Do you have a minute?" He looked to the bag I held. "We won't keep you."

"Of course." I pasted on my polite, professional smile as we moved over to the shade.

Although the outside temperatures weren't the scorch fest of summer, it was warm enough that standing around too long might work up a sweat. We stepped into the shade cast by a tree that shouldn't exist in the desert. Even I had to admit it offered a lovely reprieve, not just for us but for a few buzzing insects. I shooed off one that got too close and felt a slight sting on the back of my hand as Beau said, "I didn't get a chance to ask you last night, but you mentioned you were a freelance Transporter."

"I am." I rubbed my hand against my jeans to ease the irritation.

He nodded. "If Regal Enterprises was interested in contracting your services for runs between our LA and Vegas offices, would you be interested?"

I tamped down my burst of excitement and managed a sedate "Are you looking for on-call or scheduled deliveries?"

"Most likely both, depending on your rates."

The scheduling logistics could get tricky, but it was doable if they were willing to pay. "If you could email me the details, I'd be happy to send you a quote."

That seemed to please him. "Wonderful, if you could text me your contact information, I can get that to you Monday."

"Of course." I rearranged my bag of food and slipped my hand through the plastic handle so I could text when there was another irritating nip on the back of my neck. I batted at whatever bug, most likely a mosquito, had decided to dive-bomb me and shuffled a little farther away from the tree. Hoping I had cleared whatever insect zone existed, I opened messages. "What's your number?"

He rattled it off as he pulled out his phone.

I typed out my information and hit Send. "There you go."

A soft ding sounded, and he looked down at his screen. "Fantastic." He looked up and held out his free hand. "Thank you again for giving us a moment."

I shook his hand. "Of course. Thank you for considering me, and I look forward to hearing from you."

We exchanged goodbyes then parted ways. I headed back

to the hotel, feeling a little less anxious than when I'd set out. I was going to take this offer as a sign from the universe that I was on the right path.

I got back to the room and was pulling out containers in the kitchen when Zev joined me.

He came up behind me, his hands going to the counter, as he pressed a kiss at the back of my neck, just under my ear. "You got bit," he murmured.

I showed him the small red bump on the back of my hand. "Mosquitos."

"Hmm, they must find you tasty." He nipped my shoulder. "I know I do."

A soft chuckle escaped. "Seriously, Zev?"

"What?"

I turned my head, and he was close enough it was my turn to take a taste. When I drew back, I teased, "Corny much?"

He opened his mouth, but before he could respond, there was an audible growl from his stomach.

Grinning, I opened a container filled with rice, vegetables, and thin slices of grilled steak. I stuck a plastic fork in it then held it up to him. "Eat."

"Smells good." He took it from me then moved to my side. Leaning back against the counter, he crossed his legs at the ankle. He took a bite and gave a hum of appreciation.

I took out another container, this one with shrimp, grabbed a fork, then turned to match Zev's position. When the first forkful hit my tongue, I echoed his satisfied hum. "So good."

We spent a couple of minutes appeasing our stomachs. Once I was sure mine would leave me alone for a minute, I set aside my meal and went to pull two bottles of water from the small refrigerator. I set one next to Zev and kept the other. I grabbed my plate and strove for a casual tone. "So, I might just get a contract from Regal." I shoved a forkful of rice into my mouth.

He paused in midbite and raised an eyebrow. "Really?"

"Mm-hmm." I chewed then swallowed. "Ran into Beau Lennox and his wife, and he asked for my contact information. They're considering using me for runs between their LA office and here."

"Lennox," he repeated with a frown.

"Older guy, quiet, part of Hathaway's dinner party."

Recognition clicked. "Right. Sounds like a corporate contract, then?"

"Yep." I gave it a second, letting him take a bite, before adding, "Also got an email from Mari. The Council wants to meet next week."

He eyed me as he chewed. "Any indication which way they're going to go?"

I shrugged. "No."

Zev paused with his fork halfway to his mouth and studied me with narrowed eyes for a long moment. "You made a decision."

I wasn't surprised he could read me so easily, since he'd been there while I struggled over my options during the last few weeks. Hell, I had used him as my sounding board as I waffled between *Should I?* and *Shouldn't I?* Not once did he get impatient with me or my indecision. Instead, he asked questions as I worked through my concerns, listened with no judgement, and waited until asked to share his opinion. He let me be… me. And it struck me then, like it did sometimes, how much I loved him.

I held his gaze and said softly, "Do you know how much I love you?"

He set his food aside and reached out to tug me close.

I put my container next to his and snuggled in, relishing the feeling of being home, being safe.

"I know," he said as he held me tightly. "I love you too."

We held each other for a long moment. I listened to his heart beat under my ear, and I shared. "If the Council does offer, I won't be re-signing the contract." I couldn't tell if his sigh was one of relief or resignation, so I tilted my head back so I could see his face but couldn't read his expression. "Nothing to say?"

His lips curved slowly as he brushed his fingers along my jaw, his gaze steady. "Not my decision, babe. It's yours. You know what's best for you and your career. Although, I'll admit I'm selfishly glad."

"Why?"

"Because I know the Council, and they're like quicksand. They'll suck you under piece by piece until you're drowning. Better to stand on your own ground, where you know where to put your feet."

"Too fucking true," I murmured as I held him tightly.

TWENTY-ONE

ZEV and I were sprawled side by side on the couch, our legs propped up on the low coffee table, watching an old movie that involved a lot of explosions and impossible car chases. Well, Zev was watching. I was dozing until the lock at door clicked, and Zev hit Pause on the remote. He craned his neck as I used one hand on his chest to push up to watch the door open. Sabella and Val sauntered in.

"*Buonasera!*" Sabella's greeting was followed by the clatter of items hitting the entry table then the click of her heels crossing the tiled floor. Zev and I untwisted as she came around the end of the couch and dropped gracefully into the plush chair. "I need a drink."

"Water or something stronger?" Val asked as he angled for the kitchen.

"Water, please." She looked at the TV, where a car was frozen in midair, then back at us. "You two are too young to be watching TV on a Saturday night in Las Vegas," she chided.

"Recovering from a hex, here," Zev drawled as he lifted his arm so I could reclaim my previous position on his chest.

When her attention came to me, I said, "I'm recovering

from his being hexed, playing bait, and dealing with demonic tube socks."

My aunt blinked and looked at Zev. "Tube socks?"

"Hexed creation," he said. "Bad reptile-arachnid mix."

"Mm-hmm." She eyed me with concern. "You do look a little pale, *cattivella*. You weren't bit, were you?"

"No, but I'm pretty sure the no sleep and excitement finally caught up with me." I wasn't lying. After lunch, I'd managed to catch an echo of Zev's headache, and within a couple of hours it had been joined by a blanket of exhaustion. If my stomach had joined the parade, I would've pinned it on bad shrimp from lunch, but my stomach, so far, was fine. "Where have you two been?"

"Based upon the story running around through the police halls, having much less fun than the two of you," she said.

"Ah, you heard about Damon, then." I rubbed at my tired eyes and focused on the conversation.

"Hard not to," Val said as he handed a bottle of water to Sabella and kept one for himself. "Double homicides do cause quite the stir, especially when rumors are floating around that one of the victims was feuding with a powerful, local Family." He went over to the dining table no one bothered to use and grabbed a chair. He dragged it over and set it next to my aunt.

I groaned, thinking about what it meant that the police were linking the Hathaways to Damon. "Please tell me I'm not going to find my ass hauled in for interrogation."

"You are not going to be hauled in for questioning," Val confirmed as he sat in the chair. "However, the same may not apply to the younger Mr. Hathaway. If the police do reach out, let me know. I'll make sure they understand you and, by extension, Sabella were simply caught in the cross fire. Though I'm pretty sure that won't be a concern."

I wished I could share his belief, but prior experience taught me to proceed with caution.

Val hooked an ankle on his knee. "You two made quite the impression on Lieutenant Encinas."

"Although I do wish we had found out about Damon's demise before we spoke to Russ." Sabella took a drink from her water.

"Russ?" Zev tossed the remote onto the cushion next to him. "Who's that?"

"Russ Ekhart is the man you"—Val tipped his water my way—"put in the hospital."

"Mr. White," I murmured, putting the name to blond half of the Shed Twins. "You got him to talk?"

"Not him," Sabella said. "His partner, Dan Taylor."

The permanently grumpy punk-biker wannabe, Mr. Black, was named Dan Taylor? No wonder he stuck with Mr. Black. I reined in my distracted thoughts and shoved them back on track, trying to navigate Sabella's timeline of events. "I thought you were planning on talking to him first, before he got a chance to make bail."

"We did, but he didn't give us anything until our second visit," she said.

"Second visit?" I was officially lost, because that made no sense. Maybe I was more exhausted than I realized.

"Wait, run us through that again," Zev demanded. "You went to the station this morning to talk to the idiot in the cell, right?"

"Right," Sabella confirmed. "But he wasn't inclined to talk."

"And his name is…" Zev prompted.

"Mr. Black," I murmured as Val supplied helpfully, "Dan Taylor."

Undeterred, Zev kept going. "And the one at the hospital?"

"Mr. White," I said.

"His partner, Russ Ekhart," Val finished.

"So you went to the hospital to talk to Ekhart…"

I couldn't help but find the humor in listening to Zev wrangle Sabella and Val into untangling their story.

"No, dear." Sabella's voice carried that tone that indicated she was concerned with Zev's comprehension. Under my head, Zev's chest rose and fell with an aggrieved sigh that my aunt completely ignored. "We went to where they were holding Mr. Taylor."

Val took pity on Zev and stepped in. "However, he invoked his right to an attorney and refused to say anything until they showed. We decided to head over to the hospital to try our luck with Mr. Ekhart."

"Unfortunately, he was equally uncooperative," Sabella lamented. "In fact, he claimed that we overreacted."

I blinked. "Overreacted to them trying to kill us?"

"According to him, they were simply trying to carjack you," Val shared.

"We were in a rental." Disbelief was clear in my voice. "A nice rental, granted, but not one that could easily be offloaded if obtained through illegal means." No chop shop wanted to risk triggering an antitheft hex that most rental companies installed. "If I was still in the Gullwing, I might buy his claim, but who in the hell carjacks a freakin' rental?"

"Obviously, he was lying." Sabella waved that off. "But he stuck to that story like glue."

"Which means he's more scared of whomever he's working for than you." Zev shook his head. "What a dumbass."

Sabella glowed as if he'd paid her a compliment. "Thank you."

Val took up the story. "When we realized we wouldn't get anywhere with him, we returned to the station to talk to the chief. I was hoping Mr. Taylor's attorney would give us a few minutes with his client, but by the time we got back, Mr. Taylor was already at his hearing. Luckily for us, he was brought back to be processed and transferred to county."

"The judge denied his bail," Zev guessed.

"He did," Val confirmed. "I got the impression the judge was insulted when Mr. Taylor's lawyer no-showed."

"Oooh, I bet that pissed him off," I said, thinking how easily riled Mr. Black could be.

"Yes, he was quite upset," Sabella said with way too much joy. "So much so that he was demanding to see us as he was being brought in. The chief graciously offered us space to chat."

And I was betting that space came with a camera and a two-way mirror. "So what's his story?"

"According to him," Val said, "he and his partner were contacted via a forum on the dark web to interfere with the delivery of a classic car. They were told that the car in question was a custom build by Wilson Rides and that they were to relieve the driver of the vehicle before it reached Las Vegas without attracting the attention of the authorities. The promised fee was a hundred thousand, and they were encouraged to do whatever they needed to convince the driver to hand over the keys. They were given a twenty-thousand-dollar deposit, with the remaining balance to be paid upon assignment completion."

My mind stumbled over the proffered amount and the stupidity created by greed. All because two grown-ass men were acting like spoiled, entitled teenagers. "They were offered six figures and didn't stop to wonder why that amount was so high?"

Val shook his head. "These are not sophisticated criminals, Rory. My impression is that these two have made a career out of taking on one-off, high-paying jobs from people with more money than sense. They weren't expecting much by way of resistance, not from what they thought was simply a contracted Transporter. Especially since they'd managed to get the initial driver out of the picture. They figured you wouldn't put up much of a fight for a contracted transport, not if they made what they felt was a significant threat."

"Dumbasses," I concurred with Zev's earlier assessment.

Zev played with my hair. "If they weren't supposed to flip the cops to what they were up to, why did they decide to go after the two of you in the garage? Especially since they failed to intercept the delivery."

"Pride," Sabella said.

"Injured pride," Val corrected. "It seems they did not appreciate your response to their initial request or losing out on such a hefty payment. Since they had your name and knew where the car was being delivered, it just took a couple of well-placed bribes to valets to figure out where you two were staying and tail you. Then they waited for their chance. When you and Bella went shopping, they took it."

I refrained from repeating my earlier assessment. "Do they know who hired them?"

"All they had was a digital username," Sabella said. "But after some persuasion, Mr. Taylor shared the online account where the initial deposit was made. That information was turned over to their forensic accountant team."

That meant we might get an actual name in about six weeks. But combine that request with the fact that Evan was busy digging into Damon's hidden accounts, and I was pretty confident that when the forensics team was done, it would be Damon Innes's name behind the username and the over-the-top job offer. I just wasn't keen on waiting two months for that confirmation. If I could get that username to Evan, that two-month wait would be a memory. I was trying to figure out how to ask without inviting questions I didn't want to answer, when Zev went for it.

"Any chance of you sharing that username?"

Sabella studied him with narrowed eyes. "Why?"

Zev flicked his gaze to Val then looked to Sabella. "There's a possibility that Damon had a couple of hidden accounts tucked away."

"How strong of a possibility?" Val asked.

Zev considered him for a long moment. "Very strong."

"And you came by this information…"

"Through an anonymous source who is currently working on verifying that information."

"Can they do so in such a way as to hold up to scrutiny in court?"

"I can ask."

Val tapped his water bottle against his knee as he considered Zev. Finally, he said, "Ask. Otherwise, this could drag out for months."

Zev nodded.

There was a soft buzz, and Val frowned, shifting his weight to one hip and digging his phone out of a pocket. He checked the screen and turned to Sabella. "We've got a conference call with Xanto in fifteen minutes. Do you want to take it here or in my room?"

Sabella stood up and stretched. "Let's take it in yours." She turned to Zev and me. "Are you two in for the night, or would you be interested in a late dinner?"

Zev's arm tightened on my shoulders, and I tipped my head back to find him looking down at me.

"I'm good right here," I murmured.

He turned to Sabella and Val. "We're good for the night, but you two have a lovely dinner."

"Well, then, we're off." Sabella curled her hand on Val's arm, and he started to lead her to the door. She called back, "Have fun, you two, and don't wait up."

"We will, and we won't," I called back.

Once the door clicked shut behind them, I looked at Zev. "They didn't give you a username."

"Nope, but I'm not sure we need it." He pulled out his phone, hit his screen, and put the phone up to his ear.

I was close enough to hear Evan say, "Yeah."

"Vegas police have two men in custody, Russ Ekhart and Dan Taylor. According to Taylor, they were hired by someone on the dark web to intercept Rory's deliver to Hathaway. They took a deposit of 20K. Can you match that to Damon's hidden accounts?"

"You have other information, like the date of the deposit or a username or a forum where the job was posted?"

"Nope, but I'm betting it's in a recorded interview that went down earlier today."

"Is that so?"

Zev didn't get a chance to answer, because Evan disconnected.

"I give him until tomorrow morning," I said.

"I'm betting he'll have it before we get up," Zev countered.

TWENTY-TWO

BY NINE O'CLOCK, I was dragging ass so hard that I all but crawled into the shower, hoping it would wash away some of the exhaustion weighing me down. I think I fell asleep a couple of times between washing my hair and shaving my legs, because by the time I stepped out, the water had gone from steaming hot to mildly warm.

Still, the mirror was shrouded in steam as I wrapped the towel around myself. I grabbed a smaller one from the stack on the open shelf under the sink and started to use it on my hair. I had my eyes closed and my head buried in cotton when I heard something hit the floor behind me. I spun on a bare heel, not smart while on wet tile, because I lost my balance and had to throw out my hand to the counter before I landed on my barely covered ass. The towel in my hair slid to the floor and landed right in front of a grotesque cross of scorpion and lizard.

I froze, my Prism locking into place as my heart raced. I stared down the hexed creature that was in my freaking bathroom! "Holy shit," I breathed, not able to find enough air to call out to Zev.

It darted forward, and I stumbled back, tripped over my

pile of discarded clothes, and landed on my ass on one of the bathmats with a pained grunt. Thankfully, I managed not to lose my towel.

The creature hit the edge of it and bounced off with a shrill hiss. Using the hand not holding the towel in place and my heels, I scooted away until my back hit the door with a soft thump. The twisted creature rushed me again, totally ignoring the fact that my Prism held it back. This time, instead of bouncing off, it jabbed its ugly, needlelike tail into the barrier repeatedly in a mindless frenzy, as if not realizing it wouldn't get through.

There was a knock on the door behind me. "Rory, you okay?"

I started to answer Zev then stopped when I realized if he came in, he would be another target. "Um… I slipped on the wet tile, but I'm good." My voice came out with the tiniest hint of panic that I hoped the door would muffle.

"You sure?"

"Yeah." My relief at hearing his feet move away from the door didn't last long because the little shit that was cornering me reared back, and its form wavered then began to shift. That was not good.

"Oh shit," I muttered, frantically searching for something to trap it in. From my position on the ground, my options were limited.

My dirty clothes wouldn't do much to stop it or its tail. I could try smashing it with the hair dryer, but considering the body looked like it was armored, I dismissed that option. Then my gaze fell on the metal trash basket tucked in the corner under the sink and behind the little freak.

"Think, Rory, think," I hissed in frustration. If I moved from my position, would the thing make a break for it? If it tried, it might be able to squeeze under the door, giving it a straight shot into the suite. I needed a distraction.

Without taking my eyes off the little bugger, I tucked in

the towel edge then braced one hand on the floor near my hip as I leaned over and reached out. My fingers brushed the coiled cord of the hair dryer hanging off the counter to my left. I straightened out a leg until I could press my toes against the edge to the water closet and stretched a little farther.

This time, I managed to get a fingerhold on the cord and pull it toward me. The hair dryer slid along the counter, its weight shifting as it got closer to the edge, then it was falling. I gave up saving my modesty and lunged forward, going from hips to stomach, my face inches from the tile with my hands outstretched. I caught the dryer as it dropped into my hands, then I flipped to my back with the dryer pointed at the freaky scorpion that was rushing toward me. I hit the power button.

The unexpected blast of heat made it pause for just a moment. Long enough for me to shift the dryer to one hand and use my other to grab the wastebasket. My towel gave up the ghost as I threw the dryer at the creature then slammed the basket over it. I used both hands to hold the basket in place as it bounced off the inside, the high-pitched squeals audible even though the hair dryer was going full blast.

"Zev!"

The door slammed open, then Zev was there, chest bare, sleep pants hanging low on his hips and a ferocious frown on his face. "What the hell?" He stood in the doorway, arms braced against the frame, while shock replaced his frown.

No doubt the scene had to look strange—me, boobs out, towel barely covering my ass, leaning over a trash basket while a hair dryer spun itself in little circles. The creature hit the can, and despite the fact I was holding it in place with my weight, it shifted across the tile. "A little help, please?"

Proving how much he loved me, he didn't ask any questions. A nimbus of blue erupted around him, throwing the lines of his tattoos in sharp relief. "What's in there?"

"A twin to the little freak you found at Damon's."

Zev's frown made a comeback as he muttered a vile oath. "Where did it come from?"

"Don't know. Don't care." The can shifted another fraction as the creature slammed it again.

Zev picked up the hair dryer, flipped it off, then tossed it to the counter. "Did it sting you?"

I gritted my teeth at another vigorous hit. "No."

Zev dropped into a crouch, his attention on the metal container. "Your Prism's up, yeah?"

"Yeah." I tried to shift my weight because the edge was digging painfully into my ribs, but the freak of nature hit the side again and dragged me and the can a couple inches off to the right.

Zev's hands, lined in blue flames, grabbed the metal sides. His power rasped against my Prism like a scouring pad, just another layer to my current discomfort, but the shrill shrieks cut off, and so did the constant battering.

"Can we kill it?"

"No, but we can untether it from its maker." Zev kept his hands where they were but rose into a partial squat, his gaze scanning the counter.

"What are you looking for?"

"I need you to reach back and to your left about eight inches and grab me that toothpaste."

I awkwardly reached back and patted around until I hit the squishy tube. I grabbed it and handed it off to Zev. He used his teeth to undo the top then, with one hand, started laying out a series of lines and runes in spearmint. When all he had left was the area just under my torso, he had me shift around so he could close the circle.

He tossed the toothpaste aside and looked at me. "On three, I need you to let go and back up. Ready?"

I nodded.

"One, two, three."

I threw myself back as he sank power into the ring of cavity protection. Blue-white flames erupted, trapping the can in a two-foot-high ring of fire. I scooted back until I hit the wall by the sink and pulled my towel back in place so I wasn't flashing Zev. I rubbed at the painful ache where the edge of the can had pressed into my ribs, wondering if I'd cracked something in my zealous containment effort.

My gaze was focused on the thin white filaments that wove themselves around the basket until the metal was caught in a magical net. Once the filaments covered the can, there was another surge of magic. The white fire shifted to a pale blue and finally darkened to deep sapphire. The openings in the weave slowly tightened down.

The shrill squeals started up again, accompanied by the dull thuds as the creature fought to escape. Dents appeared in the thin metal as scorch marks bloomed under the web. I bent over with a groan as a sharp stabbing pain streaked from the sore spot on my ribs then arrowed around my chest and up the back of my neck.

"Rory? What's wrong?"

"Whatever you're doing, stop!" I gasped.

Zev's magic paused, and the agonizing claw digging into my neck did the same. "Talk to me."

I breathed through the pain, trying to think.

Somehow, whatever Zev was doing was impacting me, which meant… I reached for my magic, and the room around me lit up with indigo storms that raged outside the diamond sheen of my Prism. The metal basket caught in an incandescent net glowed blindingly bright. I had to blink a few times before I could see the twists of ugly orange that snaked from the knot of squirming yellow and greens caught in its center. Those twists stretched impossibly thin and were latched to… me.

"Oh, fucking hell no!" I shook my fist to dislodge one of those threads, which was somehow embedded on the back of my hand. It hung on, and my Prism was having a hell of time cutting it off. I twisted and turned until I found another thread that disappeared behind me. I slapped a hand over the back of my neck and felt the raised bump of what was clearly not a mosquito bite. "Son of bitch."

"What?" Zev bit out.

"That little shit has me hooked like a fucking fish," I groused, trying not to let panic get the better of me. "I can't get them off."

A predatory mask fell over Zev's face. "Where?"

"The damn insect bites, back of my hand"—I lifted the hand in question—"and back of my neck by my ear. My Prism's trying to snap them off, but it keeps sliding away."

His jaw hardened, and his eyes burned with an unearthly blue. "You've been tagged."

Only because I knew him so well was I able to recognize part of that burn was fury. "Tell me you can untag me."

"I can, but it's going to hurt like a bitch."

Of course it will. "I don't care. Just do it."

"The minute I lift this, I'm going to cut its tether to its maker, and you're going to feel it. Ready?"

No. "Yes."

He yanked the can upward and tossed it aside. The incandescent net snapped tight around the frantic creature. Earsplitting shrieks filled the air as blue fire coiled around the trussed-up scorpion. Tongues of agony wrapped around the base of my skull, and my hand felt like it was melting. I locked my teeth to hold back my screams, and I doubled over as a noxious odor filled the confines of the bathroom. Just when I thought the encroaching wave of darkness would take me under, the pain blinked out.

It was so abrupt that it took me long seconds to realize it was gone. When the room came back in focus, I was lying on cool tile, muscles quivering in relief, and gasping for breath. There was a click, then the fan above was chugging away.

Zev's face replaced the white ceiling, his hair falling around his face as he leaned over me, his hands on either side of my head. "Rory, can you sit up?"

I licked dry lips and reached for my voice. "I think so."

With his help, I managed to get upright. I leaned against him as the shift in position made my head swim for a second. On the floor where the hexed creature had been was now a smear of ash and toothpaste. The horrific smell was drifting away.

"You okay?" Zev asked from behind me.

I curled my hand around his arm that was holding me against him. "Yes?"

"Are the tags gone?"

I peeked through the door that let me see the echoes of magic and searched for the ugly orange threads, but all I could see was the faceted layer of my Prism covering every blessed inch. No threads in sight. "Yeah, they're gone."

"Good. Let's get you up."

I let him help me to my feet. I was standing there as he retouched my towel, when something red caught my eye. I grabbed his wrist and looked at it then looked at the floor. "The bracelet." Zev squatted and reached for it, but I used his wrist to tug him back. "Hold up. You're not supposed to touch it, remember?"

"Right." A flicker of blue licked up the string behind ash on the floor. He straightened, put an arm around my hips, and guided me toward the bathroom door. "Get dressed. I'll clean this up."

I tested my balance, and when I didn't topple, I shuffled out of the bathroom. While Zev cleaned up, I dug through our bags and pulled out one of his T-shirts. I was tugging it in place when a phone rang. I looked over to the nightstand, and Zev's phone was lit up.

"Can you grab that?" Zev asked from inside the bathroom.

"Sure." I rounded the bed, reached for the phone, and saw Evan's name on the screen. "Hey, Evan." I sat on the edge of the bed.

"Hey, Rory, so I was able to track that payment Zev asked about to one of Damon's accounts."

Completely not shocked, I said, "Uh-huh."

"And found out that Damon had a hell of a side gig going on."

"Side gig?" I asked, twisting to see Zev standing in the doorway to the bathroom and watching me. "Hang on. I'm putting you on speaker." I lowered the phone and hit the screen. "Okay, go ahead."

"Yep," Evan said. "Based on these hefty deposits every month, it seems Damon made bank doing a little blackmailing."

"Of who?" Zev asked as he leaned his shoulder against the frame.

"Beau Lennox."

TWENTY-THREE

HOURS LATER, after ingesting massive amounts of caffeine to deal with the late-night, early-morning discussions that involved Sabella and Val, which then resulted in a flurry of phone calls filled with legalese, I finally fell into bed. It felt like my head had barely touched down before Zev was urging me awake. He shuffled me into the bathroom and gave me another cup of coffee, then we were on our way to the police station with Sabella and Val. I was too bleary-eyed to get behind the wheel, so Val drove.

Once at the rather modern-looking building that housed the police station, we were greeted by the burly, silver-streaked chief of police and a grim-faced Lieutenant Encinas. They took our party of four through a maze of cubicles. A couple of heads popped up as we passed, but then they slid back down, barely making a ripple in the overall quiet. Guess barely nine on a Saturday morning was too early even for Sin City to get into trouble.

The chief opened a door marked Room 744 and ushered us into a narrow space. Three people were sitting in the chairs facing the two-way mirror. Two rose to their feet, but the third, a woman in a pencil skirt and fitted blouse with neatly tucked-up hair, barely looked up from her tablet.

In front of me, Encinas sent out a general greeting and Agent Hays lifted her paper coffee cup in return. She sidled through the chairs to meet us. "Morning, all. Didn't expect to see you again."

"Was a surprise to us too." A nudge at my back had me shuffling to the side and toward the chair-free sliver of space at the back of the room.

Zev followed, and we both huddled with Encinas in the open area. Hays course corrected without spilling her coffee and joined us in supporting the back wall. She left behind a cadaverously thin man with a bright smile and shock of red hair that stood on end as if he'd stuck his finger in a light socket.

As the man made his way forward, he flashed a polite smile our way, but it gained serious warmth when it landed on Val. "You know, the next time you invite me to an early-morning meet on a Saturday, it better involve clubs and a caddy."

Val chuckled as he shook the redhead's hand even as he kept his other at the small of Sabella's back. "Maybe next time." He let go of the man's hand. "Paul, I'd like to introduce Sabella Rossi-Giordano."

Paul gallantly took Sabella's hand, squeezed, then let it go. "Sabella, while I wish this was under better circumstances, it is a true pleasure to meet you."

I gave him points because he sounded sincere, not smarmy. Sabella murmured something I didn't catch, because I heard my name.

"I heard a rumor Rory there found a twin to our little critter," Hays said to Zev.

"Not a rumor," he confirmed.

"Did you leave me anything to work with?"

I stopped listening to them and paid attention to the

round of introductions and pleasantries that filled the next few minutes. I learned Paul was here representing the Attorney General's Office and the prim-and-proper introvert was a Ms. Hughes from ACRT.

There was a shift in bodies, and I spied a coffee cart tucked off to the side. I bumped Zev, who was listening to Hays, and when he looked down, I tilted my head toward the cart. He nodded, so I headed over to pour us both some.

The murmur of conversation floated around me as I reversed my route, handed Zev one cup, and reclaimed my earlier position next to him. I got a few good sips in, when the chief rumbled, "If you all wouldn't mind taking a seat."

Even though I was highly concerned that if I sat, my body would take it as permission to shut down, I moved in front of Zev and followed Encinas and Hays to the back row of chairs.

The chief stood near the edge of the mirror, facing us, his expression stern, his voice all business. "I appreciate everyone rearranging their schedules on such short notice. As I informed you earlier, based upon the information provided by Mr. Fortune, we were able tie the deposits made to Mr. Innes's account to Mr. Lennox. This gave us the necessary leverage to request Mr. Lennox's presence so we can further pursue this information. At this time, Mr. Lennox will be joined by his legal counsel and Mr. Winston Hathaway, who requested to be present as both a personal friend and business associate."

I studied my coffee, knowing that Winston's presence was allowed only because of politics. The Hathaways might not wield the fearsome influence of an Arcane Family, but their checkbook obviously had enough weight to make a dent. However, I had to wonder at Beau's arrogance of involving Winston in this. If Beau was willing to pay Damon to keep his dirty little secrets secret, why on earth would he let Winston sit in on this interview? Was he really that clueless? I was about to find out, because there was a soft buzz.

The chief checked his phone. "They're here."

He touched a spot on the wall, and a flash of power drifted through the room. The previously opaque window cleared to reveal a small conference table that held a couple of bottles of water. The table was surrounded by four padded chairs. I was vaguely disappointed by the bland, nonthreatening interrogation room. About the only thing that matched all the shows on TV was the mirror. On the other side, the door opened, and I settled in to watch.

The first person through was male, and he was looking back over his shoulder. "We appreciate you making time to meet with us this morning." He came in then held open the door. His brown hair was cut short above a heavy brow, and his square jaw was clean-shaven. He was dressed in black tactical pants and a green collared shirt. His badge winked from his belt. He waved those behind him to the empty chairs. "Please, come in. Have a seat, and we'll get started."

"Is this going to take long? I promised my wife I'd take her to a late brunch." Beau strode in, an affable expression on his face, the picture of an easygoing, helpful businessman.

It was bullshit of course, but I silently gave him kudos on his acting.

A pressed and polished fortysomething who held a leather folio followed in his wake. His sharp gaze swept through the room, and he frowned. "We're being recorded," he warned Beau. Clearly, this was the legal counsel.

"It's procedure," the first man said as he pulled out one of the chairs closest to the mirror. "Makes documentation easier." He moved the chair over to the other side of the table.

A spurt of amusement hit me at his politely offered version of "recordings don't lie."

"Well, I'm sure this will be short and sweet." Winston walked in and claimed the newly offered chair, leaving Beau and the legal counsel the remaining seats.

"Baker, I'm going to grab a chair," said a woman from the doorway, her dark hair ruthlessly constrained in a tight braid.

"Got it," said the brown-haired officer. "We'll wait for Detective Young before we get started."

"Of course," the counsel said as he settled in between Winston and Beau.

Detective Young was back in under a minute, dragging a chair in her wake. She wore a uniform similar to her partner's, except her polo was an off-white. Once she was seated, the interview began.

The two detectives didn't come out blasting. Instead, they eased into things with softball questions of name, address, and other standard questions. Then they started to pick up speed, getting into Beau's work history, how long he'd been friends with the Hathaways, whether he knew Damon Innes or Darlene Hedgerow, his whereabout in the last couple of days, and so on.

Beau, with some interjections from counsel, initially fielded the questions with ease. But I noticed as the two detectives took turns rephrasing his answers into new, more direct questions, that easygoing façade began to crack.

We were about twenty minutes into the friendly discussion when Detective Baker took his shot. Without looking up from the file in front of him, he flipped through the pages and asked, "Is there a reason why you gave Mr. Innes ten thousand dollars every month for the last four years? Well, all except last month."

Beau paled, shock evident in his gaping mouth, which he was quick to close. His fisted hand slipped beneath the table. "I don't know what you're talking about."

And just like that, the show really began. The next thirty minutes continued with escalating denials and heated warnings from counsel, who was clearly concerned with what his client had not shared.

I heard Encinas mutter to Hays, "He's going to break."

Hays nodded and kept her voice low. "Just a couple more, and he'll topple right over."

The two clearly knew how things worked, because not even three minutes later, Winston snapped, nudging Beau right off the cliff into a free fall. The detectives were relentless in laying out their undeniable trail of evidence that Beau had embezzled from Regal Enterprises.

Red-faced and seriously looking like he was on the verge of a heart attack, Winston shoved his chair back and lunged for Beau, his hands aiming for Beau's neck. Beau all but fell out of his chair then scrambled back from the imminent threat of death barreling toward him. The only thing that kept Winston from strangling his ex-friend was his legal counsel, who managed to get between the two men.

Detective Baker roared, "Enough!"

Winston stood pressed against his in-house lawyer, chest heaving, hands fisted at his side as he glared at Beau. "What the fuck, Beau?" Winston's question broke at the end, the pain of betrayal breaking through his rage for just a brief moment. "What the fuck? You told me you were done with that shit. After all those times I bailed your ass out? And you *stole* from *me*! You asshole!"

Baker joined the lawyer, and together, they got Winston out of the room even as he kept hurling dire threats.

"Mr. Lennox," Detective Young said as she walked around the table, "why don't you take a seat." She righted the chair that had toppled in Beau's bid for escape.

Slowly, shaking like a leaf, Beau sank into the chair.

Detective Young handed him a water then went back to her chair, pulling the file Baker had been reading closer.

The door opened, and the lawyer came back in and started to collect his stuff. Even before he spoke, it was clear he was rethinking his commitment. He clutched his folio in a white-knuckle grip and cleared his throat. "Detective, based upon what's come to light, I cannot, in good faith or as Regal

Enterprises legal counsel, continue to represent Mr. Lennox." He straightened and turned to Beau, who was now slumped in his chair. "You should be aware, Mr. Lennox, that Mr. Hathaway has requested an internal investigation to be opened into your financial mismanagement and that charges be filed against you."

He started to turn away then paused, looking at Beau. "I suggest, Mr. Lennox, that you invoke your right to stay silent until you can find alternate representation." With that, he followed in Winston's wake. This time, the door closed on a soft snick that sounded ominous in the tense interrogation room.

Beau looked down at the table, his shoulders hunched, his hands hidden by the table, but I was pretty sure they were shaking. There were no signs of his earlier confidence. The constant, unrelenting questions had torn that apart. Just like Encinas and Hays predicted, he was in pieces.

"Mr. Lennox"—Detective Young leaned forward, sympathy easing into her voice—"why were you paying Mr. Innes?"

Beau looked up, his face haggard, his eyes going to the folder in front of the detective. "I used to have a gambling problem, and five years ago, that problem became a serious issue that threatened my family. In order to keep them safe, I borrowed money from one of the business accounts." He shook his head and added the same excuse that every gambling addict used. "I was planning on paying it back." He stopped talking.

"But you didn't," Detective Young pressed.

He rubbed a hand over his face. "I couldn't. I was going to cash in some investments, but the stocks were dropping, and…" He stopped and tried again. "I sat in a few games, managed to recoup some of the money, but…"

I tuned out the litany of excuses that blamed everyone but the person at fault. The detective let him dig a deeper hole as he explained that Damon had found out about him dipping into Regal's bank accounts and threatened to expose him if he didn't pay up. Occasionally, when Beau was short, Damon would let the difference slide if Beau gave him dirt on Virgil, whom he hated for some reason that alluded Beau.

Young waited until his excuses ran out. "Why didn't you make the payment last month?"

"I couldn't... There were questions coming from the accounting team, and there were hospital bills from my wife's stay..."

"What did Mr. Innes do when you told him you couldn't make the payment?"

Beau swallowed hard and avoided looking at her.

"Mr. Lennox," she said, a bit sharper, "what happened when you told Mr. Innes you weren't paying?"

"He threatened to go to Winston and tell him everything. I told him to go ahead. I mean, I had nothing to give him. He'd bled me dry." He dragged his hands through his hair. "Beyond dry, actually."

"And then what happened?"

Beau finally met her gaze, his eyes red and watery, the picture of a broken man, but I couldn't find an ounce of sympathy for the idiot. "Damon gave me a choice—come up with the money by Friday night, or not only would he turn over the evidence he had of my withdrawals, he'd make sure my life was over by making it seem like I tried to kill Virgil."

Detective Young frowned. "How would he do that?"

"He mentioned setting something up so it looked like I hexed Virgil and Juls at the theater." A confused frown broke through. "Though I'm not quite sure how he was going to do that."

My eyebrows rose as the detective pressed for more. Bit by bit, the whole ugly story unfolded. Damon, in true narcissistic style, had decided that he would get one over on Virgil by stealing the Gullwing en route and leaving behind a trail that would point to Beau. Instead, I'd thrown a wrench into his plans when I handed over the car to Virgil.

That explains the death-glare treatment at the theater.

Desperate to save his own ass before Damon burned his world down, Beau tracked down Damon at Darlene's and confronted his blackmailer. That went over about as well as to be expected. While Damon laughed at him, Beau released his hexed creature then left to wait for the inevitable end. When he was sure both Darlene and Damon were dead, he went back in to retrieve Damon's phone, thinking he would be able to access the evidence.

That, of course, did not work, so Beau went to plan B. A couple months back, during one of those games he shouldn't have been sitting at, he'd shared how he hoped to make some fast cash in a big way. Someone, he couldn't remember who, had commented that there was one way to make cash like that, but it would take serious balls to see it through because the rate of survival was low.

"And why was that?" Younger asked.

"Because the job was to hurt a Family the way they had hurt theirs."

"And how were you to do that?"

Beau licked his lips. His eyes flicked to the window then back to the table. He shook his head but didn't answer.

"Mr. Lennox?" Younger leaned in when he didn't stop shaking his head. "Beau, look at me."

Slowly, too slowly, he did.

"What were you supposed to do?"

"Make Sabella Rossi-Giordano hurt the way she made them hurt."

TWENTY-FOUR

AFTER BEAU'S JAW-DROPPING REVEAL, he broke down in tears. Not that it stopped the detectives from placing him under arrest. Val asked Paul to let him stick around because he wanted a turn with Beau, mainly so he could find out who had made the request to strike out at Sabella.

Unlike the rest of us, Sabella appeared unmoved by the revelation. She did, however, agree to return to the suite with Zev and me while Val did his thing. I waited until we were back behind closed doors before confronting my aunt about her blasé approach to the threat. She'd responded, "Cara, I've spent longer that you've been alive navigating these waters. I know how to swim in the deep."

Knowing that I would get nowhere pressing the issue, I had to let it go and hope Val would be able to track the threat back to the source. I did make a mental note to reach out to Xanto and loop him in. Who knew how he would take the news, especially since we had never met? But it couldn't hurt to have more eyes on Sabella.

After lunch was delivered to the suite, I left Sabella in the front room, where she was conducting business via her laptop, and holed up in the bedroom with Zev to call Lena and Evan. Then we took turns filling them in on Beau's confession and the nebulous threat hovering around Sabella. Proving that family was not limited to blood, Evan promised to keep an eye on the darker spaces of the net, and Lena said she would reach out to her network to see if she could find any threads to pull.

Then our conversation shifted to future living arrangements as Lena finally told Evan that Zev was willing to buy her out of the condo so she had a clear shot to move in with him. A lively discussion followed as we discussed the logistics of moving, signing papers, and everything else that went into shifting households. It was when I made a passing comment about my upcoming meet with Mari that Lena asked if it was about the Council's decision, reminding me I had not yet shared where I was at with that situation.

"Yeah, guess they've come to a decision on my status."

"You think they're going to lift the ban on using Guild assets?"

"I hope so, but there's a chance they won't, which means I need to secure alternate options quick." If I was staying out of the Council's arena and they decided they didn't like the fact I wouldn't be exclusive to them, I could see them retaliate by nixing my access to the Western Arcane Guild. Though, if the Council took that route, I was fairly certain that between my previous service to the Guild and Sabella's close friendship with the Guild Director, we would find a solution.

Lena let out an excited whoop. "Tell me you aren't re-signing that contract, because I like the fact that you haven't had a sit-down with death in, like, forever!"

Zev, who was lying across the bed from me with his head propped on a hand, choked out a laugh. I met his laughing gaze and winced. Perhaps sharing about my naked time with the creature from hell could wait. "It wasn't that bad, Lena."

"No, it was worse," she said with her usual bluntness.

"Come on, Rory, give my stress levels a break and tell me you aren't going back to work for the Council."

I sighed and gave her her wish. "I'm not going back to work for the Council."

Her excited "Yes!" was followed by Evan's "You know you're going to be just fine without them, right, Rory?"

I looked at Zev, taking comfort in the solid support that stared back. "Yeah, I'm going to be fine."

We finished our conversation with plans for dinner when we got back in town. Then Zev and I ended our trip to Sin City in bed, doing things best left in Vegas.

Which brings me to now.

I was repacking my bag and tucking Umber's inks into one of the side pouches. "I need to text Umber and see when I can drop this off."

Zev, who was rolling up a pair of jeans on the other side of the unmade bed, said, "You think he has any openings?"

I stopped what I was doing and looked at him. "For what?"

"I'm thinking it might be time to get one of those Yantra tats. You know, since you're going full-out on your own."

I narrowed my eyes. "What's that mean?"

His lips curved upward as he shoved the last bit of jeans into his bag. "Well, like Lena said, you tend to court death, and since I'm sticking around, I'm thinking you just might drag me along," he teased. "Maybe we can get matching ones, say, intertwined hearts or some shit."

I threw a pillow out him. "Don't be a dick, babe."

He batted the pillow away and broke out into a full-on grin. "You know I love you."

"Yeah, back at ya!" I went back to packing my bag and, without looking at him, said in a considering tone, "You know, if we were getting matching tattoos, they'd need to be way cooler than that."

He zipped up duffle and rested his hands on top as he studied me. "You serious?"

I shoved in the last T-shirt and zipped my pack closed. "About?"

"Getting a tattoo."

"Maybe." I thought back over all that had happened in the last year and a half, how close some of those calls had come to being my last. "I mean, getting one that could offer additional protection?" I gave the idea serious consideration and shrugged. "Yeah, I think I am."

He opened his mouth to respond, but a knock on the door cut him off. "Come in," he called out.

Sabella opened the door, stepped just inside, and stopped. Her expression was hard to read, and her vibe was edgy.

I braced. "What happened?"

She drew in a breath and said, "Beau Lennox was found dead in his cell this morning."

All signs of teasing disappeared from Zev's face as he frowned. "Are you kidding me?"

She shook her head. "According to Val, when they went to transfer him, they found him in his cell on the floor. It appears he was bitten by a hexed creation."

"His or someone else's?" Zev asked as he picked up his bag and slung it over a shoulder.

"They're investigating," she said. "So it may be a bit before we know."

I picked up my bag. "So there goes any chance Val has of figuring out who targeted you."

She waved that away. "Oh, I wouldn't discount Val just yet. You'd be surprised at what he can work with."

I shouldered my bag and rounded the bed. "Mm-hmm, I'm glad you're feeling so confident."

She gave a light laugh, and as soon as I got close, she pulled me in for a hug. "Don't worry, Rory. You'll have more than enough opportunity to watch my back over the next few months."

"Why's that?"

"Well, you know me. I don't take kindly to those who think they can mess with me and mine."

Definitely getting on Umber's schedule ASAP. I gave her a squeeze and pulled back so I could see her face. "Please don't seek out trouble, auntie of mine."

She cupped my face in her warm palms and gave my cheeks a soft pat. "Where's the fun in that?" She let me go and clapped her hands. "So, are you two ready to head back? We have a flight to catch."

"In a hurry, are you?" Zev asked.

"Not at all, but I do have a couple of friends to visit before Val and I get back to dealing with the board."

With that, she turned and hustled out of the room. Zev and I did one last check to make sure we got all our stuff, then we followed her out. The porter was in the entryway, piling Sabella's luggage onto a cart.

When my phone buzzed, I checked the screen and saw Cassandra's name. "Hang on," I told Zev as I took the call. "Hey, Cass, what's up?"

"Hi, Rory. I was wondering, you up for a job?"

"Always." I grinned. "Whatcha got?"

*This marks Rory and Zev's first pit stop in the Arcane Transporter series, but if you're not ready to leave the Families behind, then pull up a seat at the Arcane's favorite bar, Wonderland, and join Cass and Grayson in **LAST CALL**.*

But if you made your way here via Wonderland and want to enjoy more of Jami's fantasy worlds, then check out SHADOW'S EDGE and binge this complete series.

Now available at your favorite bookseller!

KYN KRONICLES

Welcome to a world where the supernatural walks alongside humans, their existence kept secret behind the thinnest of veils. Now modern man's scientific curiosity is determined to rip that curtain aside, revealing the nightmares in the shadows.

SHADOW'S EDGE

Raine's spent a lifetime hunting monsters, but can she stop her prey from exposing the supernatural community one bloody corpse at a time?

SHADOW'S SOUL

When a simple assignment turns into a nightmare, can Raine and Gavin unravel old vendettas before they both pay the ultimate price?

SHADOW'S MOON

Compromise isn't in Warrick's vocabulary and Xander won't abandon the hunt. As the line between instinct and intellect blurs, will they survive the fallout?

SHADOW'S CURSE

When the queen of chaos locks horns with death's justice, Natasha and Darius set a dangerous game in motion, leading two predators into a lethal dance of secrets.

SHADOW'S DREAM

Tala can't forget the past. Cheveyo can't change it. As the dreams they shared linger, can they escape the encroaching nightmare before it's too late?

SHADOW'S FALL

A trail of missing Kyn leads a powerful new threat into Raine's backyard. Will she and Gavin be able to hold their own or fall under the weight of secrets haunting the shadows?

ABOUT THE AUTHOR

"This story is an emotional roller coaster, from betrayal, anger, fear, love…" —InD'tale Magazine

Jami Gray is the coffee addicted, music junkie, Queen Nerd of her personal Geek Squad, Alpha Mom of the Fur Minxes, who writes to soothe the voices crammed in her head. Her series combine high-stakes urban fantasy and edgy paranormal romantic suspense into books you don't want to put down. Buckle up and get ready for a wild ride through the fascinating worlds of the Arcane, the Kyn, the PSY-IV Teams, and the Collapse.

Come visit Jami's website at **https://www.jamigray.com** and stay up to date on what kind of trouble she's getting into and when you can expect to join in.

www.ingramcontent.com/pod-product-compliance
Lightning Source LLC
Chambersburg PA
CBHW060914210726
48293CB00006B/2098